Joshua

RULER, HIGH PRIEST
AND
COMMANDER OF GOD'S ARMY

Sandra L. King

Xulon Press
www.xulonpress.com

To order additional copies, call 1-866-909-BOOK (2665).

Contents

Preface

The Word of God is circular in motion. God reveals the Truth of His redemption through Yeshua/Jesus Christ slowly and progressively….a portion at a time, line upon line, precept upon precept. **(Isaiah 28:10)** God used the Old Testament scriptures to paint a picture of His redemption through His Son Yeshua/Jesus. He used the "imperfect" to paint a picture of the "perfect." The first Testament was full of earthly shadows of heavenly things. God used the visible (natural) to speak in the invisible (supernatural). **For since the creation of the world His invisible attributes are clearly seen, being understood by the things that are made, even His eternal power and Godhead, so that they are without excuse. Romans 1:20** The first Testament had a measure of grace and truth until the fullness of grace and truth came through Jesus Christ. The Law came through a servant, but grace and truth through the Son. **For the law was given through Moses, but grace and truth came through Jesus Christ. John 1:17**

When speaking to His disciples, Jesus said in **John 5:46, "If you believed Moses, you would believe Me, for he wrote about Me."** Jesus was telling His disciples that He was in the beginning, was involved in creation and was the One whom Moses wrote about. In **Luke 24:44-45,** Jesus said to His disciples, **"this is what I told you while I was with you: Everything must be fulfilled that is written about Me in the Law of Moses, the Prophets and the**

Psalms. Then He opened their minds so they could understand the Scriptures." The Law, the Prophets and the Psalms represent the whole first testament, which was written before Christ came into the world in His incarnate form. Christ's disciples only had the Old Testament scriptures at the time of Yeshua/Jesus. Jesus was opening up the Old Testament scriptures to show Himself in them to His disciples. Jesus said in **Hebrews 10:7, "In the volume of the Book it is written of Me."** The whole Bible is the revelation of Yeshua/Jesus as the Redeemer of the world. All Truth leads to Jesus because He is Truth.

Jesus is the Word of God of **Genesis 1:3** through whom God created all things. Jesus is and will always be the Word of God *(voice of God)*. Jesus is the Word/Light/Life of **Genesis 1:3**, the Word/Light/Life of **John 1:1-4** and the Word/Light/Life of **Revelation**. He does not change! He is the **"same yesterday** *(first testament)*, **today** *(second testament)* **and forever** *(Revelation)*.**" Hebrews 13:8** The scriptures began with God the Creator, the Spirit and the Word *(Yeshua/Jesus)*. The Word of God had to begin this way because these three were **"in the beginning"** before all things were created. God created by the power of His Word. Jesus is that Word. **"All things were created through Him, without Him nothing was made." John 1:3** His Word still brings life *(new)* and recreates His followers into His image and likeness. Because all things were created through Jesus as the Word, all things must return to the Father through Him by His sinless blood.

The tri-unity of the Godhead works in perfect harmony and agreement. In the first three verses of Genesis, the Father created, the Spirit hovered as if in a birthing position and the Word brought forth Light and Life. The Father gave the Son; the Son gave the Holy Spirit. This is the Godhead working in perfect harmony, unity and agreement. Another example of the harmony of the triune God is when Jesus went down in the Jordan to cleanse it of its pollution, the Holy Spirit rested upon Him. The Father *spoke* witnessing that Yeshua/Jesus was indeed **"His Beloved Son in whom He was well pleased,"** the Son Jesus *stood* and the Holy Spirit *rested*.

All Truth comes to fullness in Christ because He is Truth. Throughout the scriptures God did a "new thing" or worked in a "new way" to reveal fuller truth. As God moved through scripture revealing truth, He included previous truth in the fuller truth. An example of this is God gave the Law through Moses, but the Law was hidden in Christ. Then Christ and His Word are hidden in the hearts of His followers, not on tablets of stone. Yeshua/Jesus became the Law of Moses in the flesh. He fulfilled all of the requirements of the Law perfectly for all even its penalty of death. In so doing, Christ established the Law in Him. Revelation is the sea of fulfillment of all previous truth. We will see Jesus in all of His power and glory.

The first testament was a "shadow" of the good things to come. In order to have a shadow, there must be a substance that creates the shadow. A shadow is a faint representation of something or someone. Yeshua/Jesus is the Substance of the "shadows" of the first testament. Yeshua/Jesus fulfilled all that was shadowed and prophesied in the Law and the Prophets and Psalms. The Truth of Yeshua/Jesus is hidden in the first Testament scriptures and unveiled in the New Covenant and Revelation. The purpose of the "shadow" was to bring us to the "Substance" who is Yeshua/Jesus. **Colossians 2:17 says, "which are a shadow of things to come, but the substance is of Christ."** Speaking about Moses, the tabernacle and the high priest, **Hebrews 8:5** says they **"serve the copy and shadow of the heavenly things, as Moses was divinely instructed when he was about to make the tabernacle."** So, these earthly, temporary things pointed to an eternal, permanent Truth. That Truth is Yeshua/Jesus who is the True Tabernacle of God who not only dwelt among men, but also is the Eternal Temple *(dwelling place)* of God in the heavenly sanctuary. Christ, the Substance is greater than the shadow. No one is to receive glory and honor except Christ, so God and the Holy Spirit will *ALWAYS* glorify Jesus Christ, not the shadow (temporary). Jesus cannot and will not share His glory with anyone or anything. To do so would reduce His majesty, honor and glory as the Creator of all things with the Father. We must be careful not to glorify the temporary over the Substance who is Eternal and permanent. The first testament joins with the second testament in the revelation of Truth, but the shadows of the Old Testament must not be exalted over Jesus who is God and <u>all</u>

Truth. King Solomon and his temple in all of their majesty and glory could not touch the majesty and glory of King Yeshua/Jesus. Jesus said of Himself that One who was far greater than Solomon was here. **(Matthew 12:42)**

Joshua, which means "Jesus" in Greek and "Yahweh Saves" in Hebrew, is a shadow of the True Joshua Jesus. Joshua was not only the High Priest, he was also Ruler over God's people and commander of God's army who led God's people in warfare against the inhabitants of the Promised Land and gave them their inheritance *(reward/blessing)*. Yeshua/Jesus is our Great High Priest and Ruler who will lead us into spiritual warfare as Commander of God's Army to conquer the land and give us our eternal inheritance of eternal life with Him and the Father. Moses showed God's people the **way out** of bondage through the Red Sea, which pointed to the Red Sea of Christ's blood that sets a person free from bondage to Satan. But Joshua showed God's people **the way into** their inheritance and reward in the Promised Land. *Together Moses and Joshua represent the finished work of Jesus.*

In order to see and understand all Truth, all scripture must pass through the cross. Jesus takes it from the natural, which is earthly and temporary to the spiritual, which is eternal and permanent. Yeshua/Jesus is the Tabernacle of God. He is the brazen altar of sacrifice. He is the Word of God represented by the laver that washes us clean. He is the golden menorah as the Light of the world. He is the table of showbread as the Bread of Life and the place of fellowship. He is the golden altar of incense as our Intercessor before the Father. He is the Ark of the Covenant as the very presence of God on earth. He is the two tablets of Law as the Word of God. He is the golden pot of manna as the Divine Bread from heaven. He is Aaron's rod that budded as the Resurrection and the Life. He is Noah's Ark of Salvation and Joseph the Suffering Servant who was exalted to the right hand of the throne. He is David the shepherd in his father's field that became a conquering King with a kingdom. He is Samuel, the judge, prophet and ruler of God's people. He is Solomon as the King of peace in majesty and glory, and so on and so on. These hidden truths are Eternal in Jesus, not the ritual of the Law.

God will never go backwards. He is not a backslider! Truth must be studied in its circular motion passing it through the cross of Jesus to be fully understood. Once God's Grace and Truth Yeshua/Jesus came into the world, God will not revert back to the Law. He established the Law in Jesus and is moving forward in His plan of redemption of the world through Jesus. In Revelation, Jesus will be revealed in all of His majesty and glory in the Heavenly Sanctuary. All will be returned to the spiritual once again as it was in the beginning before Adam and Eve sinned. Adam and Eve were clothed in God's glory before they sinned, as we will be clothed in God's glory in the Heavenly Tabernacle. We will reflect the Light of the throne and the Lamb who are the Light of the Heavenly Temple. **Revelation 22:3-4**

There is a veil over the Word of God that only Yeshua/Jesus can remove. **Revelation 5:9** When Jesus died on the cross, not only was the veil between the Holy Place and the Most Holy Place in the Temple torn from top to bottom *(God to man),* the veil over the Word of God was also removed for those who love Jesus and have spiritual eyes to see and spiritual ears to hear. The whole Bible is written in symbolic language. God used what He created to speak spiritual Truth. Because God created all things, all things have a spiritual message from Him. He uses the "earthly," i.e. an eagle, a brook, a sea, a river, a tree, a dove, a blade of grass, a raven, the nation of Israel, the tabernacle, the law, the feasts, etc. to speak a Divine, Eternal Truth. **(see Job 12:7-10)**

All glory, honor, power and praise belong to Yeshua/Jesus alone. The presence of God was taken out of the temporary of the earthly tabernacles of Moses and David and the temples and put into the permanent and eternal temple of Yeshua. Yeshua/Jesus is building His spiritual temple in the hearts of those who love and serve Him.

Since Jesus is the Word of God brought to life, we must walk in the love, compassion and authority of Christ. As the Old Testament saints were **"examples"(1 Corinthians 10:11),** Jesus is the perfect example who not only shows us the Truth through His life and walk, but also will guide us into all Truth by the power of His Holy Spirit and Word. If we are walking in the Light and love of Jesus

Christ, there is no need of a Law, **"for love fulfills the law."** If we are not under His authority and His love, then we have rejected His ways and return to the Law whose penalty is death.

God has no favorites. **(see Acts 10:34-43;Acts 15:1-15; Romans 2:11)** He wants all—both Jew and Gentile— to come to His saving grace in Yeshua/Jesus. The Apostle Paul said in **Acts 15:1-15 that God who knows the heart showed that he accepted them** *(gentiles)* **by giving the Holy Spirit to them, just as He did to us** *(Jewish disciples).* **He made no distinction between us and them, for He purified their hearts by faith. Now then, why do you try to test God by putting a yoke that neither we nor our fathers have been able to bear?** *(Law)* **No! We believe it is through the grace of our Lord Jesus that we are saved, just as they** *(gentiles)* **are."** Believers in Yeshua/Jesus are to be yoked to Him, not the Law. God makes no distinction between the Jews and Gentiles. He shows His acceptance of both through the giving of His Holy Spirit and the purification of their hearts by faith. All of the patriarchs and Old Testament saints could not obey the Law completely thus coming under its condemnation and penalty. Abraham, Isaac, Jacob, Moses, Joshua, David etc. were saved by faith in the True God, not the Law. All who believe in Jesus cannot perfectly obey His Word either because our flesh gets in the way. There is only one way to the Father and that is through the sinless blood of Jesus. He obeyed the Father perfectly and completely for all of us. We must all be restored to the Father in the same way Jesus was.....by His sacrificial blood. The beauty of the grace we receive through Jesus is the double portion of His love. He not only saves us by His sinless blood, He also gave us the power of His Holy Spirit to bring us to obedience to His precious and holy Word.

To sacrifice an animal's body and blood, even if it is considered a "memorial" of Christ's perfect, complete and finished sacrifice of His Body and Blood would be an insult to His finished work on the cross. Christ established the table of bread and the cup of wine as the "memorial" of His death and resurrection. To go back to animal sacrifices would be in direct disobedience to Jesus who is God. Some of the Jews are looking forward to the day when the temple will be rebuilt and they can offer animal sacrifices again.

Unfortunately, this desire of God's people will be the very thing the Antichrist will use to deceive the Jews. **(see Revelation 13:11-18)** This Antichrist will come as a man of peace but after three years he will show his true character. Because he will bring peace to the land and will allow the Jews to build a temple, the majority of God's chosen people will be deceived. He wants political, economic and religious authority. So, peace and the temple will be his tool to deceive the Jews. Though he allows them to build a temple, he will desecrate it by setting up an idol of himself to be worshiped. Anyone who will not worship him will be killed. God will send warnings to His people to make them aware of the plans and plots of the Enemy but they must heed the warning.

As promised in the book of Daniel, God is opening up His scriptures in depth to those He has taught in the quiet, secret places as he trained up David in obscurity in the shepherd's field. God will use these trained prophets and prophetesses to correct the distortion of Truth that has taken place over the years. God told the prophet Daniel to shut up the book until the end times. It is now time for God to open His Book. The Lord is now giving deeper revelation knowledge to those who love and serve Him and have meditated upon His Word night and day, as David did. He will use His anointed ones to open the scriptures for all who have **"eyes to see and ears to hear."** In addressing His Church in **Revelation 2 and 3,** Jesus said seven times, **"He who has an ear, let him hear what the Spirit says to the churches."**

The Word of God is an embroidered work of one piece with the blood of Yeshua/Jesus woven throughout drawing it together as one work in Him. When God made His covenant promise with Abraham, He told Abraham to take a three-year old heifer, a three-year old female goat, a three-year old ram, a turtle dove and a pigeon and cut all but the birds in two and lay them side by side. **Genesis 15:9-10** Usually the covenant parties at the time of Abraham would pass between the halves indicating that they were irrevocably bound together by blood. But this time, God passes between the pieces in the form of a smoking oven *(refining fire)* and a burning torch *(light)* indicating that it was His unconditional covenant and He would perform it. Man would lay the pieces, but

God would perform the covenant. Nothing Abraham can do will bind the covenant nor anything Abraham does can break this covenant. God alone will perform it. These three animals laid side by side represent the three sections of the Word of God that shows the fulfillment of this covenant in Yeshua/Jesus. Jesus who is God passes through the two testaments binding them together by His sacrificial blood. In Genesis, it was in the darkness that the fire of God passed between these split sacrifices. Jesus came into the world when it was in darkness. He is the One who fulfilled the Abrahamic Covenant. The work was God's alone through Yeshua/Jesus. Abraham had no part in it. The dove and the pigeon were not cut because they represent the work of the Holy Spirit that unifies. There must be no division in the work of the Holy Spirit.

These three animals (flesh) cut in two and laid side by side add up to six, which is the number of flesh (man). They represent the Jew and the Gentile who are to walk side by side with Yeshua/Jesus in the center of their hearts ruling making one covenant, one faith, one body, one hope and one Lord and Father of all. **(Ephesians 4:4-6)**

This book on Joshua is written to open up the Eternal Truths hidden within which point to the True Joshua Jesus (Yeshua). Jesus Himself spoke in parables that had hidden within spiritual, eternal truths that only those who had **"eyes to see and ears to hear"** could see and understand. Like Jesus' parables, the Old Testament also had veiled truths within. These truths are brought to light through Jesus and the Holy Spirit. The Old and New Testaments are linked in the unveiling of these Eternal Truths. Christ's kingdom is **"at hand"** unfolding in the hearts of those who love and serve Him. In these end times, we must have a **love of the truth (2 Thess. 2:10)** to keep us from being deceived. Those who love the truth should also walk in love when they use the truth. Walking in truth is abiding in Yeshua/Jesus because He is Truth. When we walk in Christ-like love, we will draw others to His Truth and we will use the truth that He has entrusted us with to help set others free, not to attack them.

Joshua led God's people into victorious living against the giants of the land. The True Joshua, Jesus, leads us into victorious living against the giants of self, sin, Satan and demons. As the Father, the

Son and the Holy Spirit work and walk in perfect unity, harmony and agreement, those who love and serve Jesus are to walk in the same manner in unity, harmony and agreement without division. Joshua and Caleb were the only two out of the hundreds of thousand sons of Israel to enter the Promised Land. Both Joshua and Caleb typify Christ. Joshua also typifies the Jewish believers who will overcome and be more than conquerors through Christ, and Caleb typifies the Gentiles who will do the same. Together they represent the Bride of Christ. Jesus is raising up His spotless and pure Bride made up of both Jews and Gentiles who love and obey Him to bring in the end time harvest and conquer the land for Christ as Joshua conquered the Promised Land for God's people. Out of the multitudes Jesus taught, healed and performed miracles among, only 120 followed Him while He walked on earth, just as there were only Joshua and Caleb in the first testament who entered into the fullness of God's promise. Hopefully, in this age of grace the ratio of those who wholly follow Jesus as His Bride will increase.

There is a land to be conquered and spiritual warfare to be fought. There is only one way to victory. We must cling to Yeshua/Jesus and allow Him to love our sins to death. The battle and the victory is the Lord's. We are not our own. We were bought with a price. **(1 Corinthians 6:19)** Serving Yeshua/Jesus will also have a price—love, faith, obedience and sacrifice. We must surrender all to Yeshua/Jesus giving Him the full right to own, control and possess the land of our hearts. As Caleb destroyed the prideful, arrogant Anakim by his sword, we must allow Christ to destroy our pride by the Sword of His Word. We cannot bring others into the knowledge of the love and grace of Yeshua/Jesus until we have first conquered our flesh. We must come to Hebron the place of intimate fellowship and Christ-like love before we can come to Jerusalem, the City of God and His throne where we see Yeshua/Jesus face to face. Remember that David began his reign in Hebron, the place of fellowship and love, before moving to Jerusalem, the City of God, and bringing the Ark of God's Presence there.

If we are to conquer the land for Christ, we cannot do so by "lording it over" others in prideful arrogance, but must come "under" them in humble, servanthood lifting them up to Jesus through prayer, spiritual warfare, faith and a Christ-like love in our hearts. Jesus showed us this when He stooped to wash His disciples' feet.

Joshua, the faithful overcomer, inherited Timnath Serah, which means "the city of the sun." Those who faithfully follow the True Joshua, Yeshua/Jesus will be more than conquerors through Him and will abide with Him forever in the city of the Son where the Lamb is its light. **Revelation 21 and 22.**

CHAPTER 1

Joshua Called

God commands and encourages Joshua – Joshua 1:1-9

The names Joshua and Jesus (Yeshua) are the same in Hebrew. Moses the Lawgiver has died. Israel had to wait until Moses was out of the way in order to enter the land of promise.

The mantle of Moses fell upon Joshua. Joshua, which means, "Yahweh is salvation" in Hebrew and "Jesus" in Greek, must become leader of God's people and take them to their Promised Land *(Israel)*. New life would come after death. Where the Law (Moses) ends, Jesus (Joshua) begins. Moses brought the people **out of** Egypt *(freedom)*, but Joshua brings them **into** the land God promised Abraham, Isaac and Jacob *(blessing)*. The lifting up of the rod of Moses is type and shadow of the cross. Moses represents redemption from bondage via the Red Sea and the Law, and Joshua represents the conquest and possession of the land. Canaan, the Promised Land, is not only the place of inheritance of God's promises; it is also the place of spiritual warfare. **(Genesis 11:1-9;Revelation 17-18)** Only Jesus can redeem us and then lead us into our promised inheritance. . *Moses together with Joshua represent the finished work of Christ.* Joshua fulfilled all that God had spoken to Moses just as Yeshua/Jesus fulfilled and established in His Person all of the Law God gave through Moses. Joshua conquered all of the land and then the land and God's people rested from war. It is Yeshua/Jesus, our Redeemer, and the Holy Spirit who will bring us into our inheritance and rest. Yeshua/Jesus will conquer the land through His faithful, obedient servants as Joshua and Caleb, the two faithful witnesses and servants, conquered the land of Israel for God's people.

Moses saw the Promised Land but could not enter into it. The Law God gave Moses stopped short of the Promised Land. The Law makes a person conscious of sin and its penalty but it does not have the permanent remedy or the power to bring us to obedience or to impart eternal (spiritual) life. It is not the Law that brings life or death. It is the sin that brings death, and the power of sin is the law. **(1 Corinthians 15:56)** The Law exposes our sin and imposes the penalty, which is death. Moses fell under its penalty for disobeying God just once. God showed His people the way they must live through the Torah, but His people were never able to live up to His perfect Law. The Law was not flawed, the people were. The sinful inclination in the heart of man made them incapable of obeying the Law. God knew this so He gave the Law as a temporary means of atonement. But God had a plan for His people. He said He would make a new covenant with them through which He would forgive their sins and change their sinful nature into His nature. Yeshua/Jesus, the Perfect Paschal Lamb, ratified this covenant by His own blood. It was strictly the work of God alone. Man had no part in it. Only the sinless blood of Jesus, who lived in perfect obedience to the Law, could pay the penalty and give us the Holy Spirit to bring us to obedience. Jesus did not abolish the Law. He abolished **"in His flesh the law with its commandments and regulations. His purpose was to create in Himself one new man out of the two** *(Jew and Gentile)*, **thus making peace, and in this one body to reconcile both of them to God through the cross, by which He put to death their hostility." Ephesians 2:15-16** Jesus took upon Himself the penalty of the Law for sin for all so both Jew and Gentile could be reconciled into one body through Him. If the Spirit, which is love, is leading us we have no need of the Law.

Moses, like believers today, was looking forward to the hope and promise of Messiah. **Hebrews 11:26-27** says, **He** *(Moses)* **regarded disgrace for the sake of Christ as of greater value than**

the treasures of Egypt, because he was looking ahead to his reward. By faith he left Egypt, not fearing the king's anger; he persevered because he saw him who is invisible. Moses saw "Him who is invisible"—Yeshua/Jesus— and knew that one day he would receive his reward for his faithful service. Moses looked forward to the time of the coming Messiah and Redeemer. Moses suffered long with his people. Those of us who believe in Yeshua/Jesus, the Messiah, by faith should also be willing to suffer disgrace for the sake of Jesus just like Abraham and Moses did.

Moses stood alone with God even in his death. God was with Moses as his spirit departed. Then God Himself buried Moses. Because Moses was a mighty man of God, God probably buried him so no one could make a shrine of his burial place and worship it.

Moses appeared with Jesus and Elijah on the Mount of Transfiguration where Jesus showed three of His disciples His glory. Three is the number of "perfect witness." *(i.e. three sections of the Word and also the Trinity)* Moses and Elijah faded away leaving just Jesus illustrating that their lives and ministry pointed to Him. **(Matthew 17:3,8)** Moses represented the Law and Elijah the prophets. Jesus fulfilled both. The Law and the Prophets pointed to Jesus— the Word of God from beginning to end. The three sections of the Bible are the "perfect witness" of the redemption of the world by Yeshua/Jesus.

Moses also represented Jesus' death and Elijah His resurrection. God established patterns in the Old Testament that were fulfilled in the New. Moses and Elijah also represented the Apostles (Moses) and Prophets (Elijah) through whom, in the last days, God will reveal truth that has been distorted over the years. These anointed apostles and prophets will be filled with the knowledge of God's Word and will seek His face. Then God will use these apostles and prophets (prophetesses) to reveal Truth.

God's promise to Abraham, Isaac, Jacob, Moses, David and Joshua was both an earthly promise and a spiritual promise. Jesus came to establish both an earthly and a heavenly kingdom. Jesus takes it from the earthly to the spiritual. The two become one in Him.

Over and over in Deuteronomy, Moses told the Israelites of the necessity of walking in obedience to God's Word so they will have the abundance of life in the Promised Land *(Israel)*. Moses also told them to **"drive out the seven nations who are larger and stronger than you." Dt. 7:1** These seven nations represent the perfection of evil. Satan and his demonic powers are larger and stronger than us. They cannot be fought with our flesh. Jesus and the Holy Spirit who are within us are more powerful than the enemy and his demons. This is why God continually tells the Israelites to walk according to His commands and then they will have success in the battle. **Psalm 104:9** says, **"You have set a boundary that they may not pass over…"** Our boundary is the Word of God. Jesus (the Word) and the Holy Spirit will illuminate the scriptures for us. They will burn out the darkness (sin) in us and will also guide us in the Light (Truth).

Entering the Promised Land was a major transition for God's people. They had been looking forward to it for almost 40 years. Moses told God's people in **Deuteronomy 31:2-3** that he would not cross over the Jordan with them but that God would cross over ahead of them with Joshua. Moses was showing the people that God was their leader and that He would bring them into their inheritance. The people were not to depend upon their leader, but to depend on God Himself. Moses was a great spiritual leader but he never had to fight any battles. God had prepared Joshua to take over as leader of His people. Joshua was not only a capable religious leader as High Priest, but also a courageous military commander who would lead His people into victory over the inhabitants of the land of Promise. This, of course, is a picture of the True Joshua, Jesus, who is our Great High Priest and the Commander of God's spiritual army who will bring us to victory over the enemies of our souls.

Joshua was the second person to lead the Jewish people. The True Joshua came to earth in the form of Man in the second testament. Joshua who is now the leader of God's people is from the tribe of Ephraim **(Numbers 13:8,16)**. Ephraim was the son of Joseph and his Egyptian (Gentile) wife. He was a Jew/Gentile. Ephraim received the blessing of the firstborn son even though he was the second born. Jesus had both Jewish and Gentile blood in His flesh body. He was the descendant of David who descended from Ruth (a Gentile) and Boaz (a Jew). Joseph's father Jacob adopted both Ephraim and Manasseh as his own in order for them to receive their inheritance. These two sons came together as one with the father Jacob. Jacob crossed his hands in order to give the blessing of the firstborn to Ephraim instead of Manasseh. This was a picture of the cross of Jesus. God refers to Israel as His firstborn son *(eldest)* in **Exodus 4:22.** The firstborn son according to the Law receives the special blessing of the father. He is also made the head and authority of the family, and also receives a double portion of the father's inheritance. The firstborn son is to be dedicated to God **(Exodus 22:29-31)** and redeemed **(Exodus 34:20).** Jesus, the Only Begotten Son of the Father, fulfilled all of these requirements of the firstborn son. God told Rebekkah in **Genesis 25:23c** that her older son would serve her younger son. Israel, the elder son of God, will serve the younger Son of God, Yeshua. Jesus the Jewish Messiah adopts us as His own, restores us to Yahweh, blesses us and gives us our inheritance.

By adopting and blessing these sons of Joseph who are both Jew and Gentile, Jacob was giving them a place in the Covenant family. Jesus also adopts both the Jew and the Gentile and grafts both into the Tree of Life *(Jesus, the Giver of life)* giving each a place in the New Covenant family of God.

Ephraim is the northern tribes of Israel that God scattered throughout the earth. Ephraim represents the Bride of Christ made up of both Jews and Gentiles. God had told the Israelites that they would be the light of the world, but because of their disobedience, God must now work through **"a people who were not My people."** Both the Jew and the Gentile have been rebellious and disobedient to God. There is no pure bloodline except the sinless blood of Jesus. We cannot depend on our earthly heritage for entrance into the kingdom of God. We can only enter in through the blood of Jesus as His adopted sons and daughters. Though we have an earthly heritage from our ancestors, our spiritual heritage can only come through Jesus/Yeshua.

As captain of God's earthly army, Joshua will lead God's people in overcoming the enemy and occupy the land God promised Abraham, Isaac and Jacob. Jesus has given us victory over our spiritual enemy here on earth and will bring us to our promised inheritance when He comes to gather His Bride to Himself. We will live and reign with Jesus here on earth during the millennium. The land will be ours because Satan will be bound for 1,000 years. And, we will live forever with Him in the new heaven and new earth.

Joshua reaped the harvest of Moses' labors. **"I have sent you to reap that for which you have not labored; others have labored, and you have entered into their labors."** **John 4:38** Joshua was trained up under Moses in the same way Jesus was trained up in subjection and under the command of the Father. Joshua has been prepared through 40 years of selfless service and training in the desert. Joshua's life of faith, submission, humility, obedience and sacrifice pointed to Jesus Christ who walked in absolute obedience and submission to the Father's will. Jesus is our example. Joshua has been trained and proved loyal. Now he is ready to lead the people across the Jordan into the Promised Land. Joshua must learn the loyalty of a servant before he can be exalted to leader. Jesus came as a humble Servant willing to suffer for the sin of the world. He will come again as the exalted King of Kings and Lord of lords.

God chose Joshua many, many years before. Joshua showed his leadership skills when he was sent as one of the twelve men who were to spy out the Promised Land. Only Joshua and Caleb came back with a good report. They had faith that they could conquer the giants of the land because they had the God of Israel with them. **(Numbers 14:6-10)** Joshua's military might was tested previously when he defeated Amalek and his people with the edge of the sword in **Exodus 17:8-15.** God told Moses to **"write this for a memorial in the book and recount it in the hearing of Joshua, that I will utterly blot out the remembrance of Amalek from under heaven."** Moses was writing the Book of Law. Joshua only had the Book of the Law at the time. Joshua was to obey it fully if he was to possess the land. The earthly Joshua was not able to do this. But, the spiritual Joshua (Yeshua/Jesus) did. Jesus became the Law. He fulfilled all of it for us establishing it in Him. Those who believe in Jesus have obeyed the Law completely through Him. The entire curse of the disobedience to the Law is removed through His sinless blood and all of the blessings of the Law are **"yea and amen"** in Jesus. Even Jesus said that Moses wrote of Him. **(John**

5:46-47) Amalek represents Satan and those who do not receive Christ's saving grace. Those who have not received Jesus as Savior and Lord are blotted out of God's Book of Life. Jesus will totally destroy Satan and blot him out of our memory when we live with Him in the new heaven and new earth.

Even though Joshua did not obey the Law of God fully, God never left or failed him. God has always preserved a remnant of faithful Jewish believers in Yeshua despite their human failure to obey Him perfectly. God's grace began in Genesis and is reflected throughout all of Scripture.

Moses openly honored Joshua so the people also respected him. **(Numbers 27:18-23; Deuteronomy 31:7-8)** Moses also openly honored the True Yeshua on the Mount of Transfiguration when he stood beside Jesus with Elijah and then faded out of the picture giving glory to Jesus alone. **(Matthew 17:1-17)**

Moses gave the Law that provided atonement until Jesus shed His sinless blood. Exodus in Greek means, "way out." God showed Moses the "way out" of bondage. The eternal "way out" is through the Red Sea of Christ's blood. The book of Exodus is about the redemption of God's people. God told Moses to build Him a tabernacle according to God's instructions that **"I might dwell among you."** Then God gave Moses the Law, which included sacrificing the blood of an innocent animal for atonement for sin. Jesus is the very presence of God on earth. Jesus not only became the Law, He became sin for us in order to remove the Law's curse. The work of the Law and of redemption was His alone. **(2 Corinthians 1:20)** All of the commandments of God are kept perfectly for us in Christ. In Christ, all "Israel" is under no obligation to keep the Law. However, those who accept Jesus as Messiah, receive the covenant blessings of the Law because He has kept the Law perfectly for us.

Moses was the man to face Pharaoh and lead the people out of slavery, but Joshua was the man who would lead them into battle against the enemies of the land God gave them and possess it. Joshua was to reap the harvest of Moses' labors just as Jesus will reap a harvest from the labors of His Bride who will capture the land for Him and defeat the Enemy of peoples' souls.

The journey through the wilderness for forty years represents carnal Christians who have not matured in their faith and obedience to God's Word. They cannot enter the fullness of the promises of God in Christ because they have not been prepared and sanctified. God must prepare His people on the wilderness side of the Jordan in order for them to cross over and fight the larger battles and conquer the land. Some Christians are still in the wilderness between Egypt (world) and Canaan (the fullness of the promise). They have received Jesus' saving grace but they haven't entered into their inheritance of rest, peace and victory by faith. They will rise no higher because they are content with little. God will never give His treasure to an indifferent heart. The cost of holiness is too great for those who are like Lot and the Reubenites, Gadites and half tribe of Manasseh who chose to live close to the world. God wants His blessings cherished above all cost and sought above all earthly desires and treasures.

Crossing the Jordan represents the mature Christian who has been tried and tested and found faithful, obedient and true. The Jordan symbolizes baptism in the Holy Spirit, which empowers us for ministry. When Jesus was baptized in the Jordan River, immediately the Holy Spirit in the form of a dove rested upon Him. Jesus didn't begin His public ministry until after this. Jesus went down into the waters of the Jordan to cleanse it of its pollution. The first Adam came as a full-grown adult and fell. The Second Adam came as a babe, was nurtured and grew in wisdom and did not fall. It is matured Christians who will conquer the land for Christ and bring others into God's promised inheritance through Christ.

God had the foundation laid in the wilderness, but now he will build upon it. The Israelites under the leadership of Joshua must conquer the giants in the land and possess it. The land is God's to give, but ours to possess. Selflessness is the requirement to cross over. We are to "take up our cross" by leading a crucified life. Conforming to Christ's death is the gateway into the resurrection power of Jesus Christ. If the land of promise is to be conquered, God's people must live the power of a crucified life. The cross (crucified life) is the power of God for victory. The resurrection power of Jesus Christ is made manifest in each of His followers by the crucifixion of our flesh. There has to be a death before there can be a resurrection.

God brought Moses forth again in his resurrected, glorious body along with Elijah and Jesus on the Mount of Transfiguration in the Promised Land to introduce Jesus as the One to whom their ministries pointed. Elijah and Moses appeared with Jesus, but Elijah and Moses faded out of the picture giving all the glory to Jesus. Peter, James and John, the three Jewish disciples who drew nearest to Jesus, were the ones to whom Jesus revealed His glory. **"Draw near to God and He will draw near to you."**

The Law shows us the land of promise, but Jesus brings us into it. The Law is our tutor that brings us to Christ. **God takes away the first to establish the second. Hebrews 10:9** God took away the Law to establish Grace through Jesus Christ. He must also take away our flesh to establish His Spirit and the image of His Son in us. We must all come to the cross and crucify our flesh. If we think we can avoid the cross and thus continue to live our sinful nature and think that the law will not condemn us, we are fooling ourselves. We cannot use God's grace through Jesus Christ as a license to sin. Jesus calls us to a life of righteousness, not lawlessness. Jesus became the Law. Jesus, the True Joshua to whom the earthly Joshua pointed, established the Law of Moses in His Person by fulfilling all of its requirements for us. **"Do not think that I came to destroy the Law or the Prophets. I did not come to destroy, but to fulfill! Matthew 5:17** By fulfilling the Law, Jesus established the Law in Him. Those who follow Him are no longer under the Law but under Grace as the means of atonement through His sinless blood. **For the law of the Spirit of life in Christ Jesus has made me free from the law of sin and death. Romans 8:2** The Law is fulfilled in each of us through Yeshua/Jesus. The Law brought the penalty of death, but Yeshua/Jesus brings life and that more abundantly.

Joshua led the Israelites to an earthly rest, but Jesus leads us to our spiritual, eternal rest. **For if Joshua had given them rest, God would not have spoken later about another day. For anyone who enters God's rest also rests from his own work, just as God did from his. Hebrews 4:8-10** Joshua leading the Israelites into a better rest and victory over their enemies points to Jesus, the Captain of our salvation, leading us to victory over Satan, the world and our flesh. Once the enemies of our souls are defeated, we enter into the better rest and peace in Christ. Only Christ can crucify us. It is the work of Him alone by grace, not by any effort on our part. All He requires of us is that we have willing, submitted hearts and a hunger and thirst for righteousness.

The other side of the Jordan is a battlefield, but it is also full of blessings. Joshua has received his marching orders from God. Joshua has rallied the troops. They have been trained and equipped through their trials and tests in the wilderness. They have watched the mistakes of their forefathers and gained wisdom from them. They are now an army of unity and of Holy purpose. All must fight in unity including the Reubenites, Gadites and half tribe of Manasseh who chose their inheritance on the east side of the Jordan. They have a land to conquer and possess and it cannot be done with division.

To the Jews, the Jordan River has deep spiritual significance as well as to Christians. The Jews see it as the gateway to the homeland of Israel because it was the place of entrance after their many years in exile. To the Christian, the Jordan River represents the Holy Spirit who will bring us into our promised inheritance through Yeshua/Jesus.

To illustrate how the "natural" speaks to the "supernatural," we can use the Jordan River. The name Jordan comes from the Hebrew root word "yarod" which means, "to descend." Yarden means "descender." Jesus descended from heaven to redeem mankind. After His crucifixion and resurrection, Jesus ascended to the Father and the Holy Spirit descended. The Jordan symbolizes the Holy Spirit.

The Jordan begins at Mount Hermon and travels down about 20 miles to the Sea of Galilee, which is the place that Jesus lived most of His life on earth and was the primary region of Jesus' ministry. (**Matthew 2:22**) Galilee means, "circle." Jesus is the "circle" of the Word of God. Jesus chose disciples from Galilee (**Matthew 4:18,20**) and performed many miracles there. The people of Galilee received Him. (**Matthew 4:25**) In **John 4:1-3,** Jesus sought refuge from the Pharisees in Galilee as we are to seek refuge in Him and the full circle of His Word. **Matthew 27:55** says that women ministered to Jesus in Galilee.

Mount Hermon is thought to be the mountain that Jesus was transfigured upon as He stood with Moses and Elijah. Mount Hermon is sometimes called "ice mountain" because of its snow-capped peaks. It is the highest mountain in the area. The whiteness and purity of the snow coupled with the brilliance of the sun shining upon it would give off glory and reflect light. Mount Hermon is referred to as Zion *(God's holy mountain)* in **Deuteronomy 4:48.**

The Jordan continues flowing from the Sea of Galilee *(representative of Jesus)* and empties into the Dead Sea, which is way below sea level and thought to be the hottest spot on earth. So the Jordan flows from the highest mountain into the depths of the Dead Sea. Christians begin at the Dead Sea, dead in sin because of the sin of Adam. When we come to Jesus at the Sea of Galilee, He will take us higher until we reach the very presence of God in all of His glory at Mount Hermon (Zion).

Jordan River

The Jordan is approximately 120 miles long. There were 120 disciples in the Upper Room when the Holy Spirit descended in power at Pentecost. The number 120 is the number of the beginning of life in the Spirit. **(Acts 1:5)** It also represents the end of all flesh. **(Genesis 6:3; Dt. 34:7)**

The Jordan is the place of separation. It is at the Jordan that the wheat *(matured believer)* is separated from the chaff *(believer who is close to the world)*. The Jordan was where Abraham and Lot separated. Both Abraham and Lot were believers in the True God. However, Lot chose the Jordan Valley close to Sodom, but Abraham chose the higher places of Canaan. **(Genesis 13:10-11)** Lot represents a backslidden believer or nominal Christian.

It was at the ford of Jabbok, a tributary of the Jordan, that Jacob sent all of his wives and children across. Jacob was left alone on the other side where He wrestled with the Angel of the Lord *(Jesus)* for a night. After rendering Jacob lame by dislocating his thigh *(representing the breaking of Jacob's will and the surrendering to God's will)*, God changed his name to Israel. **(Genesis 32:22-28)** Jacob must now lean on God for his strength. Jacob, the sinner, is now called Israel, "one who strives with God."

God told Joshua, **"Arise, go over this Jordan, you and all this people, to the land which I am giving to them – the children of Israel. Every place that the sole of your foot will tread upon I have given you, as I said to Moses." Joshua 1:2-3** It's a done deal! God has already given them the land. All Joshua and the people have to do is have faith, obey God's Word and walk in unity. God's first word to Joshua is "arise." In other words, he must get up and move. God has already given Joshua the land, but he has to step into his inheritance. Every place that the sole of their feet treads upon is already theirs because God has given it to them.

Jesus walked the land of Israel during His time on earth and shed His blood there. For this reason, the land of Israel is Holy. Our Savior's blood is in its earth. Jesus purchased not only the land of Israel by His blood but also the whole earth. Jesus gives victory to those who love, obey and serve Him over every enemy. Followers of Jesus have a piece of the land that God has given to them to conquer for Christ. Each individual Christian is a part of a mighty whole – brooks that together become a mighty river of life with Jesus as our Commander. The Promised Land represents our full inheritance in Christ. The gateway to this land is the death of self and sin. **Likewise you also, reckon yourselves to be dead indeed to sin, but alive to God in Christ Jesus our Lord. Romans 6:11** Our flesh must die that we might live the fullness of the life that Christ has for us.

God promises Joshua three things:

1. land **(Joshua 1:2-4)**
2. His presence **(Joshua 1:5)**
3. He would keep His Word **(Joshua 1:7-9)**

When God speaks, what He says will happen. When He speaks His words will come to pass because He is Truth. God speaks from perfect, infinite wisdom. If He makes a promise, He considers it done because He speaks from the perspective of eternity, not of time.

The "east" is the place of God's glory. **(Gen. 3:24;Mt. 24:27;Rev. 7:2)** Across the Jordan is a new land *(promises and blessing)* and new battles *(spiritual warfare)*. God assures Joshua that He will be with Him as He was with Moses. God will do His part, but Joshua must do his part. The Great Encourager tells Joshua to:

1. **"be strong and courageous."** Joshua is to have faith in God which gives strength and courage.
2. **"Be careful to obey all the law My servant Moses gave you"** God tells Joshua that success will come if he is obedient to His Word. Joshua must obey all of God's Word **"turning neither to the left of to the right"** – no compromise.
3. **"Do not let this Book of the Law depart from your mouth; meditate on it day and night, so that you may be careful to do everything written in it. Then you will make your way prosperous, and then you will have good success." Joshua 1:8** Joshua needs the "written Messiah" – the Law – to lead God's people into their inheritance. Joshua must keep the Word of God in His mouth and meditate on it day and night. **(see Psalm 1:3)** Victory would come through

the power of God and obedience to His Word. If Joshua and the people obey God's Word, they will be prosperous and will have good success. We will see that Joshua failed to do this when he didn't seek God's counsel and went out on his own strength and failed. When they sought God and His counsel and obeyed His Word, they were successful. Faith and obedience brings blessing. If we are to walk in the blessing of the Lord, we must speak God's Word, meditate on it, read it and personally apply it to our lives. God will make a way to cover the earth with the Good News of His salvation through Jesus through His dedicated servants in preparation for His return.

4. **"Be strong and courageous. Do not be terrified; do not be discouraged, for the Lord your God will be with you wherever you go.v9** Joshua's need to be strong and courageous without fear knowing that God is with him is so important that God reiterates it.

Jesus, the True Yeshua, was the only One to walk the earth who perfectly obeyed God's commandments. He came to do the will of the Father. As a result, Jesus purchased the land and gave victory over the enemies through His sinless blood. However, we must be prepared for the battles. Jesus gives us all of His power and authority to tread on serpents and scorpions and conquer the land for Him. **"Behold, I give you the authority to trample on serpents and scorpions and over all the power of the enemy, and nothing shall by any means hurt you." Luke 10:19** "Serpents and scorpions" represent Satan and his demonic powers. We must not underestimate the power of the enemy. Flesh cannot defeat him. Jesus and His Holy Spirit who is within us can defeat Satan and his demons. However, it must be done Christ's way in obedience to His Word, not by the ways of the flesh. Christians are to conquer **"every place that the sole of our feet tread upon"** through Jesus and His Word. Faith and obedience coupled with courage will claim the land for Christ. He has placed Satan and his demons under our feet! We are the head, not the tail. Moses grabbed the serpent by the tail, but Jesus cut off His head (put Him to death). We don't serve the Law, but Jesus who defeated Satan at the cross of victory.

Having been assured of God's presence and being encouraged to go forth by God, Joshua calls his leaders to go through the camp and tell the people to sanctify themselves because within three days they would cross over the Jordan **"to go in to possess the land which the Lord your God is giving you to possess."** The chain of command is as follows:

1. God commands Joshua
2. Joshua commands the leaders
3. The leaders command the people

Joshua 1-12 which is about Joshua and God's people conquering the land of Israel is a period of seven years. The rest of Joshua's life was spent ruling the nation of Israel and dividing up the land.

CHAPTER 2

Preparation for Crossing the Jordan

Prepare and sanctify yourselves – Joshua 1:10-11

God had been supplying manna from heaven up to this time. Now the Israelites must gather provisions for themselves. Mature Christians do not need to be spoon-fed. They feed and meditate on the Word themselves allowing the Holy Spirit to teach them. Of course, God also uses anointed teachers, apostles, prophets, evangelists and pastors to lead us into all truth.

Moses in **Deuteronomy 8:1-2** tells the Israelites to be careful to obey all of God's commandments and reminds them of how the Lord led them all the way in the desert for 40 years to humble them and test them in order to know what was in their heart and whether or not they would obey His commandments. **"He humbled you, causing you to hunger, and fed you with manna, which neither you nor your fathers had known, to teach you that man does not live by bread alone but by every word that comes from the mouth of the Lord." Dt. 8:3** God let them become hungry so they would see their need of His Divine bread. Divine Bread feeds our spirit. Just as we need the nourishment of bread and water to feed our natural man, we need a daily intake of Divine Bread to feed our spirit man.

Before crossing the Jordan, the Israelites must not only have the provision of the Word in their hearts and in their mouths, the people must sanctify themselves. Sanctification brings glorification. David loved God's Word. So much so He wrote the longest **Psalm 119** on the excellencies of the Word of God. When David went to battle Goliath, he chose five smooth stones from a brook. **(1 Samuel 17:40)** We must begin in the brook before we can cross the river at flood stage. The waters of a brook trickle over the rocks so even a child can walk across. God's children must begin in a brook as a child and must be matured until they unite with all other Christians as a mighty river of life that floods the earth with the Good News of salvation through the blood of Jesus. Smooth stones have been in the water a long time and have had their rough edges washed off. This represents the washing and removal of our flesh so the Holy Spirit will be established within us and we will go forth in the image and likeness of Jesus. Jesus operated both with love and compassion and also in courage and strength. A rough stone will wobble and sometimes miss its target, but a smooth stone will be precise in hitting its target. Goliath had four sons. David had a stone for each one of them. David used a God-made weapon *(a stone)* not anything of man.

The five stones David used against the giant Goliath also represents the fivefold ministry gifts Christ gives His Church – **apostles, prophets, evangelists, pastors and teachers to prepare God's people for works of service, so that the body of Christ may be built up until we all reach unity in the faith and in the knowledge of the Son of God and become mature, attaining to the whole measure of the fullness of Christ. Then we will no longer be infants, tossed back and forth by the waves, and blown here and there by every wind of teaching and by the cunning and craftiness of men in their deceitful scheming. Instead, speaking the truth in love, we will in all things grow up into him who is the Head, that is, Christ. From him the whole body, joined and held together by every supporting ligament, grows and builds itself up in love, as each part does its work. Ephesians 4:11-16** The work of the fivefold ministry is to equip believers to become the greatest army ever to mobilize for the invading, liberating and occupying of this earth. This army will be one of unity and of Holy purpose. Selflessness, love of the brethren and obedience to the Word will be the criteria for God's spiritual commissioning. All acceptable work flows from a heart filled with a fervent love for Jesus that spills over to others.

Though Goliath was full of pride and arrogance and boasted for 40 days, David was fearless because he knew the battle was the Lord's and He would give him the victory. After all, God had trained David in the shepherd's field against the bears and the lions. It was in the shepherd's field that David had drawn near to God in a close, intimate relationship. Now he was ready for the larger battle against the giant in the land. First David prophesied the victory. When the Philistine came and drew near to David, David did not run away but instead ran forward to meet Goliath. Then he took a stone and slung it and it sunk into Goliath's forehead making him fall facedown to the ground. This is type and shadow of Jesus' work on the cross that rendered Satan lame. Like David did Goliath (**1 Samuel 17:51**), Jesus will eventually cut off Satan's head putting him to death forever. In the days of David, giving the head of a conquered foe was a sign of victory. Jesus gained the victory over the Enemy of our souls at the cross, and He gives those who love and serve Him the victory through Him. David cut off Goliath's head with Goliath's own sword. Jesus will turn Satan's sword of accusation, condemnation and evil used against God's own people back onto his own head. Satan will reap what he sowed.

The Israelites must wait three days before crossing. We must not get ahead of God. God must prepare the way for us before we can cross over and be victorious. In those three days, the Israelites are to sanctify themselves and gather provisions for themselves. This was each individual's responsibility so they could collectively cross over the Jordan a pure, prepared and unified spiritual army of God marching in order and in obedience to God's commands given through Joshua. This, of course, is a picture of Jesus and His Bride who in purity, unity and preparedness will conquer the land and defeat the enemy for Christ.

The great multitude in white robes in **Revelation 7:9** is Christ's purified, unified, powerful and worshipping Bride who will usher in Yeshua/Jesus. Jesus prayed that His body of believers would all be one and that they would be full of His glory in **John 17:21-26. (see also Ephesians 4)** Jesus wants us to repent of everything worldly and fleshly and live in complete abandon to His will and to unity of purpose.

The Third Day

"**Within three days you will cross over this Jordan….v1** The third day represent resurrection power. Jesus' fleshly body was lying dormant in the grave for two days and was resurrected on the third day. His Body of believers will also be raised in resurrection power on the third day. *Jesus' ministry began on the third day at the wedding at Cana.* At the end of the Gospels, *Jesus is resurrected on the third day conquering death and the grave.* "**The first will be last, the last first.**" Jesus' flesh died, but His spiritual body lives on eternally with the Father in majesty, authority and power. As Adam was clothed in God's glory before he sinned, Jesus who is without sin will return to His glory in the heavenly sanctuary. God's whole plan of redemption through Yeshua/Jesus is to bring us back to our originial condition before sin in Genesis. He wants us clothed in His glory once again. Yeshua/Jesus provided the way through His sacrificial blood, His Spirit and His Word. Yeshua/Jesus will restore us glory upon glory until we reflect the Father who is love. The third day represents new levels of faith and wisdom. God's people will launch out into the deep waters of His Word and move where they have never gone before. The third day is the day of His power, strength and authority coming through His Body. **Psalm 110** is about the day of Christ's power in His Body to rule over Satan and his kingdom. God is bringing forth the third day power in His Bride. She will be a Warrior Bride pure and courageous. His Bride will come forth in the **beauty of holiness from the womb of the dawn.v3** Remember that the women went to the tomb of Jesus on the third day just before dawn and the tomb was empty! He was resurrected. We who love and follow Yeshua/Jesus will be reborn by His Light and His Spirit until His resurrection power is made manifest in each of us. We will be clothed in His glory, power and light.

"**Your troops will be willing on your day of battle, arrayed**

in holy majesty…" Psalm 110:3 The third day Body of Christ will be willing to go into battle and must be arrayed in garments of holiness. If Christ's Bride sanctifies itself and goes forth in Christ's resurrection power, it will be a time of great victory. **The Lord will extend His mighty scepter from Zion. V2** Christ's united, purified Body will go in the authority and power of Jesus/Yeshua who sits at God's right hand and who extends His authority from God's Holy mountain. The earthly king extended his golden scepter to Esther as she stood in the inner court prepared and cleansed for his presence. It was then that the king invited her into His inner chamber. Holiness will bring us into the presence of King Jesus.

This three-day wait represents the three years of the purification of Israel in the last days. After three days, God raised up the salvation of Israel – Jesus Christ. The harvest of the earth in the last days will be done when the Jordan *(Holy Spirit)* is at floodstage. It will be a time of great tribulation and adversity, but it will also be a time of great Light and victory. **(Rev, 12:15-16)** Christ's army must be prepared for the battle to come. **Jeremiah 12:5** says, **"If you have run with the footmen, and they have wearied you, then how can you contend with horses? And if in the land of peace in which you trusted, they wearied you, then how will you do in the floodplain of Jordan?"** We must be strengthened in the Lord and not grow weary in the battle.

Joshua and the Israelites crossing the Jordan are type and shadow of Jesus and His Bride who has sanctified herself and moved into a nearer and dearer walk with her Lord. She arises, *(goes up higher)* flooding herself with the Holy Spirit and the light of the Word, allowing its cleansing hand and entering into the Lord's favor. The spiritually immature cannot inherit the land. Ministers have to prepare the people to take up their inheritance, as well as train God's people in spiritual warfare. Christ's Bride is a "warrior bride." God will speak to His Bride face to face as He did to Abraham, Moses, Jacob, David, Deborah, Elijah, Elisha, Gideon, etc.

Hosea 6:1-3a shows us that after two days, God will revive us *(breath new life into us)*, and on the third day He will raise us up into His presence. **After two days, He will revive us, on the third day He will raise us up, that we may live in His sight** *(presence).*

Let us know, let us pursue the knowledge of the Lord. The two days represent the 2,000 years of grace. God is going to pour out His Spirit upon those who love Jesus before He comes to ingather His Bride. The two spies Joshua sent to Canaan to spy out the land hid in the hills for three days before returning to Joshua with their report. The three days the two Jewish witnesses spent in the hills represents the harvest of Israel *(Gentile)* and Judah *(Jew)* on the third day. The two mighty witnesses of God's power and glory in Revelation also lie in the streets three days and are resurrected after three and a half days. **(Rev. 11:8;11:11)** Jesus walked in His ministry on earth for 3 ½ years before His death, burial, resurrection and ascension.

Esther prepared herself for 12 months before being presented to the king. Twelve is the number of Divine government. When Jesus comes to take His glorious and spotless Bride home, we will live and reign with Him. As Esther prepared herself to come before the king, Jesus is preparing His Bride so He can present her without spot or blemish to His Father. Esther is a story of the respect and royal procedure that an earthly Queen paid to an earthly King. It pointed to the respect and royal procedure that Christ's earthly Bride must give to its Heavenly King Jesus. Esther did not "assume" that her position of chosenness allowed her to barge into the king's chamber and expect his approval. On the third day Esther **"put on her royal robes and stood in the inner court of the king's palace. Esther 5:1** Esther made herself ready and then stood before the king. She prepared herself with myrrh, which is a sign of burial—the death to self. Then she prepared with a season of bathing in sweet fragrance, which is figurative of sacrifice in **Leviticus 26:31.** A sweet fragrance is also figurative of cleansing and gifts. Sacrifice and cleansing is a sweet aroma to God. Christ, of course, was the ultimate sacrifice and sweet aroma to God. The Lover in the Song of Songs, who is a type and shadow of King Jesus, described His Bride as one who was set apart for Him filled with the sweet aroma of spices, frankincense, myrrh and aloes. **(SOS 4:12-15)**

Esther was willing to risk her life for God's people. The Bible says that we who love Jesus must **"present our bodies a living**

sacrifice to Him." This is the fragrance that invites the deepest levels of intimacy. Esther was prepared both for intimacy and for war. Then the king invited her into his chamber. Christ's Bride must also enter into His Chamber, the Most Holy Place. We begin at the brazen altar of sacrifice representing Christ's atoning blood. Then we proceed to the laver representing the cleansing of His Word. Next we enter into the Holy Place where the Golden Candlestick representing the Light of the World (Jesus) will shine upon the Bread of His Word giving us revelation knowledge and wisdom. At the golden altar of incense we offer intercessory prayers and prophetic proclamations before the veil into the Most Holy Place. This moves us into the third section of the Tabernacle of Moses where the Ark of God's presence is the only piece of furniture. David, who represents Jesus as the Shepherd in His Father's field who became a Conquering King, also had a tabernacle that housed only the Ark of the Covenant where the presence of God's glory rested upon the mercy seat. Instead of the ritual sacrifices and silence of Moses' tabernacle, David offered the sacrifice of thanksgiving and praise to come before the Ark of God's presence. David's tabernacle typified the heavenly tabernacle of Revelation where the whole host of heaven sing praises and worship to King Yeshua/Jesus.

The Ark in Moses' tabernacle contained the two tablets of Law, representing the two testaments of the Word, the golden pot of manna representing the Divine Word (Bread) – Jesus—, and the rod of Aaron, the High Priest, representing the resurrection power of our Great High Priest Jesus. The Most Holy Place is where we see Jesus face to face as John the Revelator did. John was the Apostle whom Jesus loved. The books John wrote showed the love and grace of Jesus. John had a very, close and dear relationship with Christ. So much so that Jesus revealed the things that were to come to John in Revelation. John was the only male who stood at the cross with the women when Jesus was crucified.

We have been made holy through the blood of Christ, but we have to put on the royal wedding robe through cleansing and preparation. Esther is a type and shadow of the Bride of Christ. Esther presented herself before the king prepared, cleansed and dressed in royal robes ready for intimacy. It was on this third day that Esther received the king's favor. He placed a royal crown upon her head and made her Queen. Then the king gave a great banquet in celebration. This represents the wedding celebration after Jesus has united with His Bride when He comes again. King Jesus has held out the golden scepter of His Word of authority to His Bride. Those who humbly draw near to Him through obedience to His Word and faith and paying proper respect to His Word will be like Esther and her king. Esther gained true favor in the sight of the king, as we will if we follow her example before coming before King Jesus. The Spirit and the Word will prepare us to be ready when Jesus comes if we obey it.

Haman, the wicked, deceitful destroyer was also destroyed on the third day. The third day of Christ *(resurrection power)* is the seventh day of God *(spiritual perfection)*. It will be on the 7th Day, the Day of the Lord, that Satan will be destroyed forever. **Do not forget this one thing, that with the Lord one day is as a thousand years, and a thousand years as one day. 2 Peter 3:8** The Lord spoke creation into existence for six days and rested on the 7th day based on His finished work. God's Word has been speaking for almost six thousand years, representing the first six days of creation, in an attempt to restore all people back to the Father (Creator) through the Son. The 7th will be the 1,000 year millennial reign of Christ. Satan will be destroyed on the last day before the new heaven and new earth is ushered in.

It was on the third day of creation that the earth burst forth through the waters bringing forth life. This is symbolic of resurrection. Jesus burst forth through the waters between heaven and earth bringing forth spiritual life.

We see a pattern, which began in Genesis, continuing here in Joshua. Preparation, cleansing and crossing over the Jordan will empower us, destroy the Enemy and conquer the land. The enemies of Jesus will fall before His sanctified, glorious Bride because the King of glory will be with them and lead them just as Joshua will lead God's people across the Jordan into victory. After being prepared and cleansed like Esther and the Israelites led by Joshua, Christ's Bride will go forth in the resurrection power, faith, courage, and obedience of Joshua. His Bride will have a heart of love for her Bridegroom and His people, the spiritual sight and swiftness of an eagle and the power, boldness and majesty of a young lion. Victory will be hers.

Esther stood close to the king in His sight, but not too close waiting for him to call her forth. The Lord told Joshua to keep a distance of 2,000 cubits between the people and the Ark of God's presence. **(Joshua 3:4)** These 2,000 cubits also represent the age of grace during which Jesus is preparing His Bride. Though we love Jesus, we must be ever mindful that He is holy. We must walk in deep reverence, faith, love and humility behind God's presence (Jesus). It is these heart attitudes that will help us see God and follow after Him. We must not become so "familiar" with Jesus that we lose our reverence and awe of His power and holiness. The place of God's presence is holy ground. We are to be holy as He is holy. **"May He strengthen your hearts so that you will be blameless and holy in the presence of our God and Father when our Lord Jesus comes with all his holy ones." 1 Thessalonians 3:13 It is God's will that you should be sanctified...that each of you should learn to control his own body in a way that is holy and honorable....4:3-4**

The same is true with His Word. We must not get too familiar with His Word that we think we already know all there is to know and thus have the tendency to lay it down and go no further. "Good" is always the enemy of "best." You cannot plumb the depths of God's Word. It always has green pastures. God will take you as far as you want to go in it, but it will require a humble, teachable heart and meditating on His Word night and day.

The Lord's Body of believers began in power in Acts and it will end in the resurrection power of the Lord's Holy Spirit just before He comes for His Bride. In the latter day rain, Christ's Bride will operate in the resurrection power anointing produced by the glory of God.

The resurrection power of the third day anointing is also illustrated in the story of Lazarus. **(John 11)** Mary, Martha and Lazarus were Jews. Mary and Martha received and believed in Jesus before Lazarus. Jesus was welcomed in the home of Martha, Mary and Lazarus. He had been a frequent guest. Lazarus did not believe in

Jesus until after he was resurrected from death. **(see John 12:1-2)** Martha, Mary and Lazarus each had an intimate relationship with Jesus, although each of their relationships with Jesus was different. In this story, Mary and Martha are seeking Jesus. A seeking soul and a seeking Savior will always meet! Those who seek Him will find Him. **Luke 11:9**

So, when Lazarus was sick, they sent a message to Yeshua to come. Jesus didn't come right away. Even though Jesus loved Mary, Martha and Lazarus, He waited two more days before He went to them. Jesus would use this situation to reveal Himself as the Resurrection and the Life, even of Israel whom Lazarus typifies. Hidden within this story is the hope of resurrection life. Jesus resurrected Lazarus in the "natural" just before His own resurrection. Jesus throughout the Gospels illustrated in the "natural" what would soon take place in the "spiritual" in Him. This resurrection of Lazarus took place just before Jesus' death on the cross and resurrection.

When Martha saw Jesus, she said, **Lord, if you had been here, my brother would not have died. But I know that even now God will give you whatever you ask."** Jesus said to Martha, **"Your brother will rise again." Martha answered, "I know he will rise again in the resurrection at the last day." Jesus said to her, "I am the resurrection and the life. He who believes in Me will live, even though he dies; and whoever lives and believes in Me will never die. Do you believe this?" John 11:21** Martha saw Jesus' resurrection life as sometime in the future. But, Jesus is saying that His resurrection life is in Him now! **"Yes, Lord,"** she *(Martha)* **told Him, "I believe you are the Christ, the Son of God, who was to come into the world."** Martha knew this great truth at a time when women weren't expected to have revelation knowledge! Mary reacted in a different way when she saw Jesus coming. Mary said the same thing that Martha did but first she fell at His feet reverencing and worshiping Him. Both Martha and Mary believed in Jesus' ability to "save" from death, but Mary added reverence, worship and humility to her faith. It was Mary's faith, humility, reverence and worship to Jesus coupled with her sorrow for her dead brother that moved Jesus to act. **"When Jesus saw her** *(Mary)* **weeping and the Jews who had come along with her weeping, He was**

deeply moved in spirit and troubled." John 11:33 Jesus understood Mary's love and heart intent. She was not judgmental or condemning. Instead she illustrated both her love for Jesus and her love for her brother through her tears. Jesus also wept. He shared in their sorrow for their dead brother. Lazarus was not only physically dead; he was spiritually dead. He had not accepted Jesus into his heart as His Savior. Like Jesus and Mary, we are to weep for those who are dead in sin. Mary placed herself in the right place in humble reverence before Jesus and also had the right heart toward her physically and spiritually dead brother.

It was on the third day that Jesus spoke His Word calling Lazarus forth and Lazarus was resurrected from death to life. The power of His Word took away the corruption and decay of Lazarus' flesh bringing him forth into new, resurrected life. This was the last thing Yeshua/Jesus did before His own resurrection defeated death. Jesus set the bound Lazarus free by His Word. Then He told His disciples to **"Loose him and let him go." John 11:44b** Jesus used His Word of authority to resurrect Lazarus from the dead, but His disciples also had a job to do. It was Jesus and the power of His Word that resurrected Lazarus but it was the work of His disciples to loose him by removing the graveclothes. Those who love and serve Jesus and His Word will also use the power of His Word and Spirit to set the captives free from the graveclothes of their flesh as Jesus did Lazarus.

"Lazarus, Come forth!" The story of Lazarus is a true account and literally happened in the natural, but it has a deeper meaning and spiritual truth. There are seven miracles of Jesus in John. This is the seventh—the crowning miracle – resurrected life. Jesus saves the best for last. This miracle takes place in Bethany, which means "house of affliction" or "place of unripe fig." Bethany is a town on Mount Olive. **(see Luke 19:29)** It is about two miles from Jerusalem, the Holy City. Jesus left this earth on the Mount of Olives and will return to the Mount of Olives in power and glory. Bethany is on the fault line that will split the Mount of Olives when Jesus sets his feet on it at His second coming. Therefore, it is the place of separation and where Jesus will resurrect the nation of Israel by showing Himself to them as the Anointed One of God who has power over life and death at the very place He resurrected Lazarus. Jesus called Lazarus forth before His own resurrection. He will call His Bride to Himself before the final resurrection. As Lazarus' body of flesh had begun to decay, there will be great rotting, death and destruction during the Great Tribulation.

Jesus came to Bethany, the "house of affliction." Jesus meets us at our deepest need at God's timing. Because Jesus tarried, hope was dying in the house at Bethany. They thought He had come late! But Jesus was right on time! Jesus waited two days before going to Lazarus' tomb. These two days represent the 2,000-year age of grace. It was on the third day that Jesus spoke His Word of power and called Lazarus forth to life. It is the power of the Word of God anointed by the Holy Spirit that will bring people from spiritual death to spiritual life in Jesus, the Living Word.

Martha, Mary and Lazarus were put to the test for the "glory of God." God was going to use this situation to testify of Jesus' resurrecting power. In like manner, our faith will be tested to teach us to listen to His Word and heed His voice so others will see the glory and power of God in our lives. In this miracle, Jesus not only manifests His power to bring those who are dead back to life, He also manifested His love.

Martha and Mary represent the Bride of Christ. Martha was the one who served and Mary was the one who adored Yeshua/Jesus and listened to His Word. Lazarus represents the remnant of Jews who are saved through Yeshua/Jesus. All together Mary, Martha and Lazarus represent the full Body of Christ *(Israel)*.

Long before the Law was given to Moses at Mount Sinai, the third day had spiritual significance. Jacob's debt was paid and he was set free from his father-in-law Laban on the third day. **(Genesis 31:22)**

The third day was also important in the days of Moses. In **Leviticus 7:17**, the flesh of the peace offering had to be burned with fire on the third day. God told Moses in **Exodus 19:10-12** to tell the people to **Go to the people and consecrate them today and tomorrow** *(2 days)*. **Have them wash their clothes and be ready by the third day, because on that day the Lord will come down on Mount Sinai in the sight of all people. Put limits for the** people around the mountain and tell them, **"Be careful that you do not go up the mountain or touch the foot of it. Whoever touches the mountain shall surely be put to death."** God is saying the same thing here to Moses and the people as He said to Joshua. God's people must set themselves apart for God for two days. They must cleanse themselves to be ready for the third day because God's glory will come down on Mount Sinai on that day. They are not to get too close to the mountain or to go up on it or they will be put to death. The place of God's presence is Holy. Nothing unclean can touch it or death will come.

The rite for touching a dead body in **Numbers 19:11-12** says that if a person touches a dead body, he shall be considered unclean for seven days. **"He shall purify himself with the water on the third day and on the seventh day, then he shall be clean."** This is the third day cleansing again. On the 7th day, the day of the Lord, we will be perfected.

The third day was important in the life of David. It was on the third day that David was informed that Saul was dead. **(2 Samuel 1:2)** Saul was the unholy king. Saul represents Satan. Satan began as Lucifer, an anointed cherub in the throne room of God. Saul also started out anointed and good, but then fell into pride and rebellion like Lucifer. God created Lucifer, but Lucifer created Satan!

David, God's mighty King and Warrior, was anointed three times. This represents the triune God who lives within the hearts of all who follow Jesus. With Jesus as our Commander, we will be more than conquerors over the flesh, the world and the devil.

Like David, Elijah prophesied God's victory at Mount Carmel against the prophets of Baal. He spoke it and it was so. Elijah told the people to pour water around the trench of the altar three times. The altar and trench were soaked in water representing the Word of God and His Holy Spirit. Then the fire of the Lord came down and consumed the burnt offering, the wood, stones and the dust and licked up the water. It was an acceptable sacrifice to God. Then Elijah and the people seized the prophets of Baal and killed them giving Elijah victory over the enemies of God.

All of these pointed to Jesus who was raised in resurrection power on the third day. **(Luke 9:22;Luke 13:32 ......"and the**

third day I shall be perfected.")

Jesus illustrated the need for cleansing when He washed His disciples' feet. In the days of Jesus, the people wore sandals so their feet were dusty and dirty. A host would provide a basin of water so his guests could wash and be refreshed. To place our feet into the basin of Jesus means that we are placing the dirt and filth of our sins into His hands for cleansing. We cannot cleanse ourselves. Jesus said, **"If I do not wash you, you have no part in Me." John 13:8**

Joshua and the people are to cross the Jordan River at flood stage on the third day to possess the land God is giving them as their inheritance. The river was wide and deep and the enemies were fierce and strong on the other side, but the Israelites have been prepared, cleansed and unified for the battle. There were blessings on the other side of the Jordan also. The land was also full of milk and honey. Milk represents the pure Word of God **(see 1 Peter 2:2)** and honey represents its sweetness in our mouth and in our hearts. **Psalm 19:10** shows us that honey is figurative of God's Word; God's blessing in **Exodus 3:8, 17** and wisdom in **Proverbs 24:13-14.** The prophet Isaiah says in **7:15** that Jesus will eat **"curds (made from milk) and honey, that He may know to refuse the evil and choose the good."** Curd is the protein rich part of coagulated milk. As the Word of God, Jesus is the richest and sweetest part. He is the one who coagulates all others together.

There is much unoccupied land in the Word of God because people don't put the time and energy into studying it. We show Christ we love Him not only through faith and obedience, but also in studying His Word so we **"may know Him and the power of His resurrection, and the fellowship of His sufferings, being conformed to His death." Philippians 3:10** It is the pure Anointed Word of God in our mouths, our hearts and our actions and our leading a crucified life that will bring us across the Jordan, defeat the enemy and conquer the land.

Moses couldn't enter the Promised Land because he represented the Law, which he broke in his disobedience at Meribah. **(Numbers 20:7-13**) Because Moses broke the Law, he fell under its condemnation and penalty. The Law gives us a Divine standard of holiness, but it can't help us attain that standard. Only the power of Christ's blood, Holy Spirit and Word can do this. Without these, we can view the land but never enter it. Canaan is a type and shadow of the land of rest, peace and abundance of life we have in Jesus Christ. Moses the lawgiver could not bring rest and peace. Moses could not plant the Spirit of obedience in God's people. Only Jesus (Yeshua) the True Joshua could. And, only the True Joshua (Jesus) could bring rest and peace in the hearts of His followers. Joshua could offer God's people an earthly rest, but Jesus gives us eternal rest. **Indeed, was it not all who came out of Egypt, led by Moses? Now with whom was He angry forty years? Was it not with those who sinned, whose corpses fell in the wilderness? And to whom did He swear that they would not enter His rest, but to those who did not obey? So we see that they could not enter in because of their unbelief. Hebrews 3:16-19** Because of their sin, they forfeited their rest. There is no rest in sin. **Therefore, since a promise remains of entering His rest, let us fear lest any of you seem to have come short of it. For indeed the gospel was preached to us as well as to them; but the word which they heard did not profit them, not being mixed with faith in those who heard it. For we who have believed do enter that rest, as He has said: "So I swore in My wrath, they shall not enter My rest," although the works were finished from the foundation of the world. For He has spoken in a certain place of the seventh day in this way: "And God rested on the seventh day from all His works"**..............God's rest on the 7th day of creation was not because He was weary and in need of rest because God is all powerful and without end. It was rest based on His finished work. When Jesus gave up His spirit on the cross, He said, **"It is finished."** His was a finished work. It need not be repeated. Jesus accomplished all that He had to accomplish on the cross. Faith in Jesus and His finished work brings all who love and believe in Him rest and peace. We rest upon His finished work. The work of redemption will be completely finished on the Lord's Day in Revelation with eternal rest and peace. The seventh day of rest in Genesis represented the perfect creation sanctified and at rest. The 7th Day of the Lord in Revelation will restore creation back to its original condition in Genesis. All will live in the presence of God in peace and harmony forever. **For if Joshua had given them rest, then He would not afterward have spoken of another day. There remains therefore a rest for the people of God. For he who has entered His rest has himself also ceased from his works as God did from His. Let us therefore be diligent to enter that rest, lest anyone fall according to the same example of disobedience. Hebrews 4:8-11** True rest did not come through Moses or Joshua but through Christ. We rest in His finished work, not in our works. Jesus is the last Word. Those who love Jesus are to examine their condition. The Word shows us our condition because it **pierces even to the division of soul and spirit......And there is no creature hidden from His sight, but all things are naked and open to the eyes of Him to whom we must give account. Hebrews 4:12-13** We are accountable to the written Word of God whose Author is the Living Word Jesus. God must conquer the sin in our hearts in order for Him to inherit the land of our hearts completely.

With Jesus as our Commander, His Word as our guide and His Spirit of power we will take possession of the land for Christ. In Christ, God made a way for us to pass through the center on dry ground. Jesus is the Word, the Way and the Center through which we must pass from spiritual death to spiritual life.

Joshua is now 85 years old yet God tells him, **"Take possession of the land the Lord your God is giving you for your own." Joshua 1:11** Eight is the number of a "new beginning" and five is the number of "grace." The Israelites *(God's people)* under the leadership of Joshua *(Yeshua/Jesus)* are embarking on a new beginning in a new territory by God's grace.

Unity of Purpose – Joshua 1:12-18

If the land is to be conquered and possessed, all Israel must be unified to fight against the occupants of the land of promise. No one can go his own way. The Reubenites, Gadites and one-half tribe of Manasseh asked Moses to give them a portion of land on the east side of the Jordan. They chose an "easy" inheritance outside of Israel, the land God promised Abraham. All too often believers get comfortable where they are and want to stop and take their inheritance outside of the fullness of God's blessing. They don't want to take the next leap of faith and obedience to bring them into the fullness of their inheritance in Christ. These 2 ½ tribes really didn't want to go and fight with their brothers, but God said that they must in order to get their chosen inheritance on the east side of the Jordan. They must fight in unity with their brother Israelites until the Promised Land is fully conquered. Then they can return to their wives and families who had to remain on the east side of the Jordan during the warfare. Victory can only come through unity. The Apostle Paul gave an individual sevenfold walk of unity to the Church at Ephesus, followed by a sevenfold walk of unity for Christ's Body. **(Ephesians 4:1-6)** As individual believers in Jesus, we are to:

1. **walk worthy of the calling with which you were called**
2. **with all lowliness** *(humility)*
3. **and gentleness**
4. **with longsuffering**
5. **bearing with one another in love**
6. **endeavoring to keep the unity of the Spirit**
7. **in the bond of peace.**

As to the Body of Christ:

1. **There is one Body**
2. **one Spirit**
3. **one hope of your calling**
4. **one Lord**
5. **one faith**
6. **one baptism**
7. **one God and Father of all, who is above all, and through all, and in you all.**

God is a God of harmony and agreement. The triune nature of God works in perfect unity, harmony and agreement. The two testaments of the Word also walk in unity and agreement. **(see Amos 3:3)** Therefore, God's people are to walk and work in the same way.

These two and a half tribes had fertile land, had gained herds (wealth), and had gained many descendants on the east side of the Jordan. They did not want to give these material gains up to cross over the Jordan. They had one foot in the world and one foot in God. Like these 2 ½ tribes, Lot also had gathered much wealth. Instead of choosing the high places, Lot chose the plain (low place) of Jordan near Sodom. **(Genesis 13:10-11)** Lot's choice was the easy one. But Abram chose the way of sacrifice, hard work, peace and grace. Abram went up for the higher, deeper life. The land that Abram saw was a far larger and richer blessing than his natural eyes could see. But Lot walked by sight. Lot's choice of the land was well watered and fertile. He could gain more wealth there. Lot wouldn't have to dig wells, as Abraham would have to do to obtain water in the high places of Canaan. Grace and hard work go hand in hand. It is those who are willing to study and dig into God's Word and are willing to lay down their lives in service to God who will be taken to the higher places and will unearth the deep springs of water buried within the Word. The fullness of the blessing in Christ is also larger, richer and deeper than most see. Jesus has a special inheritance chosen specifically for each one of us as His gift to each of His children. However, He must prepare us to receive the blessing. Everyday of the wilderness wandering of the Israelites was a lesson. God was taking away something of their flesh and adding more of His Spirit and ways. Though the land looked beyond the reach of the Israelites across the Jordan, with God all things are possible. It is the eyes of faith that see the fullness of the blessing of God in Christ Jesus.

Lot "**looked up and saw the plain of Jordan.**" Lot walked by sight, not by faith. He also walked in self-will. He didn't seek the Lord's counsel as to where He would have him settle. Instead, Lot walked toward an unclean world and then eventually dwelt in it. **2 Peter 2:7-8** says that Lot was a **"righteous man,"** who was tormented day by day by the wicked deeds of the inhabitants of Sodom but he preferred to stay there and become wealthier rather than take a stand against evil. Lot compromised his convictions for wealth. Lot's life ended in shame because of his incestuous relationships with his daughters. Instead of wealth, Lot ended up living in a cave, destitute, drunk and without sense. **The devil comes to steal,**

kill and destroy. Lot represents carnal Christians. Lot's life was full of compromise and wrong choices, which he paid for dearly.

Lot and Abram had to separate because of strife and jealousy between their herdsmen. **(Genesis 13:7)** Carnal Christians bicker and fight over ministries, doctrine, music, and each other. Paul called the brethren at Corinth "carnal" because of their divisions and strife. **(1 Corinthians 3:1-3)** Carnal Christians pray, go to church, help others and believe but they don't want to dedicate their whole heart, mind and soul to God in His service without compromise. It's not enough that we just open our eyes and see the land, or just to hear the Word, we must let it take root in our hearts and then live it. Instead of fighting, Abram was a peacemaker and offered Lot the first choice of land. **"Blessed are the peacemakers for they shall be called sons of God." Matthew 5:9** Abram was willing to take whatever land God would give him. Abram walked by faith in God.

It wasn't long after Lot settled near Sodom that Abram had to rescue him from the hands of the enemy. There was a war in the land, and Lot was taken into captivity. **(Genesis 14:1-12)** Even though Lot was greedy and had chosen the wrong way, Abram went with his **"trained servants"** to rescue his nephew. **(Genesis 14:14)** This is the attitude followers of Jesus must have toward a weaker brother or sister who has fallen into sin. Many Christians condemn and judge a brother or sister who have fallen but God says we are to fight the enemy for our brother or sister and rescue him. Then we are to bring him or her back into a right relationship with God. **Genesis 14:14-15a** says that he took trained servants who were born in his own house to save Lot and set him free. Untrained servants who are out of the house of God will not be successful in spiritual warfare. Those who are faithful and matured in their walk with God will be the victors. Abraham was willing to lay down his life for his nephew. Jesus tells us that we are to lay down our lives for others. **(John 15:13)**

Though Lot was saved from God's judgment at Sodom, his life was eventually destroyed and empty. Because Lot was so close to the "world" (Sodom), he was easily tricked by his daughters who fed him too much wine and then had intercourse with him. He is the father of the Moabites and the Ammonites through his daughters.

The Moabites were responsible for the most carnal seduction in Israel's history. **(see Numbers 25)** The Ammonites were responsible for human sacrifice to Molech **(see Leviticus 18:21).** As we can see, the sins of the father are visited down upon generations. Lot not only lost everything because of his worldliness, he also caused God's people much pain because the Ammonites and the Moabites were enemies of the Israelites. Our sins have an effect on others. The scriptures say that the Ammonites were cruel **(Amos 1:13),** prideful **(Zephaniah 2:9-10),** callous **(Ezekiel 25:3-6)** and idolatrous **(1 Kings 11:7).** The Word says that the Moabites were equally as bad. They were idolatrous **(1 Kings 11:7),** wealthy **(Jeremiah 48: 1,7),** superstitious **(Jeremiah 27:3,9),** satisfied **(Jeremiah 48:11)** and proud **(Jeremiah 48:29).**

Lot was a backslidden believer. Lot could have received the same blessings and legacy that Abram did. It was available to him. Instead, he made the wrong choice of walking too close to the world and it cost him the fullness of the blessings of God. Abram, on the other hand, received a land, seed and blessing. We must count the cost and choose to follow Christ. We must choose to put Him in the center of our life or we will, like Lot, slip further and further away from the fullness of the blessing that is our in Christ Jesus. Like Abram, we must be willing to leave all behind and go to a land that we do not know (new territory) by faith and obedience to God.

These 2 ½ tribes of the Israelites also made the choice to live close to the world. It too cost them. They failed to realize that there were enemies in that land also and because they were outside of the will of God for them, the Reubenites were eventually enslaved by Assyria **(2 Kings 15:29).** The half tribe of Manasseh was unfaithful to God and prostituted themselves to the gods of the people of the land. **(2 Chronicles 31:1)**

Though the half tribe of Manasseh was fewer in number, they had the largest territory on the east side of the Jordan. Manasseh was the firstborn son of Joseph and his Egyptian (Gentile) wife who didn't receive the blessing of the firstborn. Instead it was given to Ephraim, the second born. We can see why God chose Ephraim over Manasseh. The tribe of Manasseh was divided even on the land they would settle in. One half of the tribe settled on the east side of the Jordan and the other in Israel.

These two and a half tribes had found their rest outside of the land of Israel, but now they must fight with their brothers so they too can have rest in the land God promised them. If the other tribes were to suffer defeat, these two and one half tribes would also be subject to attack and defeat. Unity is strength and will bring the victory and rest to all. This speaks of Jesus' army of Christians who must do spiritual warfare against the enemy of all who don't know Him. We must help the weaker person to win the victory over the sin in their lives that has them bound. We are all Israel who believe in Jesus Christ. Israel means "one who strives with God." Those who have received the Son of Promise are those who strive with God for His spiritual kingdom. There is only one tree with two branches (Jew and Gentile) and Jesus is the root. Both Ephraim (Gentile) and Judah (Jew) are grafted into this tree because they have all disobeyed God. But Jesus, the root of the tree, restores them all, grafting them in again. **(see Romans 11:11-32)** Therefore, neither human, nor the nation of Israel nor Christ's Church can take any of the glory that belongs to Christ alone. We are all sinners and deserve God's judgment. But because of His great love for the crown of His creation, mankind, God sent Yeshua/Jesus to earth to redeem God's children back to Him. All – both Jew and Gentile— need to lay down their pride and biases and let Jesus be God and receive all of the glory and honor and power.

1 Chronicles 5:18 shows us that the sons of Reuben, the Gadites and the half tribe of Manasseh were skillful in war. So Joshua tells them that they must go before the others armed for battle. No doubt all of the tribes of Israel had remembered the suffering in the wilderness caused by their disobedience. They have learned the value of obedience and unity, so they agree to do whatever Joshua commands. Joshua tells the Reubenites, Gadites and half tribe of Manasseh that **all their fighting men, fully armed, must cross over ahead of your brothers. You are to help your brothers until the Lord gives them rest, as he has done for you, and until they too have taken possession of the land that the Lord your God is giving them. After that, you may go back and occupy your own land, which Moses the servant of the Lord**

gave you east of the Jordan toward the sunrise. Joshua 1:13-15
They are willing to follow Joshua and obey all of the commands of
the Lord. They even encouraged Joshua to be strong and courageous and asked the Lord to be with him as He was with Moses.
They told Joshua they would put to death anyone who rebelled
against his leadership. Sin brings death!

Joshua has his army in place and the people cleansed, prepared
and unified. God organized the Israelites just as He organizes His
Church. God sends each person into the Church for the leaders to use
and develop their talent. If there is no organization, and the leader
overlooks anyone, the Body will be weakened. In order for God's
army to be effective, every person must be in his or her place using
his or her God-given gifts and moving under the commands of their
Pastor for the common good of all. Without God's order consolidated
in strength and unity, the power is broken and paralyzed. Unity is
power! The enemy knows this which is why he is always trying to
cause jealousy and division in Christ's Body. No power in hell can
stand against a church led by a Godly Pastor and marching in unity,
faith and obedience and living for the common good of all.

Joshua has set up the chains of command and all Israel agree to
do whatever he says, **"only the Lord your God be with you, as He
was with Moses. 1:17** In other words, they were agreeing to obey
as long as Joshua was in the Lord's will as Moses was. Moses was a
loving, humble yet disciplining, persevering, forgiving, long-suffering servant of God who obeyed God's Word. He even told God that
he was willing to be blotted out of the Book of Life if God would
not destroy His people because of their sin. He also graciously
accepted his fate of not being able to enter the Promised Land
because of his one act of disobedience to God. Moses was truly a
servant of God and a great leader of His people. It is important for
believers to understand that we are not to follow an unholy leader in
Christ's Body. We must be sure that the Lord is leading him according to His Word.

Joshua sends two witnesses (spies) to the Promised Land

Joshua has the assurance of obedience and unity. Joshua has

raised up "giant killers" because he had the faith to be a "giant killer." Now he will spy out the land. To the enemy, these two were seen as "spies." But to Rahab, the Gentile prostitute, they were "witnesses" of Israel's God of saving grace and power.

Joshua had been one of twelve spies 40 years previous who had spied out the Promised Land. Only Joshua and Caleb returned to Moses with faith that they would be able to conquer the giants of the land with the power of God on their side. God has sent Jesus and the Holy Spirit as well as the two testaments of His Word as witnesses of His grace and power in the land today.

Joshua and Caleb, the two faithful witnesses, represent the Bride of Christ made up of faithful Jews and Gentiles. Joshua was an Ephraimite whose father was a Jew and mother a Gentile *(Jew/Gentile)*. Joseph, the father of Ephraim and Manasseh, lost his Jewish identity in Egypt. He was given an Egyptian *(Gentile)* name and an Egyptian wife who birthed his two sons. The Egyptian Pharaoh gave Joseph the name Zaphnath-Panneah which means "the revealer of secrets or the abundance of the life." Joseph had two identities. He was born a Jew but became a ruler in the gentile land of Egypt *(representing the world)* with a new name. Jesus came into the world with His earthly name. He also has a heavenly name known only to Himself. **"He has a name written on Him that no one knows but He Himself." Revelation 19:12** Eventually Joseph was reunited with his Jewish family and his Jewish identity. In like manner, the Church of Jesus Christ also lost its Jewish identity. Judaism is the foundation of Christianity. In order to fully understand the New Testament scriptures, we must understand the Jewishness of the Old Testament. Like Joseph in Egypt, God will bring Christ's Body back to its Jewish foundation and identity.

Caleb was a Gentile who crossed over the Red Sea with the Israelites and joined the tribe of Judah *(Gentile/Jew)*. Joshua and Caleb represent the two houses in **Ezekiel 37:15-20** that must become one "Israel" before Christ comes again to renew the earth. Israel means "one who strives with God." There is an earthly nation of Israel which points to the spiritual nation Israel of Jewish and Gentile believers in Yeshua/Jesus. This will take place completely in Revelation. Jesus will reveal Himself to 144,000 pure Jewish men whom God has set apart for this purpose. These converted Jewish men will evangelize the earth to Jesus Christ during the tribulation. God began with Gentiles and Jews and He will end with Gentiles and Jews. The Word of God goes full circle.

God's Word speaks in three tenses: past, present and future. The events of Revelation are in the future. Believers, both Jew and Gentile, should be presently uniting right now on earth as one house under the Son. Every believer is either of the house of Judah (Jew) or the house of Ephraim (Gentile). These two houses become one house under the headship of Jesus Christ. Bloodline does not guarantee you a place in Israel. Only faith in the True God and the blood of Jesus Christ does. Abram was a Gentile idolater when God called him out of Ur of Chaldee (Babylon) to go to a land he did not know. God's selection of Abram had nothing to do with his bloodline. Abram was called because of His faith in the True God. He was willing to go because He believed God was true to His Word. God is calling His people Israel to come to His saving grace through His Son Jesus Christ.

Caleb was the son of Jephunneh a Kenizzite, which was a Canaanite tribe. **(Genesis 15:19)** Caleb, a Gentile, identified with God's people and became a Jew in the tribe of Judah. Jesus came to earth through a Jewish woman. By identifying with Christ, Gentile believers identify with the Jew also. God requires that **"every word be established by two or three witnesses." Dt. 19:15** A matter is established through the mouth of two or three witnesses. God established His redemption of mankind through His Son Jesus Christ through the three witnesses of the three sections of the Word of God. The two testaments of the Word of God point to the third section of Revelation where we see the throne room of God in all of its glory. The first testament prepared the way for the second testament that prepared the way for Revelation.

Joshua and Caleb established the witness of God's ability to defeat the enemies of the Promised Land and conquer it forty years hence. Caleb along with Joshua also wandered in the wilderness for 40 years in selfless service to Moses and God's people. Three times in **Joshua 14:8,9** and **14** it says that Caleb followed the Lord **"wholly and fully."** Caleb was wholly abandoned to the will of God. He knew the mind of the Lord and fulfilled all that the Lord required. The Bible says that Caleb had a **"different spirit."** Caleb had unfaltering and strong faith. To follow God faithfully, wholly and fully means that we may have to walk over many a thorny road in a land full of giants. But, God is mightier than all of our foes and He will give us the victory. Caleb because of his faithfulness inherited the choicest piece of the Promised Land – Hebron. Hebron is one of the most interesting and beautiful places in Palestine. It is a highly elevated place overlooking a wide area of country. Hebron was not only beautiful; it was full of fruit. Hebron represents the mature Christian who radiates the beauty and grace of Christ and is full of the fruit of the Spirit. Hebron was originally called Kirjatharba, which means "city of the strength of Baal," but God turned it into Hebron, which means "friendship" or "fellowship." God can take a heart that is controlled by the devil and transform him into a "friend of God." Arba *(representing the flesh)* must die before Hebron can be won. Self-will must be slain before love can reign in the land of our hearts. Then we will bear much fruit for Christ's kingdom. Hebron is the choicest spot in the land of promise, but it is also the hardest won victory. Pride and self-will do not die easily.

Although Caleb has been faithful, obedient and courageous throughout the wandering in the wilderness, his fight of faith is not over yet. He must conquer the giant inhabitants of Hebron. The giants were the largest in this portion of the land, but Caleb had giant faith in God to defeat these giants so he could have his inheritance fully. It is the mature in the faith who can take on the biggest giants and be victorious. The mature, steadfast faith of Joshua and Caleb is the faith that Jesus is calling His Bride to so they can gain the fullness of their inheritance in Him and bring others to Him. Caleb was tried, tested and found faithful. Caleb would not take anything less than all God had for him. Now, He will receive His reward – God's highest and best —- a Christ-like love, peace and joy in the Promised Land. The "best" is when you go from the friend of Christ to the Bride of Christ. **"And it shall be, in that day,"** says the Lord, **"that you will call me 'My Husband,' and no longer call Me 'My Master'."** This is a deeper union than the Master and the servant. As the Bride, we are wedded to Him heart to heart in such intimacy that we will never leave Him.

We must be aware that at every stage of our growth, the devil will try to stop our advance. When the devil starts growling at you the loudest, you can be sure that there is a Hebron *(a choice piece of the land that God wants you to conquer for Him)* just around the corner.

It is when we obey God that we please God. **John 14 says three times: "Whoever has my commands and obeys them, he is the one who loves me. He who loves me will be loved by My Father, and I too will love him and show Myself to him."** This is the special love of Jesus and the Father for the obedient, faithful heart. Jesus' disciples were so pierced by this statement that they asked Him again about it, so He repeated the same promise except in stronger language. Many of His disciples walked away from Him at this point because this was such a hard teaching. Jesus even looked at His twelve apostles and asked if they were going to leave Him too.

God's grace saves the sinner, but there is a deeper, richer grace that sanctifies and fills us with all the fullness of God. Grace is humble. The lower it goes, the more it can ask and receive. This grace can also rise, as our Lord Jesus Christ did, from the depth of humiliation into the highest place of glory. The depth of our humility, obedience and faith in Jesus determines the extent to which we as individual believers will rise.

Rahab and the inhabitants of Jericho had been given a period of grace before God's judgment would come. Forty years had passed since the deliverance of the Israelites across the Red Sea. Forty is the number of probation and testing. The Israelites too had been under God's disciplining and testing hand for forty years in the wilderness. Only Joshua and Caleb would cross over the Jordan from their generation. Why? Because the fear, unbelief, grumbling and complaining of the others would have brought discouragement and defeat. They would have thought it impossible for the people to cross over the Jordan at flood stage. Their unbelief brought them death. God had to remove them. **"Without faith it is impossible to please God."** But God has raised up a generation full of faith and willingness to obey their leader Joshua. It is these who will conquer the land of promise and defeat the enemies of God's people. The rest of the Israelites perished before reaching the Promised Land because of their unfaithfulness and disobedience to God. But Joshua and Caleb had the honor of crossing over the Jordan to the Promised Land because of their faith and loyalty to God and His people. Moses sent twelve spies but 10 came back with a report full of fear. However, two – Joshua and Caleb — came back with a report full of faith. This pointed forward to the division of the tribes of Israel during the time of Solomon's reign. (**1 Kings 12:17-21**)

The 10 and 2 represent the 10 northern tribes who split from the two tribes of Judah and Benjamin, which eventually became one tribe. Judah means "praise" and Benjamin means "son of the right hand." These two will bring all to unity and into the presence of God. The tribe of Judah and Benjamin pointed to the uniting of the Jew and Gentile in Christ's Body. It is the united Church (Israel) that must seek the lost to bring them into salvation in Jesus and unity of the brethren once again. Jesus said He came for the lost tribes of Israel. (**Matthew 15:24**) These are the 10 tribes that were scattered throughout the nations. They have intermarried until their Jewish roots are indistinguishable. Ephraim represents these "lost sheep." All of humanity is descendants of Noah *(Gentile)*, Abraham, Isaac and Jacob *(Jews)*, either through the good seed or the evil seed. Abraham and Jacob had both Jewish and Gentile wives. Isaac, the Promised Son, was the only patriarch to have one wife from his father's house. Isaac pointed to Jesus, the True Promised Son, who will only have one wife – His Bride made up of saved Jews and Gentiles who love Him.

Joshua will only send two spies into the land of Canaan (Israel) to check out the situation. Jesus and the Holy Spirit came to earth to witness of the Father's love and grace. These two spies prefigure the witness of Jesus and the Holy Spirit and also the two witnesses in Revelation who come to the land of Israel to witness of Christ in power and with many signs and miracles just before the full judgment of God is spilled over the earth. (**see Revelation 11:1-14**) These two witnesses in Revelation will testify of Christ before mighty kings and rulers at a time when great wickedness surrounds them like the time of Jericho's fall. Because of the deception and apostasy that exists in the earth, these two witnesses will be hated by multitudes. These two mighty witnesses will be killed in

Jerusalem and their bodies will be left in the street for three days. Their dead bodies will be abused for the entire world to see. After 3 ½ days, they will be resurrected to eternal life and the entire world will be watching.

Just as Jesus/Yeshua sends His followers out two by two as His witnesses, Joshua sends these two spies to Canaan (Israel). These two Israelite spies witness to Rahab, a vile Gentile prostitute, and save all who are in her house just before God's wrath is to be poured out on Jericho. God sends the two powerful witnesses of Revelation to witness to the Harlot Church and the world just before His full wrath is poured out over the earth. Since God's Word speaks on many levels, these two witnesses could be the end time Bride of Christ made up of Jews and Gentiles who operate in the resurrection power of Jesus and His Holy Spirit. John the Baptist who was a Jew came in the spirit and power of Elijah to prepare the way of the Lord by preaching repentance and baptism (cleansing). In like manner, these two witnesses in Revelation will also come in the power of Elijah and Moses to prepare the way of Christ's return.

Jericho is a picture of the condemned world today that refuses God's saving grace through Jesus Christ. Jericho was the first stronghold to be captured. The city of Jericho represents pride. God must break our pride first before He can shape and mold us into the image of His Son. The breaking of our pride (Jericho) is the gateway to the fullness of the land of blessing, which is ours in Christ. God gives grace to the humble. Jericho is well fortified as pride always is and its inhabitants were giants. Pride is the root of all sin.

The two spies also represent the two witnesses (*testaments*) of the Word of God that will bring people to salvation through Jesus Christ. The Anointed Word scans the earth drawing people to new life in Christ. When the Word is mixed with the oil of God's Holy Spirit, it has resurrection power, which will bring people from spiritual death to spiritual life through the mouths of His Jewish and Gentile believers in His Son. **(see Zechariah 4:11)**

Rahab the prostitute is a picture of a sinner saved by faith and grace. Though she is a vile sinner, she believed in Israel's God and was saved. There is no sin that God won't forgive if we come to him in confession, repentance and humility.

CHAPTER 3

Rahab, A Gentile Sinner Saved by Grace

Joshua 2:1-24; Joshua 6:17-25; Hebrews 11:31; Matthew 1:5

The story of Rahab shows that salvation was extended to the Gentiles. Rahab was saved and became a member of Israel. The covenant Rahab made with the two Jewish spies showed that God's covenant to Israel is extended to the Gentiles. It was the "scarlet cord" that sealed the covenant so Rahab could enter into "Israel." All who wed the Jewish Messiah Yeshua/Jesus enter into "Israel," through the scarlet cord of His blood.

God in His sovereignty led the two Jewish spies to Rahab the Gentile prostitute's house. God knew her heart and knew that Rahab was the only one in the city of Jericho who heard about His powerful deliverance of the Israelites across the Red Sea, and believed in Him. The Israelites had seen God's deliverance at the Red Sea first-hand, but Rahab heard and believed in the power of God without sight. Jesus said in **John 20:29, " Because you have seen me, you have believed; blessed are those who have not seen and yet have believed."** Rahab believed in blind faith! She was a sinner under condemnation. God had condemned Jericho and all within. However, God always warns His own before the judgment takes place. The two Israelite spies gave her warning of God's impending judgment. Rahab's faith put to work would save her.

Rahab's house was on the wall of the city so it would be a good place from which to escape if needed. She was also a prostitute so there must have been an influx of men coming in and out of her house so the two spies might just blend right in and go unnoticed. Unfortunately, however, **someone told the king of Jericho that some of the Israelites had come into the city to spy out the land. So the king of Jericho sent this message to Rahab: "Bring out the men who came to you and entered your house, because they have come to spy out the whole land." Joshua 2:2-3** Jericho and its king represent Satan and the world who are in rebellion against God and His people. Time was running out for Jericho and its inhabitants, including Rahab. God's judgment was coming soon just as our world is full of sin and facing eternal judgment. God gave Rahab a chance to be saved. The king of Jericho saw the two men as spies, but Rahab saw them as messengers even though their message was one of judgment. Rahab feared the power of Israel's God. **The fear of God is the beginning of wisdom.** Rahab could have turned these two Israelites over to the king of Jericho and probably would have received a reward. Instead, because she knew that the True God had sent them, she risks her life to save them.

The two spies also represent the remnant of Israel that believes in Messiah Yeshua and is saved. Rahab represents the Bride of Christ. These two are Christ's representatives on earth. They are His hidden treasure that He will use to draw others into His saving, loving arms. Rahab's house became a place of safety and refuge for her Jewish visitors, just as Christ's Church should be a place of refuge and safety to all those who enter in. Rahab tells a half-truth when the men of Jericho approach her about the two Israelites. She admits that they came to see her, but says she didn't know where they were from. Next she out and out lies! She tells the men of Jericho that the Israelites left at dusk before the city gate was closed. She tells them that if they hurry they might catch up with them. In other words, she sent them in the wrong direction on a wild goose chase! Some would ask why God honored her lie. Keep in mind that Rahab is not yet saved so her flesh and the devil, who is a liar, rule her. God in His sovereignty can even work through the unsaved. Her works in protecting God's people showed God that Rahab was going to obey and be saved. Though still a harlot eventually she would respond to God's Word and His standard of holiness. God's power and Word changed her heart. Rahab, the harlot, became the wife of a Jew and is listed in the genealogy of Christ. Rahab, the harlot, became Rahab the Bride of a Jew!

Rahab put her faith into action. **"Faith without works is dead."** She knew that God had given His people the land and she also understood the power of God to save. The book of James uses Rahab as an example of a person who not only believed in God but also acted upon what she believed. **(James 2:25)** She was prepared to face the wrath of the king of Jericho and its people to protect and hide God's people. She hid the two Jews in the highest place in her house *(roof)* under the stalks of flax that were laid out for drying. Flax would be used to make white linen. White linen is symbolic of purity and righteousness. **(Revelation 3:4-5;6:11;7:13-14;19:8, 14)** Jesus hides us in His heart until He brings us to perfection. In Ezekiel's vision in **40:2-3, God took him to the land of Israel and set him on a very high mountain, on whose southside were some buildings that looked like a city. He took him there, and Ezekiel saw a man whose appearance was like bronze, he was standing in the gateway with a linen cord and a measuring rod in his hand.** This is Jesus whom Ezekiel saw standing in the gateway to the city measuring the temple of God with a rod and a white cord. Followers of Jesus are the Temple of God. Jesus will bring us to purity either by the gentle nudge of His Holy Spirit or by His rod of correction. We must allow His cleansing hand. He will take us to the highest place if we have faith and obey. In Ezekiel's vision, Jesus' appearance was like bronze. Bronze is shiny and reflects light. It is an enduring metal capable of withstanding tremendous heat. Jesus, the Light of the world, withstood the full wrath of God's judgment for each of us on the cross of Calvary. No human could have withstood God's full wrath. Only Jesus, who is God, could. In **Revelation 1:16**, John the Revelator describes Jesus as **"the sun shining in its strength** *(blinding light).* Bronze is used to describe Jesus in Ezekiel because Jesus had not yet completed His atoning work. In Revelation, gold is used to describe the heavenly sanctuary and Jesus. Gold is symbolic of the Divine.

The men of Jericho went in pursuit of the two Israelites on the road that leads to the ford *(shallow crossing)* of the Jordan. As soon as these pursuers went out, the gate to the city of Jericho was shut. The Israelite spies were safe for the night. **Before the spies lay down for the night, she went up on the roof and said to them, "I know that the Lord has given this land to you and that a great fear of you has fallen on us, so that all who live in this country are melting in fear because of you. We have heard how the Lord dried up the water of the Red Sea for you when you came out of Egypt, and what you did to Sihon and Og, the two kings of the Amorites east of the Jordan, whom you completely destroyed. When we heard of it our hearts melted and everyone's courage failed because of you, for the Lord your God is God in heaven above and on the earth below." Joshua 2:10-11** This was exactly the message the Israelites wanted to hear. They were encouraged and assured because the giants of the land feared them and their God. The inhabitants of Jericho had heard of God's power, deliverance and defeat of the enemy at the Red Sea and it put fear in them. The Canaanites understood that if God could part the Red Sea, He could open up the Jordan at flood stage for the Israelites to cross over and surround the city of Jericho and defeat its inhabitants too. Rahab knew that if God's power could save the Israelites from Pharaoh, He had the power to save her too. She confessed her faith by saying **"for the Lord your God is God in heaven above and on the earth below."**

Rahab's act of kindness in hiding the Israelite spies is a shadow of the mercy of God through the covering of the blood of Christ as our righteousness. Rahab's act of kindness now makes her bold to ask for a favor in return. She goes up to the Israelites in darkness to profess her faith in God and ask them to make an oath (covenant) to her that they will show kindness to her family because she has shown kindness to them. **(see Joshua 2:12)** This is the theory of sowing and reaping God established in **Genesis 1:11**. This covenant oath will assure her of her salvation. She asks that they swear to the Lord that they would spare the lives of her family and all who belong to them after the Lord had given them the land. An oath spoken before God must not be broken. The two Israelites made an oath saying, **"Our lives for your lives! If you don't tell what we are doing, we will treat you kindly and faithfully when the Lord gives us the land."v13** This is an oath of covenant love witnessed by God. Jesus gave His life for ours. He must possess the land of our hearts and remove any obstacles.

Rahab asked them for a **"sure sign"** that they would do this. The men told her that their oath that she made them swear to before God will not be binding on them unless Rahab ties **"this scarlet cord in the window through which she let them down, and unless you have brought your father and mother, your brothers and all your family into your house. If anyone goes outside your house into the street, his blood will be on his own head; we will not be responsible. As for anyone who is in the house with you, his blood will be on our head if a hand is laid upon him. But if you tell what we are doing, we will be released from the oath you made us swear."** Notice that the Jews gave the scarlet cord to Rahab, the Gentile, not the reverse. The scarlet cord represents the atoning blood of the Jewish Messiah, Jesus Christ.

Rahab must do three things:

1. She must tie the scarlet cord in the window of her house to identify her as a believer in Israel's God. This scarlet thread also identified the way of escape.
2. She must bring her family and all who want to be saved into her house, and they must remain there. This is the same requirement that God gave Moses regarding the Passover just before they were leaving to cross over the Red Sea.
3. She must not reveal the plans of God's people to anyone.

Rahab agreed. Only Rahab could break the oath. The Israelites were bound to it because it was spoken in the hearing of God. In like manner, Jesus will never break His covenant oath of love and salvation because, as God, He is bound to it. However, believers can walk away from it. The oath between Rahab and God's people would be broken if she revealed their plans to the enemy or if she and all who wished to be saved did not remain in her house during the attack. If anyone left her house and was killed, the guilt would be theirs not God's people. Rahab's house was built in a "rock" wall. Christians must come to the sure foundation of the Rock, Christ, and then remain in God's House for safety.

The scarlet cord would mark the same window from which the Israelites escaped as the way of escape for Rahab and all in her house also. This is the Jew *(two spies)* and Gentile *(Rahab)* who will be saved by the scarlet cord of Christ's atoning blood. The scarlet cord represents the atoning blood of Jesus Christ. The scarlet cord that Rahab hung in obedience to the Jewish spies was her saving grace. It identified her as a believer and moved her from condemnation to salvation and justification. Rahab's scarlet cord was a sign of her faith and trust in God and His Word through His messengers. Rahab was saved by faith **(Hebrews 11:31)** and identified with God's people. This scarlet cord of Christ's atoning blood is woven throughout the Word of God. God's Word is an embroidered work making it one work without divisions. Just as the Father, Son and Holy Spirit are one and work in perfect agreement, so too the Word of God is in three sections but is one work with the atoning blood of Jesus woven throughout. Some examples where the scarlet thread is used in scripture are:

1. The high priest's robe was an embroidered work of five threads, one of which is scarlet representing the atoning blood of our Great High Priest Jesus. The other threads were blue representing His heavenly origin; white representing Christ's purity; gold representing Christ's divinity and purple representing Christ's royalty as King of kings and Lord of lords. **Exodus 29:5**

2. The scarlet thread was also in the embroidered curtains on the inner walls of the Most Holy Place in the tabernacle Moses built in the wilderness according to God's Word. The veil that was the entrance into the Most Holy Place had the other four threads with angels of gold embroidered in it also. The other four threads (gold, blue, white and purple) were also used in the curtains of the inner sanctuary of the Most Holy Place. **(Exodus 36:8)** However, only four of them were used in the

gate into the inner court and the door into the Holy Place. No gold thread was used because it represents Divinity and God's Divine presence. God's Divine presence was in the Most Holy Place. The angels in the veil before the Most Holy Place of God's presence represent the seraphim (angels) who guard the golden throne of God's presence in the heavenly sanctuary.

3. In **Proverbs 31:21** which is about the Godly woman and represents the Bride of Christ, it says, **"When it snows, she has no fear for her household; for all of them are clothed in scarlet."** In other words, when the storms come, she has no fear because all of her household is covered with the atoning blood of Jesus and He will protect them.

4. In **Leviticus 14:4,** the Lord instructs Moses to **take two live clean birds and some cedar wood, scarlet yarn and hyssop** to cleanse a diseased person. The cedar wood represents the cross of Christ; the scarlet thread represents His atoning blood and the hyssop represents the cleansing of His Word by His Spirit. In **Psalm 51:7,** hyssop is typical of spiritual cleansing. **Purge me with hyssop and I shall be clean.**

5. In the same chapter of **Leviticus, verse 49,** these same three things are to be used to cleanse a house of mildew. Mildew also represents sin and stagnation.

6. In **Numbers 4:7-8,** the Lord told Moses and Aaron to first spread a blue cloth over the table of Presence, place the utensils on the table and then spread a scarlet cloth over them. Blue is the heavenly color representing God's heavenly glory and home. The red cloth represents the atoning blood of Christ that covers all those who receive it.

7. In **Genesis 38:28-30,** the scarlet thread identified Jacob as the one who would receive the blessing of the father. Jacob was the second born, not the first. This, too, points to the blood of Jesus Christ that brings us to right relationship with the Father and thus His blessing in the second covenant.

8. In **Nahum 2:3,** the soldiers of the Lord are red (*human from the root word for Adam, adami*), and the warriors are clad in scarlet. God is sending His army against the Ninevites. This army dressed in scarlet typifies God's spiritual army who are

dressed in the atoning blood of Jesus. In **Revelation 19:13,** Jesus is dressed in a **"robe dipped in blood and His name is called the Word of God."**

9. In the **Song of Songs 4:3,** the Shulamite says that her lover has lips like a thread of scarlet. This is the atoning blood of Jesus that is woven throughout the Word of God (lips of Christ).

10. In **Matthew 27:28,** they put a scarlet robe on Jesus and then twisted the crown of thorns in His head. Jesus wore the scarlet robe of His atoning blood and the crown of thorns that was the first Adam's punishment for sin *(curse)* at His crucifixion where **He became sin for us that we might become the righteousness of God in Him.** We are established in His righteousness because of His sacrificial blood. However, if we want the fullness of the blessing that is ours in Christ Jesus, we must put on our white linen robes of righteousness by walking in obedience to Him.

The atoning blood of Jesus is the scarlet thread that binds the Word of God together as one finished work.

Rahab let these two Israelites down by a rope through a window in her house, which was built on the city wall. Rahab, the Gentile, showed these two Israelites which way to go for safety. Jesus shows us the way. He says in **John 14:6, "I am the way......no one comes to the Father except through Me."** There is no other way to God except through the atoning blood of Jesus Christ. All must come to the Father by the same way Jesus did, by His blood. The way was not completed until Jesus not only shed His blood on the cross, but also sprinkled it seven times in fulfillment of the Law. The seven sprinklings of Christ's blood are:

1. His circumcision on the 8th day.
2. His sweat turning to blood in the Garden of Gethsemane.
3. The lashes on His back.
4. The crown of thorns on His head.
5. The holes in His hands.
6. The holes in His feet.
7. The wound in His side.

It was after He both sprinkled His blood seven times in fulfill-ment of the Law and then shed it pouring it out over the land that He ascended to the presence of the Father. As the Gentile Rahab showed these two Jews the way to safety, Christians are to also show others, including the Jews, the way to safety through Jesus Christ.

Rahab told the Jewish spies that they must hide for three days in the high places (mountains) until the pursuers return to the city of Jericho. Then they will be safe and can go their way. Here we have the three days again representing cleansing and resurrection power. These two spies had been in a land polluted with sin and idolatry. They must hide themselves in a high place and be cleansed. Then they can go their way.

Rahab understood what she must do to be saved. She obeyed and immediately tied the scarlet cord in her window. Then she went to bring others into her house so they could be saved also. Followers of Christ are called to bring others into His saving, loving arms for safety. All who trusted Rahab and remained in her house were not killed. Those who trust in the Lord Jesus Christ and remain in Him and His house will never die but have eternal life. Faith in Christ brings salvation to the house. **Acts 16:31: "Believe on the Lord Jesus Christ, and you will be saved, you and your household."**

Now Rahab would wait patiently for the Israelites to conquer the city and its inhabitants and then return for her. This, of course, typifies Christ returning for His Bride. The spies would come again to gather her and her family just as Christ will come again to gather His faithful followers. **(Hebrews 9:28)** Rahab must live by faith and patience. She had to watch as the Israelites marched around the city wall blowing trumpets for six days. Six represents the efforts of man. But on the 7th day, the people marched around the city seven times, the trumpets sounded, the people shouted a great shout and the walls of Jericho came tumbling down. Man with God brought the victory. Rahab's house, which was on the wall of the city, was the only section of the wall that did not fall. God protects those who come to Him in faith and obedience. Jesus will also come with a shout when the trumpet sounds. Rahab's house was on a sure foun-dation—faith in God. After Rahab and all of her house were safely out of the city, Joshua ordered all within the city to be destroyed by fire. God will also protect His own when He shakes the earth and sends His wrath of fiery judgment and destroys the world. **(1 Thess. 1:10;5:19;Rev.16)**

The people of Jericho were destroyed, but Rahab was delivered from God's judgment. Not only was she saved from destruction, she attended a wedding, her own to a Jew. This is her blessing given for her faith and obedience

The account of the destruction of Jericho and its inhabitants by God's people and Rahab points to the final judgment of Revelation and the wedding feast of those who love Jesus. **(Revelation 19:7-9, 17-19)**

A brief summary of Rahab's faith, salvation and works follows:

1. She was a sinner under condemnation.
2. She heard and had faith in the power of God for salvation and deliverance.
3. She believed God's Word. **"I know that the Lord has given you the land."**
4. She put her faith to work.
5. She was willing to lay down her life for God's people.
6. She made an oath with God's people identifying with them and their God.
7. She obeyed all that they told her to do to be saved.
8. She applied the scarlet cord to her window as her way of escape.
9. She brought all who wished to be saved into her house of refuge and safety.
10. She was delivered from God's judgment.
11. She waited patiently for God's people to return to get her and all those in her house.
12. She receives her blessing. She was married to a Jew and is listed as a descendant of Christ.

Rahab was truly a picture of salvation through the atoning blood of Jesus Christ and the reward of those who faithfully love, serve and obey Him. This gentile harlot entered into the nation of Israel just as gentiles are granted salvation through Yeshua and enter into spiritual Israel. As Rahab became a part of the royal family by marrying a man from the tribe of Judah, those who follow Christ, the lion of the tribe of Judah, will become a part of the royal Bride of Christ. Rahab and her Jewish husband are a type and shadow of the Bride of Christ made up of both saved Jews and Gentiles.

CHAPTER 4

Crossing the Jordan – Joshua 3

Crossing the Jordan accomplished the same things the cross of Jesus Christ did: 1) it brought glory and honor to God; 2) it exalted Joshua (Yeshua) as leader of God's people; 3) it encouraged and empowered God's people; 4) it put fear into the enemy of God's people 5) it brought victory over the enemy; 6) it brought God's people into their inheritance; and 7) it gave them rest and peace in the land after the battles were won. Crossing the Jordan meant that God's people were committed to God and to the battles ahead. They would no longer fight in the flesh but instead would be obedient to God and His ways and put their faith and trust in God to win the battle.

God told Abraham that the Israelites could not inherit Canaan because **"the sin of the Amorites had not reached its full measure." Genesis 15:16** The time has now come. The wickedness of the idolatrous nation has reached its full measure so the judgment of God has come, just as God had done with Sodom and Gomorrah. God's people would be the instrument of God's judgment upon this wicked nation.

Because of Rahab's report, the spies return to Joshua saying, **"Truly the Lord has delivered all the land into our hands, for indeed all the inhabitants of the country are fainthearted because of us. Joshua 2:24** It was the wickedness of the Canaanites that prompted God to give Israel the land not any righteousness on

Israel's part. Israel had been rebellious and fearful throughout the journey through the wilderness. Any unfaithfulness on the part of Israel in the land of promise will be dealt with also. However, God will never completely abandon the Jewish people. His correction and discipline is redemptive not vengeful. God will draw His people Israel into a relationship with His Son Yeshua/Jesus. In like manner, God will not give Christ's followers the land based on any righteousness on their part. The giving of land is strictly God's gift because it is only His to give. It is only in Christ that we have our righteousness. Jesus imputes His righteousness on all who receive His grace by faith. All, both Jew and Gentile, have sinned and fallen short of the glory of God. Both have to be grafted into the tree that is supported by the root Jesus Christ, the tree of life. **(Romans 11:16-24)** Jesus is the tabernacle of God that is with mankind and the door through which one must pass to receive eternal life. Jesus is also the two pillars in front of Solomon's Temple. He is Boaz as our kinsman-redeemer and strength. He is Jachin, which means "He shall establish" because He will establish His Temple and kingdom in the hearts of His followers.

No nation or people can claim the glory because salvation was strictly the work of God alone through His Son Jesus/Yeshua. For any human, nation or body to try to claim the glory is to take the glory, majesty and honor away from Jesus/Yeshua. All glory and honor and power are His alone for He was the Lamb that was slain for the sins of the whole world. **Revelation 5:8-12**

The flooding of God's Holy Spirit and Word symbolized in the Jordan River will bring Christ's Body into His fullness and draw others to salvation and freedom in Christ, the Living Word.

God's people are at a crossroad at the Jordan. They can either turn back or move forward with God. Joshua had the monumental task of getting 2 million people with all of their belongings and livestock across the Jordan. The only way Joshua could accomplish this is if God's presence was with him. Jesus said, **"For without Me you can do nothing." John 15:5**

God's miracle at the Jordan River showed His people that love, faith and obedience to God brings blessing, but it also showed the power of Israel's God to the other nations also. As we who love

Jesus walk in His ways in obedience to His Word, those who don't know Him will be drawn to Him through us. We lift Jesus up *(glorify Him)* by walking in faith and obedience to His Word and Will. Our words, actions and thoughts will reflect His glory and bring honor to God.

It was at the time of the barley harvest in spring when the Israelites were to cross the Jordan River. The barley harvest was the first harvest. The wheat harvest came later. Springtime represents "new life." Barley was used to make the bread of the poor. **"Blessed are the poor in Spirit, for theirs is the kingdom of heaven." (Matthew 5:3)** This was the first beatitude Jesus taught His disciples in His sermon on the mount. Barley is the symbol of lowliness *(humility)*. In **Judges 7:13,** God used a Midianite's dream of a loaf of barley bread falling onto their tent to affirm to Gideon that God would give him the victory over the Midianites who were the enemies of God's people. God works through the humble spirit. God wanted a leader who would trust Him for the victory, walk in humility, obey and worship Him. Gideon was His man. And Joshua is God's man who will take His people across the Jordan into their promised inheritance.

Then Joshua rose early in the morning: and they set out from Shittim and came to the Jordan, he and all the children of Israel, and lodged there before they crossed over. Joshua 3:1 Shittim means "thorns" symbolizing sin and curse. God's people must leave the place of thorns (sins) to go to Jericho, which means "his sweet smell." Followers of Jesus are to put off sin and put on the sweet fragrance of Christ. It is the sweet, humble fragrance of Christ that will defeat the Enemy and conquer the world to Jesus.

Shittim is also known as "Acacia Grove." Acacia wood was the only wood used in building the Tabernacle in the wilderness. It is an incorruptible wood, which signifies Christ's incorruptible humanity. The acacia wood used in the tabernacle was also covered with pure gold indicating Christ's Divinity. Acacia means "scourging." Jesus was scourged before being crucified. Like Jesus, Christians begin at the cross of Jesus Christ and then proceed through the wilderness journey until they are matured enough to cross over the Jordan to the higher land (call).

It is a time of great transition for the Israelites. They are about to enter into a new territory with new experiences, new possessions, a new life, new food, new songs, new battles, new joys and a new inheritance. There is an order God's people must follow, however. Joshua *(Yeshua)*, the High Priest, will receive God's commands. He will give them to the people and the people must obey. As High Priest and Commander, Joshua will cross the river first with the Ark and the priests. Then the people must follow from their God-assigned positions. **(see Numbers 2)** Joshua was the first to enter the river and the last to leave it. **The last will be first and the first will be last.**

God had Joshua hidden under the leadership of Moses for many years without recognition preparing him for such a time as this. Now Joshua will receive His reward. Joshua's faith, patience, willingness to serve and his allowance of God's refining process qualified him for this tremendous work. God exalts those who are willing to serve Him without recognition. God honors those who honor Him through their lives, their words and their actions. Jesus, the True Joshua, said, **"If any man serve Me, him will My Father honor."** The Israelites will move to higher ground with a new commander and new leaders. God had been preparing these leaders in secret and now brings them forward to lead the people into new territory. By faith, Joshua will lead the Israelites to their promised inheritance just as faith in Jesus brings us into the fullness of our inheritance in Him. The third day Bride of Christ will be led by those God has been preparing in secret. These anointed men and women will lead others into the deeper things of God and will lead the Bride of Christ into the end time harvest of souls before Jesus comes to take us home to our Promised Land.

Both Moses and Joshua crossed a body of water on the 10th day of the 1st month. **(see Exodus 12:3;Joshua 4:19)** The 10th day of the 1st month was the day Jesus entered Jerusalem to be crucified. It was also the day that the Passover Lamb was set aside for use three days later at the Passover meal. Jesus was the lamb to be slain when He entered Jerusalem in fulfillment of the Law. At the very same hour that the Passover Lamb was being slaughtered for the Passover meal, Jesus shed His atoning blood on the cross. The walls of

Jericho also fell on Passover, just as Satan was defeated at the cross of Jesus Christ.

The Israelites are about to undertake a tremendous work. There are stepping stones that God's people must follow. Joshua understood that this was a spiritual battle, not a physical one. God would win the battle but they had to be prepared spiritually for God's power and presence. Since they were going to war, you would have thought that Joshua would tell them to sharpen their swords and bring out their shields. But Joshua tells God's people that they must sanctify themselves.

1. ***They must be consecrated (set apart) to God and sanctified***. **"Without holiness no man shall see the Lord."** The Israelites cannot take any "baggage" (sin) with them across the Jordan. Sin must be left on the other side, behind them. The Israelites must sanctify themselves. God will not tolerate sin. There is no freedom in sin. Sin prevents the establishment of God's kingdom and destroys those whom God loves. So, for His peoples' sake, sin must be removed. It is the consecrated and sanctified who will see the Lord. Before entering the new land, all must be healed and delivered of their past. **"But one thing I do, forgetting those things which are behind and reaching forward to those things which are ahead, I press toward the goal for the prize of the upward call of God in Christ Jesus. Therefore, let us, as many as are mature, have this mind......Philippians 3:13-15a** Cooperation with God's will and Spirit is essential for victory.

David cried out to the Lord over his tremendous sin against Him, **"Create in me a clean heart, O God; And renew a steadfast spirit within me. Do not cast me away from Your presence....Psalm 51:10** David knew God in such a near and dear way that he had to confess his tremendous sin against him in order to be renewed and restored into right relationship with the Lord. David was afraid his sin was so grave that God would remove His Spirit from him. He asked God to renew a steadfast Spirit in him. David also did not want to lose the close relationship he had with the Lord. It would be devastating to David to be cast away from God's presence. He knew that humbling himself before God and seeking His forgiveness would restore his joy. **"Restore to me the joy of Your** salvation, and uphold me by Your generous Spirit. Then I will teach transgressors Your ways, and sinners shall be converted to you."vv12-13** David also knew that in order to reach the lost, he must be cleansed and walk close to God. Likewise, those who will bring in the end time harvest to Christ must be holy. The unholy cannot enter into the Promised Land.

At the Red Sea, the Israelites were delivered from bondage. At the Jordan, they must put the self-life to death before crossing over. It was after God's people sanctified themselves that God would **"do wonders among them." Joshua 3:5**

2. *They must follow the Ark of God's Presence.*

Ark of the Covenant

God will make a way where there seems to be no way. The pillar of cloud and fire that led God's people through the wilderness is now replaced with the Ark of the Covenant. The Ark of the Covenant was in the Most Holy Place in the tabernacle in the wilderness. The Shekinah glory of God rested over the mercy seat between the cherubim on top of the Ark. The Ark represents the power, glory and presence of God. In the wilderness the pillar hovered over the camp of the Israelites in times of rest. But when God's people moved (marched), the cloud always went before them.

The Ark of the Covenant was made of pure gold symbolizing the Divine. Inside the Ark of the Covenant were the two tablets of law, the golden pot of manna and Aaron's rod that budded. Jesus

Christ is the Living Ark of God's Presence on earth. The two tablets of Law represent Jesus as the Divine Bread (the Word of God) and Aaron's rod that budded represents Jesus' transforming and resurrecting power. All three things hidden in the Ark of God's Covenant are hidden in Jesus Christ. He is the Word of God from beginning to end. He is the Divine Bread of Heaven and He is the Resurrection and the Life.

In Genesis after the sin of Adam and Eve, the two cherubim guard the throne of God with a flaming sword indicating God's judgment. **(Genesis 3:24)** But in the Most Holy Place of the tabernacle, the cherubim are united as they look down at the atoning blood of the slain lamb over the mercy seat indicating God's mercy and grace. This atoning blood of the slain lamb in the first testament pointed to the perfect, sinless blood of Jesus Christ in the second testament that was slain for the propitiation of the sins of the whole world. Heritage cannot give a person a place in God's kingdom. Only the sinless blood of Jesus can. Jesus sends us out into the world as His representatives two by two.

As God's presence and power went before the Israelites in the wilderness, His presence and power must also go before His people to lead the way over the waters of the Jordan. Jesus passed through the waters between heaven and earth preparing a straight path to God's throne for His followers. Jesus told His disciples that **if He went to prepare a place for them, He would come again to receive them to Himself, that where He was they may be also.** Christians must prepare the way of the Lord by sanctifying themselves. Jesus is returning for a Bride without spot or blemish.

When Jesus was about to celebrate the Passover Meal with His disciples, He sent them to the city of Jerusalem (God's Holy City) where they would meet a man carrying a pitcher of water. **(Mark 14:13)** That was the man Jesus told His disciples to follow, that he would take them to the place prepared for the Passover meal. This man represents a believer *(an "earthen vessel— pitcher)"* that carries the water of His Word and Spirit. **"Wherever he goes in, say to the master of the house, "The Teacher says, where is the guest room in which I may eat the Passover with My disciples?" Then he will show you a large upper room furnished and**

prepared; there make ready for us. Mark 14:14-15 The man or woman of God who is filled with the water of His Word, the anointing of His Spirit and resides in the high place (upper room) that has been cleansed and prepared for Jesus is the place where Jesus will fellowship and share His Supper *(commune with)*.

Jesus has prepared a place for us in heaven, but we must be prepared on earth to receive it....**that He might make known the riches of His glory on the vessels of mercy, which He had prepared beforehand for glory, even us whom He called, not of the Jews only, but also of the Gentiles? Romans 9:23-24** Jesus will also lead us to the waters of death of "self." Then He will stand in the center of our hearts, as the Ark stood in the center of the Jordan, as we walk until we reach our end. Jesus will then bring us to the other side into our promised inheritance of life eternal with Him in rest and peace. Sanctification releases the Holy Spirit and brings rest.

It is thought that the very place where the Israelites crossed over the Jordan was the place where John baptized Jesus. Jesus went down bodily into the dirty, turbulent waters of the Jordan to sanctify it of pollution so we could pass over to the land God promises us without hindrance. Jesus walked on water while on earth because He is the bridge between heaven and earth. The waters didn't have to part for Him because He has all power and authority over nature and all of creation.

Moses asked the Lord to allow him to enter the Promised Land but God refused. **(Deuteronomy 3:23-26)** God had prepared and set apart Joshua *(Yeshua/Jesus)* to lead His people into their inheritance. The Law cannot bring us into God's land of promise. Only Jesus, the True Joshua, can. Moses died under the penalty of the Law God gave him. But Yeshua/Jesus bore the curse of the Law for us.

God told Joshua *(Yeshua/Jesus)* to tell the priests to **"take up the Ark of the Covenant and pass on ahead of the people." Joshua 2:6** The people were not to enter the Jordan until the Ark had been lifted up ("take up") and had gone before them. Jesus said, **"And I, if I am lifted up from the earth, will draw all peoples to Myself." John 12:32** The first thing that was "lifted up" in the scriptures was Noah's ark. It was lifted up by the floodwaters. Noah obeyed all of God's Word and was saved from God's wrath. Noah's ark of safety was a type and shadow of Jesus, the True Ark of Salvation *(safety)*. Moses lifted up his rod and the waters of the Red Sea parted and the Enemy of God's people was defeated. Moses' rod was a shadow of the cross of Jesus Christ that defeated the Enemy of His people forever and opened the windows of heaven that poured the Holy Spirit down upon earth. Jesus had to be lifted up on the cross first before the waters of His Holy Spirit could be released over the earth. As we lift Jesus up before the world by walking in His will and ways, He will draw others to Him through us.

The pillar of cloud and fire was God-made and God-moved. But now the Ark that is manmade through God's Word and man-moved at God's direction replaces the pillar. It was after Moses built the Ark in complete obedience to God's commandments and then placed it in God's designated place in the tabernacle that the glory rested upon the mercy seat. It is the heart that is obedient to God's Word that God's glory will rest in. The glory of God that rested in Jesus was brought forth externally for three of His disciples to see on the Mount of Transfiguration. Not only was Jesus' glory revealed to the three Jewish disciples who drew nearest to Jesus, Moses and Elijah's glorified bodies appeared with Him. This must have been a source of comfort to Peter, James and John who were Jews knowing that Moses and Elijah were with Jesus in His glory. It must have reassured them of their own resurrection some day.

Zion is a mount within the city of Jerusalem. Zion represents the place of God's presence and glory. Like Zion is a mount within the Holy City of Jerusalem, Christ's Bride is a faithful and pure Body within His church who are filled with the glory of God. Zion not only represents God's dwelling place, it represents the Bride of Christ and a spiritual place that God will establish within His Church. These will be those with clean hands and pure hearts. Receiving Christ as your Savior is the first act of faith. Yielding to His Lordship is the next stage. It is this yielding to Our Master Jesus that brings sanctification and glorification. The glory of the Lord will cover His Bride just as the first man Adam and woman Eve were clothed in God's glory before they sinned. God is continually striving with man to bring him back to his original condition before sin. He wants His own clothed in His glory.

At the Jordan River in **Joshua**, the priests must take the first and definite step of faith into the waters of the Jordan carrying the Ark of God's Presence on their shoulders. Shoulders are the place of strength and government. That which comes from the Head of the Kingdom must rest on the shoulders of the Body. We must become subject to His government and Word and submitted to His Will. As each of Christ's followers are fully submitted to the Headship of Christ, then we will function in His spiritual authority. Stepping out of ourselves and into Christ and His fullness is the first step His followers must take so they can carry Jesus to others. Only God can do this work by His Spirit and Word. **(Romans 8:13)** All followers of Jesus – male or female, Jew or Greek *(Gentile)*—are both **"priests and kings."** As we do our job of lifting Jesus up to the world through our words, our actions and our deeds and wait for His leading, we will bring others into His rest and peace in the land of God's promises. When the priests stepped into the rough, muddy waters of the Jordan, the water upstream stopped at Adam to allow God's people to cross over. Adam was 20 miles upstream. **(Joshua 3:15-16)** It was probably an earthquake that stopped the flow of the Jordan. God controls nature. The original sin of Adam stopped up the flow of God's Holy Spirit and separated him from God's presence. But Jesus, the Second Adam, released the flow of the waters of His Holy Spirit again by becoming sin for us and removing the curse God made on the earth in Genesis. God supernaturally stopped the floodwaters at Adam so all of His people could cross over to the other side. This, of course, is type and shadow of Jesus who withheld the waters of God's wrath so all could be restored to the Father by His blood.

The Jews couldn't defeat the enemy and conquer the land until they crossed the Jordan. The Jordan represents the empowerment of the Holy Spirit. God did not act until they stepped into the water. When they took the step of faith, God opened a new way for them to go to a new land. Jesus held back the raging waters of God's judgment at Adam so we could pass over a straight path as we follow Him into the very presence of God. God not only parted the waters, His presence waited in the center of the river in power until all who would cross were over because His people **"had not passed**

this way before.'' As the priests did their job of carrying the Ark of God's presence *(Yeshua/Jesus)* before the people, the waters were held back. The priests not only went before the people carrying the Ark of God's presence, they stood with it in the center of the river until all had crossed over. Ministers are to lead the way over the Jordan ushering in God's power and presence in preparation of the latter rain that will bring in the end time harvest. The Gospels of Jesus Christ stand in the center of the two testaments drawing them together as one by His sacrificial, sinless blood. Just as the priests didn't leave their place in the center of the river until all others crossed over, Jesus will not leave or forsake His own until all who will have crossed over into the fullness of His blessing and inheritance. The Ark was the first to enter the river and the last to leave the river. It went before them to prepare the way and guide them across, and then it went behind them to protect them. Jesus said, **"I am the Alpha and Omega, the Beginning and the End, the First and the Last." Revelation 22:13** He is the only way to the Father. Jesus said, **"No one goes to the Father except through Me. John 14:6** Jesus is not only the Beginning and the End, He is the Center and the Dry Ground through which we must pass to go to the other side. Jesus is **"all in all."** Jesus went to the Father before us and is guiding us. He is also our Protector. With Jesus in our hearts ruling, He will bring us into our inheritance. He will also use us to bring others into His saving, loving arms.

God's presence was in their midst, but the priest and the people also had a job to do. Christ has given the fivefold ministry gifts to mature His Body into His Bride. These leaders must know the way themselves first by studying and rightly dividing His Word of Truth and then obeying it. Christ's leaders must not deviate from the Word of God in any way. God told Joshua that he must not let the Word of God leave his mouth. He must speak it at all times, and he must meditate on it night and day turning neither to the right nor to the left. God's leaders must not only be full of faith, they must be persistent in following the Word of God.

Joshua told his leaders that when they saw the priests carrying the Ark, they were to move **"out from their positions and follow it." Joshua 3:3** Every person in Israel walked one foot after the other behind the Ark of God's Presence in order of their positions. The Ark had the Law hidden within. Joshua and the Israelites had to march behind the laws of God hidden in the Ark until the Living Word of God, Jesus, was revealed. Now, we must march behind Jesus in obedience to His Word in order to obtain the fullness of our inheritance in Him.

God had specifically placed each tribe in their position in the camp. They were to move in order of their positions keeping a distance of 2,000 cubits from the Ark. By keeping the Ark a distance in front of them, every person could see it for himself. The leaders would not block their view. They would know whom they were following. Every step of the way each person would keep their eyes fixed on God and His commands and follow Him. Looking to Joshua (Yeshua/Jesus) and in faith, the priests and the people obey and the waters were held back so they could pass through on dry ground. God's people must follow the Ark as followers of Jesus must follow Him, not leaders. He is our example – the Sinless One. There are no obstacles to our entering into our promised inheritance in Christ except our own flesh. Jesus positions His anointed leaders in His Body. We are to move with the power of God in our assigned positions. Jealousy over gifts cannot enter into Christ's Body. God is the Giver of gifts. Anyone who is jealous over another's gift and causes dissention in the Body of Christ is not rejecting the person, but the God who gave the gift.

The priests were directed to take up the Ark, but they weren't told how they would cross the river. They must trust God and Joshua (Yeshua). After the priests stepped into the Jordan, they were to **"stand"** and wait for God to move so they could follow Him. God had given His Word and the people must stand upon it until God performs His Word. God's Word binds Him to action because His word is Truth. Our flesh and senses deceive us, but God's Word is infallible and eternal. The Apostle Paul says that followers of Christ are to put on the whole armor of God and **"having done all, to stand. Stand therefore, having girded your waist with truth, having put on the breastplate of righteousness, and having shod your feet with the preparation of the gospel of peace; above all, taking the shield of faith with which you will**

be able to quench all the fiery darts of the wicked one." **Ephesians 6:14-16** We must be bound to the truth of the Word of God in the center of our being. We must also have holiness around our heart. And, we must use our faith to quench the arrows of the wicked one. The shield is the only piece of our spiritual armor that is movable. As we move in faith against the darts of the devil, we will defeat him.

The Ark eventually ended up in the Temple. We are to receive Jesus, the Living Ark of God's Presence, into the houses of our hearts. Our hearts become the Temple of God with Jesus ruling and guiding us. Jesus says, **"Follow Me."** Jesus shows us the way. **"I am the way, the truth and the life."**

As the Ark remained in the center of the river and then followed behind the Israelites to finish the work it had begun, Jesus remains with the Father until the Father tells Him it is time to finish the work. During the age of grace, Jesus is sitting at the right hand of the Father resting and interceding on our behalf. But in Revelation, Jesus is standing and walking *(moving and taking action).* When the events of Revelation are completed, we will cross over the Jordan and receive our promised inheritance of life eternal with Jesus and the Father in rest and peace. **"The priests remained standing in the middle of the river with the Ark until everything the Lord had commanded Joshua was done by the people."** **Joshua 4:10** The priests did not move from the middle of the river until the people did everything the Lord had commanded Joshua *(Yeshua).* God and Jesus are waiting for His Body to complete the work He has called them to do before God finishes His work of redemption and the destruction of evil.

The crossing put fear in the hearts of the enemies of God's people on both sides of the Jordan. **"They no longer had the courage to face the Israelites." Joshua 5:1**

3. *Twelve chosen leaders, one from each tribe of Israel, are each to take a stone from the middle of the Jordan from where the priests stood as a memorial of God's presence and power for future generations.* Prior to this, the 12 leaders of God's people were the twelve sons of Jacob, chosen by heritage. But now Joshua chose the 12 who would lead God's people across the Jordan and

into battle against the enemies. These 12 leaders and stones of remembrance would teach future generations by the **"word of their testimony"** regarding God's miraculous work in bringing them across the Jordan River into their promised inheritance. Jesus, like Joshua, chose 12 apostles to develop His kingdom on earth. These 12 apostles walked and talked with Jesus and used the **"blood of the Lamb"** and the **"word of their testimony"** of what they had seen and heard Jesus say and do to bring others into His spiritual kingdom on earth. There had to be twelve apostles of Jesus as well as 12 leaders of the 12 tribes of Israel because 12 is the number of Divine Government.

The riverbed of stones represents hardened hearts. God removed His peoples' hardened hearts and transformed them into vessels of compassion, love, faith, obedience and victory. These twelve leaders were to go to the Ark in the middle of the Jordan and take up a stone on their shoulder to serve as a sign among them. They must never forget what God had done for them. The shoulder is the place of burden bearing, strength and government. Jesus carries the government of God's kingdom on His shoulders. The Head is connected to the Body. What comes from the Head of God's Body, Yeshua/Jesus, flows down to His people. With Him as the Head, Yeshua/Jesus has placed the government of God's kingdom on earth on the shoulders of His people.

The 12 Israelite chosen leaders are to bring each of their stones back to the place where they were to stay for the night. *(darkness)* In the light of day, Joshua would then erect a monument to God with these stones as a remembrance to future generations of God's awesome power, love and wonderful works. Christ's living stones operate in the Light. There were twelve stones but only one monument. Christ's Body (Temple) is built with the living stones of His "priests and kings" knitted together as a memorial of God's marvelous grace and love. God used stones made by Him to mark the place where His presence stood, not an elaborate monument. Nothing of man would get the glory. The softening of our hardened hearts by the Spirit and the Word will make us a memorial of God's majesty, love and grace. These twelve stones also represented the twelve leaders of Israel who were the gateway to Christianity.

These twelve leaders and twelve stones became the 12 apostles of Jesus, the majority of whom were Jews, through whom God continued the building of His spiritual kingdom. As Christ's living stones, believers are buried with Him in the river of His Holy Spirit and Word and will arise with Him in His resurrection power in victory. These stones were hidden under the waters of the Jordan but were resurrected into a memorial to God and the people. As we hide Jesus and the waters of His Word and Spirit in our hearts, we are resurrected into new life in Him. This new, resurrected life of Christ in us will be a memorial to others of God's saving and transforming power and deliverance from the Enemy of our souls. It will speak to others as a testimony to Christ and His deliverance and all-consuming love and grace.

Joshua took 12 stones and set them up in the center of the Jordan where the Ark of God's presence stood. The number 12 is the number of Divine government and apostolic fullness. Jesus Christ is the True Ark of God's Presence and the Divine government of God's kingdom rests upon His shoulders. *These 12 stones in the middle of the Jordan identify us with Christ's death.* When the waters of the Jordan subsided, this altar made of stones was visible to all. The 12 stones taken from the Jordan by the 12 leaders of the tribes of Israel were set up as an altar to God at Gilgal in Israel (the Promised Land). A "stone" in scripture is the symbol of strength and stability. An "altar" is the place of reconciliation, ransom, redemption and sacrifice to God. These 12 stones setup as an altar at Gilgal symbolize Yeshua/Jesus who is the Rock of salvation and the altar of sacrifice and redemption at the cross. The cross of Yeshua/Jesus identifies us with spiritual circumcision by removal of the flesh. *These twelve stones set up at Gilgal identify us with Christ's circumcision on the cross and His resurrection.*

Followers of Christ must carry Jesus to those with hardened hearts by living and walking as He walked. We are His stones of remembrance of His delivering, sanctifying, victorious power. We are not to forget His benefits. We must never forget the cost of our freedom—the cross. Jesus, the True Joshua and Living Stone, will build His Temple with living stones—his followers — as a monument to God and to others. **(1 Peter 2:2)** These twelve chosen men would be responsible to help Joshua govern and lead God's people. These twelve stones represent Christ's twelve apostles who were the living stones who would lead and build His spiritual kingdom on earth. Joshua erected a memorial in the center of the Jordan at the place where the Ark of God's Presence stood. Twelve stones were taken out of the center of the Jordan where the Ark stood. Then Joshua put them back into the Jordan erecting them as an altar to God. Those who follow Jesus are taken out of the world and established in the heart (center) of Christ. Jesus will build His Temple in the hearts of those who love Him as an altar to God.

After the land of our hearts is conquered, a new stage of our work begins. With Jesus in the center of our hearts ruling, the waters of the Holy Spirit and the Word will flood our souls and draw others to Christ. We must take possession of the land through the spreading of the Good News of salvation through Jesus Christ by our actions, our words and the life of Christ in us. We must not only conquer the sin in our hearts, we must also claim God's promises as our own. We must experience the fullness of Christ's blessing, enter into it and live it. We must abide in Him and build a holy habitation for Jesus in the land of our hearts. And, we must tend and feed His sheep and His field here on earth. Then He will be the real owner of the land of our hearts and will use us to build His kingdom on earth.

"Work out your own salvation with fear and trembling, for it is God who works in you to will and act according to His good purpose." God has a special design and purpose made especially for each of us. If we will love and submit to Jesus through obedience, He will embroider that purpose into our lives until it is uniquely and beautifully ours. Then He will knit us together as a "coat of many colors" who have the favor of God through His Son as its binding. The love of Christ **for** His Bride and the purity of Christ **in** His Bride are terrifying to Satan and his kingdom of darkness.

"How long will you wait before you begin to take possession of the land that the Lord, the God of your fathers, has given you?" Joshua 18:3 No doubt God is asking followers of Jesus this same question in this day and hour. How long will we wait before we take possession of the land for Christ?

As these twelve men ruled and reigned with Joshua, God's chosen ones in Jesus will rule and reign with Him. Leaders in Christ's Body must carry the government of God's house on their shoulders as Jesus did. Our actions will either bring honor or dishonor to Christ.

God began with the twelve sons of Jacob in establishing the spiritual nation of Israel. In Genesis, the twelve sons of Jacob were chosen because of their heritage. Now in the book of Joshua, God tells Joshua to choose twelve leaders from the twelve tribes of Israel who will rule and reign with him over God's people. Then in Judges, God did a new thing by exalting twelve judges over Israel and then a king in 1 Samuel. When Jesus came to earth to redeem mankind, He chose twelve apostles to establish His kingdom. In Revelation, there are 24 elders seated around the throne. **(Revelation 4:4)** These 24 are the 12 leaders of the tribes of Israel and the 12 apostles combined. The 12 leaders of the tribes of Israel were the gateway to Christianity. The 12 apostles represent the foundation of Christ's Temple, with Jesus as the Head and Chief Cornerstone. When the four living creatures gave glory, honor and thanks to God, these twenty-four elders would fall down before Him in humility and worship and lay their crowns before Him saying, **"You are worthy, our Lord and God, to receive glory and honor and power, for you created all things, and by your will they were created and have their being." Revelation 4:10-11** God does not share His glory with anyone. All that we are and all that we have are because of Him. Leaders in Christ's Temple must be careful not to draw glory to themselves. We must **"cast our crowns"** before Jesus because He alone is worthy of all honor and glory and praise.

Jesus/Yeshua is building His Kingdom in the hearts of those Jews and Gentiles who willingly offer themselves a living sacrifice through obedience to Him. His kingdom is **"at hand"** unfolding within the hearts of His true followers. The Gentiles are grafted into Israel's tree. However, Israel must also be grafted into their own tree through Jesus Christ because of their disobedience. Only His sinless blood can atone for the sins of all. All, both Jew and Gentile, are sinners who must be saved by grace through Jesus Christ. Neither have any place for pride in their chosenness because salvation is strictly the work of God alone through Jesus Christ. We do not choose Him; He chooses us. **John 15:16**

This memorial of God's greatness and power in parting the waters of the Jordan for His people to cross over was a visible sign of remembrance that the Israelites were to teach their children about God's awesome power and faithfulness to His people. This memorial will be a visible witness to all generations of the awesome power of the invisible God of Israel. **Joshua 3:10** describes Israel's God as a **"living God."** He is a God that acts and performs great miracles for His people, not like the dead gods of the people of the land. It is through the visible that the invisible can be seen. The "natural" speaks in the "supernatural." The invisible God became visible in Jesus. Those who follow Jesus have the memorial of the cross as a remembrance of His mighty deliverance, love, power and victory. The cross of Jesus must be forever memorialized before our eyes. All of our works must be under the atoning blood of Jesus and accomplished with holy hands. We must set up a memorial to Jesus in our hearts, remembering His tender grace and mercy as well as His power and might. We must teach it to our children not only through Biblical instruction but also through our actions. **"Train up a child in the way he should go, and when he is older he will not depart from it."** If those of us who follow Jesus don't teach our children about God, then the devil will be more than willing to teach them his ways. The busyness and claims of the world in the lives of some keeps them from taking time to remember God's goodness and mercy or for prayer and worship or study of His Word.

These 12 Israelite leaders are to put up these stones to keep God and His mercy and power in the remembrance of all generations. They must do so as "one man" – in unity. They are in the Promised Land strictly because God opened the way. To forget God and His mercy is a condition of the heart that must be corrected. We are here because of Him. We must never forget or take His mercy and grace for granted. God said that Israel had forgotten Him and went after her lovers *(idols)* in **Hosea 2:13.** An idol is anything we love rather than God. The cross of Jesus Christ is in the midst of the two testaments to remind us of God's goodness, mercy and grace in His delivering power.

Jesus told His disciples to celebrate communion as a remembrance of His delivering power by His shed blood on the cross. As we humbly remember His grace and mercy through His suffering on the cross, we approach His communion table in holiness and thanksgiving for His saving grace. The remembrance of God's marvelous work at the cross and the things He has done for us in the past will increase our faith, and we will trust Him to take care of us now and in the future. As we pass through our rivers of difficulty and tests, we are to put Jesus in the Center. When the floodwaters of our difficulty passes, we will see how Jesus was always in the midst carrying and guiding us through. It is by looking back at the marvelous works God has done for us in the past that increases our faith and trust in Him to take care of us now and in the future.

These twelve stones were taken out of the Jordan as Christ's "living stones" *(believers)* are washed in the "Jordan" of the outpouring of His Holy Spirit and Word and then brought into their full inheritance of peace, rest and possession of the land.

4. _They must be circumcised at Gilgal._ All of God's people must begin at the cross. The flesh must be crucified. God instituted circumcision as a sign of His covenantal relationship with Abraham. **(Genesis 17:11)** Circumcision is the cutting away of the flesh around the organ that produces life. Circumcision represents the death of the flesh. It also symbolizes the shed blood of Jesus Christ, the One who gives spiritual life. Jesus shed His blood and His flesh on the cross at Calvary. The cross was His spiritual circumcision. He was raised in an incorruptible, glorious body. Every Christian must return to the cross and crucify his or her flesh. When our flesh is rolled away at Gilgal, we are free from the bondage of sin.

The circumcision instituted by God with Abraham was an external act that had an internal meaning. God wants to circumcise our fleshly, hardened hearts creating hearts of love and compassion. **(Dt. 10:16:Dt. 30:6;Jer.4:4;Rom. 2:28-29)** The Israelites have crossed the Jordan as one body, but now individually they must crucify their flesh and offer the blood atonement of God's covenant. Because we are crucified with Jesus, we must put off the body of the sins of the flesh. **Colossians 2:9-14: For in Him dwells all the**

fullness of the Godhead bodily; and you are complete in Him, who is the head of all principality and power. In Him you were also circumcised with the circumcision made without hands, by putting off the body of sins of the flesh, by the circumcision of Christ, buried with Him in baptism, in which you also were raised with Him through faith in the working of God, who raised Him from the dead. And you, being dead in your trespasses and the uncircumcision of your flesh, He has made alive together with Him, having forgiven you all trespasses, having wiped out the handwriting of requirements that was against us, which was contrary to us. And He has taken it out of the way, having nailed it to the cross.

For forty years the Israelite males had not been circumcised because of the disobedience and unbelief of their fathers. They were out of covenant with God, so they must now individually renew their covenant with Him through circumcision. The place of their circumcision was called Gibeath Haaraloth, which means "the hill of foreskins." It was a heap of flesh. God's people are to be a marked people who live differently than the world. Before the sword *(Word of God)* can be used to defeat the enemy, it must first be used to cut off our flesh. The Israelites must gain victory over their flesh before they can gain victory over the enemy. The Holy Spirit touches our innermost being with the sharp knife of His Word circumcising our flesh life and establishing His Spirit and life in us. The crucifixion was Jesus' "Gilgal." It was His spiritual circumcision and the shed blood of atonement that brought life out of death. After Joshua had all of the males circumcised, God said, **"Today I have rolled away the reproach of Egypt from you." Joshua 5:9** Egypt represents the "world" and bondage. Their renewed covenant with God, illustrated by their obedience in the circumcision of the flesh, took away all of their blame or discredit before God. God's people were once again sealed and in right relationship with God. Jesus accomplished this once for all at the cross. Our reproach was rolled away at Calvary. If we serve a crucified Savior, we must lead a crucified life. God's order is salvation, sanctification and then glorification. In order for Jesus to become real to us, we must first become real with Him. We must open our hearts to His light and let

Him love our flesh to death. Jesus not only wants to protect us, He also wants to perfect us! It is this that protects us. **Jesus said in John 12:24, "Most assuredly, I say to you, unless a grain of wheat falls into the ground and dies, it remains alone; but if it dies, it produces much grain** *(fruit)*. Believers must die to self in order to bear fruit. What must die in us must die so the life of Christ will live in us. Our flesh is an enemy of God and of ourselves. It must go! It is better to let the Holy Spirit put our flesh to death now than the birds later. **(see Revelation 19:21...and all the birds gorged themselves on their flesh.)**

David removed the reproach of Israel by killing the Philistine Goliath who had taunted them and boasted for 40 days. **(1 Samuel 17:26)** The story of David and Goliath in the "natural" is a shadow of the "supernatural" defeat of Satan by the lion of the Tribe of Judah, Yeshua/Jesus.

The place of circumcision, Gilgal, is close to Mount Gerizim and Mount Ebal, the place of blessing and cursing. **(see Deuteronomy 11:30)** It is at these two mounts that God's people choose either blessing through obedience or cursing through disobedience. Gilgal is the place of choice and separation. Each person must choose either blessing through obedience to God or cursing through disobedience to God. As Joshua was about to die in **Joshua 24:15,** he called God's people to unity and warned them of the consequences of violating their covenant with God and disobeying His commands. **"Choose this day whom you will serve, whether the gods your forefathers served beyond the Jordan River, or the gods of the Amorites, in whose land you are living. As for me and my house, we will serve the Lord"** Each individual believer must make this choice.

Gilgal was Joshua's home base as he and God's people capture the inhabitants and take possession of the Promised Land . **(see Joshua 10:6-15; 10:43 and 14:6)** The True Joshua, Jesus, came to earth to remove the curse and take possession of it. We can choose blessing through Jesus or cursing without Him. In **Micah 6:5,** God told the Israelites to remember their journey from Shittim to Gilgal **"that you may know the righteous acts of the Lord."** Remember that Shittim means "thorns" and Gilgal means "rolling" signifying freedom. Jesus rolled away our reproach at the cross by conquering death and the grave. As we obediently follow our leader Jesus, our sins are rolled away and we are resurrected into new life – His life – in us.

In **Judges 2:1-3,** the Angel of the Lord *(who is Jesus)* went up from Gilgal to Bochim *(means "weeping"),* saying, **"I led you up from Egypt and brought you to the land of which I swore to your fathers; and I said, 'I will never break My covenant with you. And you shall make no covenant with the inhabitants of this land; you shall tear down their altars.' But you have not obeyed My voice. Why have you done this? Therefore I also said, 'I will not drive them out before you; but they shall be thorns in your side, and their gods shall be a snare to you."** Jesus is the Deliverer of God's people and the One who brings God's people into their inheritance. Jesus is the same yesterday *(Old Testament)*, today *(New Testament)* and forever *(Revelation)*. Jesus will never break His covenant with His people, because He is God. But, His people can walk away from His covenant through disobedience, rebellion and idol worship. **(see Rahab)** If we are out of God's will or in disobedience to His Word, we are in danger. God gives us the boundaries of His Word to keep us protected. When Jesus had to pronounce woes over Jerusalem, He wept. It was the heart of a suffering Savior who wept over His people whom He came to save but who rejected Him.

This external circumcision at Gilgal represents the internal circumcision of the heart. **(Romans 2:29) Joshua 5:8** says that after the whole nation had been circumcised, **they remained where they were in camp until they were healed.** God holds us in the palm of His hand until His work is done in us. Before we can move forward in victory, we must first be healed of our past. Believers are to remain with our brothers and sisters until each are healed of their pain, shame, sickness, guilt etc.

The Law God gave Moses for the Passover stated that no uncircumcised males are allowed to celebrate Passover. **(Exodus 12:48-49)** To be uncircumcised means you are unclean and out of covenant.

Gilgal, the place of circumcision of the flesh, is the place where

Joshua and God's people camped and launched all of their battles *(spiritual warfare)*. At Gilgal, the flesh has been circumcised and the blood shed. Christ's spiritual army must return to Gilgal, the place of circumcising the flesh, before they go into spiritual warfare. Spiritual warfare must be done God's way, not the way of the flesh.

The Israelites have renewed their covenant with God. God's people are now prepared to celebrate Passover. In **Micah 6:5,** God puts His people in remembrance of their journey from Shittim, which means "thorns" to Gilgal, which is the place of removal of the flesh before going into battle. **"Remember your journey from Shittim to Gilgal that you may know the righteous acts of the Lord."**

5. *They are to celebrate Passover.* The sacrificial death of the innocent lamb of Passover memorialized the salvation from death of the Israelites in Egypt and new life on the other side of the Red Sea. This pointed to Yeshua/Jesus the perfect once-for-all sacrificial Lamb for the sin of the world. **For Christ our Passover is sacrificed for us. Let us, therefore, celebrate the feast, not with old leaven, nor with the leaven of malice and wickedness, but with the unleavened bread of sincerity and truth. 1 Cor. 5:7-8** Passover represents a time of revival. When the nation of Israel strayed and then returned to righteousness, they celebrated Passover and a new commitment to God. We must all return to the cross of Yeshua/Jesus and circumcise our flesh before going into spiritual warfare.

God's people crossed the Jordan on the 10th day of the 1st month. This is 5 days short of a full forty years since they had left Egypt. The Israelites had not celebrated Passover throughout their journey in the wilderness. Five is the number of "grace—" *(atonement, life, cross and the fivefold ministry given by Christ to His Bride).* There were five wounds in Jesus on the cross. There were a total of five pieces of furniture in the Holy Place and the Most Holy Place – the golden candlestick, table of showbread, golden altar of incense, Ark of the Covenant and the mercy seat and these last two were one. Jesus fed the multitudes with five loaves, which symbolize the Bread of life who is Jesus. God in His grace has let them enter Israel in time to prepare for Passover four days later. They are to remember the miracle of their redemption in the Passover meal. This meal identified God's people with their deliverance and redemption at the Red Sea. This is the third Passover the Israelites have celebrated. The first was before their deliverance from bondage in Egypt. **(Exodus 12:1-28)** The second was at Mount Sinai just before God's people broke camp and moved toward Canaan. **(Numbers 9:1-5)** Now in **Joshua,** the Israelites are in a new land with a renewed covenant. They have been circumcised. They will celebrate Passover applying the blood sacrifice remembering God's delivering power and redemption before going into battle to inhabit the Promised Land.

At His last Passover meal, Jesus instituted the Lord's Supper, which identifies us with Christ's sacrifice. We remember His redemption and claim its benefits. **1 Corinthians 11:27-29** shows us that we are to examine ourselves before partaking of the body and blood of Jesus in communion. **Therefore, whoever eats this bread or drinks this cup of the Lord in an unworthy manner will be guilty of the body and blood of the Lord. But let a man examine himself, and so let him eat of the bread and drink of the cup. For he who eats and drinks in an unworthy manner eats and drinks judgment to himself, not discerning the Lord's body.** Before partaking of the Lord's body all known and unknown sin must be confessed. We must be pure as Christ's body is pure. If we take communion with known, unconfessed sin in our lives, we drink judgment upon ourselves. Do not take remembrance of Christ's redemption by His body and blood through communion lightly. Like the Passover Meal commemorates the redemption and deliverance of the Israelites at the Red Sea, communion is a memorial feast commemorating Christ's redemption of mankind through the Red Sea of His blood. We must come to this meal with pure hearts and with reverence.

The memorial stones of remembrance represent the **"word of their testimony"** and the Passover Lamb represents **"the blood of the Lamb."** **Revelation 12:11** shows us that Satan and his followers are defeated by the **"word of our testimony"** and the **"blood of the Lamb."**

Four things spiritually prepared the Israelites for the conquest and victory:

1. circumcision (removing the flesh)
2. memorial stones (testimony of God's delivering power)
3. Passover (blood of the Lamb)
4. new food (fruit of the Spirit and deeper truths of the Word)

As the Red Sea crossing preceded the defeat of Pharaoh and his army, the crossing of the Jordan preceded the defeat of the Canaanites in the Promised Land. The Israelites didn't possess the land after crossing the Red Sea, but they did after crossing the Jordan. **Hebrews 10:36....after you have done the will of God, you may receive the promise.**

It was at Passover when the walls of Jericho fell. The walls of Jericho had to come down so the Israelites could conquer the Promised Land. The blood of Jesus, the True Passover Lamb, will bring down the walls of stone around our hearts so He can possess the land and make us more than conquerors through Him.

There were seven great Passovers in scripture. The first Passover was in Exodus just before God delivered the Israelites from the enemy and bondage in Egypt. *(Deliverance from the Enemy and bondage)*

The second Passover placed God's people in Israel. **Joshua 5:7** This Passover gave them the land God promised to Abraham, Isaac and Jacob. On the first day of the Feast of Unleavened Bread, they ate the fruit of the Promised Land. On the last day of the Feast of Unleavened Bread, Jericho fell. "Unleavened" means without sin. Jesus, the Sinless One, was resurrected on the first day of the Feast of Unleavened Bread and will destroy Satan and the world's system on the last day of the Feast of Unleavened Bread, just as Jericho fell on that day. *(Inheritance of the Promised Land)*

The third Passover celebrated at Gideon's lead set God's people free from the Midianites and restored them back to God. **Judges 6:19** *(Restoration and victory)*

There were three Passovers first and then the building of the Temple of Solomon. These three Passovers represent the birth, death and resurrection of Yeshua/Jesus who builds His Temple in the hearts of His faithful followers.

The fourth Passover was in the days of Hezekiah after the

temple was built. The Israelites had fallen into idolatry under the rule of Ahaz. This is type and shadow of the great falling away of the elect in the last days. The Israelites had walked away from God just as we can walk away from Jesus. Hezekiah offered the sacrifice of Passover to cleanse the nation. Hezekiah sought revival and restoration of God's people. First the people had to sanctify themselves. **(2 Chronicles 29:17)** Then the Passover sacrifice was offered. When we walk away from Yeshua/Jesus, we must return to the cross and sanctify ourselves of sin and idolatry just as the Israelites had to offer the blood of the lamb at Passover. We must open the door of our hearts and allow the Word and the Spirit to cleanse them. Christ will never turn away a repentant heart. *(Revival and restoration)*

The 5th Passover was that of Josiah. **(2 Chronicles 35:1)** Josiah was a king who did right in the sight of the Lord. Josiah destroyed all of the false idols, restored true temple worship, purified the land and the people and had the people renew their covenant with God. This Passover was a great celebration. **The Passover had not been observed like this in Israel since the days of the prophet Samuel; and none of the kings of Israel had ever celebrated such a Passover as did Josiah, with the priests, the Levites and all Judah and Israel who were there with the people of Jerusalem. 2 Chronicles 35:18** The Israelites had gone backwards. They were carrying the Ark of God's presence around on their shoulders after God had given David the instructions for the more permanent house of the Ark in the temple. The Lord told Solomon in **2 Chronicles 7:16, "I have chosen and consecrated this temple so that my Name may be there forever. My eyes and my heart will always be there.** Solomon's temple is type and shadow of the heavenly sanctuary where Yahweh and Yeshua live and reign forever in the hearts of His followers. Because the Israelites were in disobedience carrying the Ark on their shoulders, Josiah told them to **"put the sacred Ark in the temple that Solomon son of David king of Israel built"** and to **"prepare yourselves by the directions written by David king of Israel and by his son Solomon. 2 Chronicles 35:3-4** *(Renewed covenant and true temple worship)*

The 6th Passover was celebrated at the time of Ezra at the dedication of the newly restored temple. **Ezra 6:19** This was the third restoration of the temple. *(Rebuilding and restoration)*

The 7th Passover was the death of Yeshua/Jesus. He is the last great Passover Lamb to which all others pointed. Jesus said, **"Destroy this temple, and I will raise it again in three days." John 2:19** The listeners thought that Jesus was talking about the earthy temple of Herod which stood in Christ's time, but Jesus was talking about His body the true, indestructible Temple of God. Jesus was prophesying of His death and resurrection. He used the earthly temple to illustrate a supernatural truth.

As Joshua led God's people into a life of faith, blessing and possession, Jesus will lead us into the abundant life of faith, blessing and possession of the land. The miracle of crossing the Jordan with Joshua leading according to God's Word was evidence of his willingness to obey God and serve His people. Therefore, God exalted Joshua before all the people. Joshua has done all that God commanded him. Because the True Joshua, Jesus, obeyed all of the Word of God perfectly and served both Jew and Gentile, He was exalted to the throne of God after His finished work on the cross. Jesus paved the way for all to be restored to the Father.

After all the people crossed over the Jordan, then Joshua told the priests carrying the Ark to come up out of the Jordan. When Jesus came up out of the Jordan, the Holy Spirit rested upon Him. Sanctification releases the Holy Spirit.

As Joshua was raised up quietly under the supervision of Moses, God is raising up a company of people in the secret places with Joshua hearts to lead His Bride into possessing the land in these end times. This will be a time of great transition in the Body of Christ. These obedient leaders who have been raised up like David in the shepherd's field will be exalted into leadership positions in Christ's Body. They will take God's people to places where **"they have not been before."**

Manna ceases – New Food

The day after the Israelites celebrated Passover, they ate the fruit of the new land. First the circumcision of the flesh, then the shed blood of the Lamb, and finally the fruit! Up to this time, God's people had only eaten the manna provided by God. Now they have new food – the produce of the land, unleavened bread and roasted grain. "Leaven" represents sin in scripture. Unleavened bread symbolizes sinlessness (purity). Roasted grain has had the chaff removed and is roasted by fire. This roasted grain represents believers who have been refined by fire. The fruit of the Spirit is the by-product of these refined, matured believers. **But the fruit of the Spirit is love, joy, peace, longsuffering, kindness, goodness, faithfulness, gentleness, self-control. Against such there is no law. Galatians 5:22** If believers are walking in this way, there is no need of any law because love fulfills the law. True agape love brings in the fruit of the Spirit. Against such, there is no law.

The fruit of the vine (grapes) grows in clusters. So, too, the fruit of the Spirit is a cluster. We must walk in all of these nine attributes. Love is listed first. If we are walking in love, all of the others will follow. Followers of Jesus must also grow together as a cluster attached to the True Vine. **(John 15:1-5)**

God will no longer supply manna. His people must now gather their own food in this land. Mature believers need not rely on pastors to feed them all of the time. Mature believers must search out the deep, nourishing fruit of God's Word for themselves.

God had promised His people a **"land of wheat and barley, vines and fig trees, pomegranates, olive oil and honey; a land where bread will not be scarce and you will lack nothing; a land where rocks are iron and you can dig copper out of the hills." Deuteronomy 8:8-9** Now, after offering the blood of the Lamb, circumcising their flesh and eating new food, God's people finally can taste the fruit of the land with its abundance and blessing!

The various foods of the Promised Land symbolize the following:

1. Wheat = godly ones *(matured Christians)*
2. Barley= poor in Spirit *(humility)*
3. Vines and fig trees = *fruit of Spirit (Jesus)*
4. Pomegranates=fruitfulness, joyfulness
5. Olive oil = Holy Spirit anointing
6. Honey = sweetness of Christ and His Word

7. Rocks of iron = strength; inflexible authority
8. Hills of copper = endurance and strength
9. Bread not scarce = abundance of the Word of God

Nine is the number of the Holy Spirit. There were nine gifts of the Holy Spirit in **1 Cor. 12:1-11** and the fruit of the Holy Spirit in **Galatians 5:22-23** was nine in number. Nine is the number of "finality, fullness and fruitfulness." It can be the finality, fullness and fruitfulness of both the Divine Spirit as well as Divine judgment.

Waters of the Jordan parted three times in scripture.

The waters of the Jordan were parted three times:

1. <u>for Joshua</u> *("Yahweh saves")* and the Israelites **(Joshua 3:14-16)**
2. <u>for Elijah</u> *("Jehovah is my God")* **(2 Kings 1:8)** and
3. <u>for Elisha</u> *("God is Savior")* **(2 Kings 2:14)**.

Three is the number of the Godhead, the Perfect Witness. The waters of the Jordan represent the death, burial and resurrection of Jesus. When Jesus removed His garment of flesh, He crossed over the waters between heaven and earth to the throne of God. In the book of Joshua, the waters of the Jordan were gathered in a heap so the Israelites could cross over into the Promised Land. Jesus will come again to gather His own in a heap to take them to the Eternal Promised Land.

Elijah: *"Jehovah is my God"*

Elijah parted the waters of the Jordan, brought rain in drought, increased food supplies, performed miracles even resurrecting the life of the widow's son, pronounced judgments on kings and destroyed enemies by the power of God.

Elijah took his mantle (garment of power and authority of the prophet), rolled it up and struck the Jordan River and the waters divided in the center to the right and to the left so Elijah and Elisha could cross over. **(2 Kings 2:8)** Most of God's prophets were prophets of judgment. They were not the most popular men. When they struck with the Word of God, the true believers received it, but the false did not. This separated the true from the false.

The Gospels of Jesus Christ pass through the two testaments drawing them together by His blood and His Holy Spirit. Elijah struck the waters of the Jordan, but Jesus went down into the Jordan bodily to cleanse it of pollution and prepare the way for all to cross over. As the Word of God, Jesus washed the Jordan and immediately the Holy Spirit was released. It is the washing of the water of the Word that brings forth new life – the life of Christ in us.

Elijah represents the Prophets. Jesus, the Mighty Prophet, was reflected in both the life of Elijah as well as Elisha. The Law and the Prophets reflected the life of Jesus through the "natural" which had the reflection of the "supernatural" Jesus in their midst.

Elisha represents Jesus as the double-portion anointing. As Elisha received a double-portion of Elijah's anointing, Christians receive a double-portion through Jesus. We not only have Jesus in our hearts, we have His Holy Spirit to illuminate His Word and give revelation knowledge and guidance. These two will perform miraculous works through His people.

Elijah was humble and compassionate as reflected in the story of the widow of Sidon *(a gentile)* **(1 Kings 17:8-24).** However, he also spoke judgment against the evil in the land. **(1 Kings 17:1)** Jesus too was full of compassion and humility, but He also spoke judgment against the self-righteous, hypocritical, arrogant and prideful Pharisees and Sadducees. Like Jesus, Elijah was a messenger of judgment but he was also an angel of mercy. He was both a hero and a humble servant of God who performed great miracles because of his loyalty to God and His people, his faith and his obedience.

Elijah witnessed of the holiness required by God in a wicked age as the Law and the Prophets show us the standard of holiness of our God. Elijah preached conviction of sin and repentance as the condition for God's forgiveness and mercy. The backslidden Israelites needed to be awakened from their spiritual slumber and idolatry. Elijah was God's man. He would expose the wickedness of Ahab and Jezebel who were leading God's people into idolatry and evil.

John the Baptist later came in the same "spirit of Elijah" preaching confession, repentance and baptism to prepare the people for their Savior Jesus/Yeshua. God will not pass by sin. We must confess and repent of it. Jesus wept over Jerusalem and His people Israel because He saw the terrible judgment that was coming to them because they had rejected God's saving grace through Yeshua/Jesus. This is the heart of a loving Savior weeping over His own people Israel. **"If you had known, even you, especially in this your day, the things that make for your peace! But now they are hidden from your eyes. For days will come upon you when your enemies will build an embankment around you, surround you and close in on every side, and level you, and your children within you, to the ground; and they will not leave in you one stone upon another, because you did not know the time of your visitation." Luke 19:41-43** Jesus is not only grace; He is also Truth. As Truth, Jesus cannot withhold the truth from any man. The very Presence of God in Yeshua had visited His people, but their own arrogance and pride of understanding and their desire to hold onto the legalism of the Law blinded them to the Truth *(Yeshua)* who was walking in their midst. As hard as it must have been for Jesus to speak these words to the very ones He came to save, He spoke it nonetheless. As God's mighty Prophet, Jesus had to warn His people. His weeping over Jerusalem showed His heart of love toward them. Jesus didn't delight in their downfall, He cried over it. Jesus tells us that we too are to speak the truth **in love**, not condemnation and judgment. Jesus didn't come the first time to condemn, but to save. He also sends His followers out into the world not to condemn but that He can save them through us.

Elijah, the prophet of judgment, prophesied of:

1. the drought that would come upon the land because of disobedience and idolatry **(1 Kings 17:1)**
2. of Ahab's destruction **(1 Kings 21:17-29)**
3. of Ahaziah's death **(2 Kings 1:2-17)**
4. of the plague that would inflict the people of Judah because they had played the harlot like the house of Ahab.

On Elijah's last day before his translation *(resurrection)* without death, he and Elisha went from Gilgal to Bethel and onto Jericho and then to the Jordan. Elijah would return the way he came. **The last will be first, the first last.** In like manner, Jesus returned to where He came from – the throne of God.

Let's take a look at these four places:

1. *Jordan River* – place of the anointing of God through the empowerment of the Holy Spirit. We die to our own will, wishes and plans and surrender to the will of God. At the Jordan, we take up our cross (crucified life) and follow Jesus. It is at the Jordan that we die, submit, wait and obey. The life and power of God only comes through the death of our own will. It is this life that will reflect the greater glory of God and Jesus. Elijah after crossing the Jordan was taken up *(resurrected)* by God's power into the very presence of God in a whirlwind. The Jordan represents the Holy Spirit and resurrection power.

2. *Bethel* – means "house of God." It is the place of prayer, worship and the teaching of God's Word. These three will bring you into God's presence and resurrection power.

3. *Gilgal* — place of circumcision of the flesh. We die to self and put on Jesus Christ.

4. *Jericho* – place of spiritual victory and the gateway to possession of the Promised Land.

The prophet Samuel established schools of prophecy at Bethel, Gilgal and Jericho. Elijah and Elisha obviously emanated from Samuel's schools.

Like Jesus did with His disciples, Elijah met one last time with the prophets to advise, encourage and assure them before his resurrection. With the True Joshua, Jesus, leading us across the Jordan River and on to Bethel, Gilgal and Jericho, He will take us to the higher Christian life. Before leaving this earth, Elijah asked Elisha if there was anything he could do for him. Elisha boldly asked for a double portion of his power and authority. The only way Elijah could grant Elisha's request was if Elisha saw Elijah transported by the power of the Holy Spirit as he was taken up. Jesus' disciples also could not receive His power and anointing until He was resurrected. Christ's disciples had to first see Him resurrected before He could give them His power and anointing at Pentecost. It is those who keep their eyes fixed on Jesus who will receive great power and authority in His Name.

Some people thought that Jesus was Elijah. Jesus said in **Luke 9:18, "Who do the crowds say that I am?"** His disciples answered saying, **"John the Baptist, but some say Elijah, and others say that one of the old prophets has risen again."** Then Jesus said to them, **"But who do you say that I am?"** Peter answered, **"You are the Christ." Mark 8:29** Flesh and blood did not reveal this to Peter. It was revelation knowledge given through the Holy Spirit.

Exit Elijah who represents the Law and the Prophets. Enter Elisha who represents Jesus. Jesus did not begin to teach until John the Baptist was put in prison. When John the Baptist's ministry ended, Jesus' began. In like manner, Yeshua/Jesus will not come again until the ministry of the two witnesses of Revelation is finished.

Elisha: *"God is Savior"*
Elisha, who was an intimate, loyal friend to his master, would not leave his master Elijah's side. **(2 Kings 2:6)** He would go wherever Elijah took him. This, of course, pointed to those who love and follow Jesus. We must never leave our Master's side and go wherever He leads us. The power of Elijah was transferred with his mantle of authority and power as Christ's power and authority are transferred through His robe of righteousness to all those who love and serve Him. Elisha tested his power in the Spirit by striking the Jordan in the reverse order. Jesus reversed the order of the Old Testament, which Elijah represented. Elisha demonstrated his power before the priesthood of Israel who were watching from afar. They were the witnesses of the transference of God's power from Elijah to Elisha. God's power was demonstrated through the nation of Israel and its chosen men of God in the Old Testament. That power was transferred to Yeshua/Jesus when He came to earth through a Jewish woman in His incarnate form.

God performed seven miracles through the mighty prophet

Elijah. However, He performed fourteen miracles through Elisha. Elisha's miracles closely resemble the life and work of Jesus. Two of Elisha's miracles were at the Jordan: 1) He commanded the Syrian *(gentile)* general Naaman to wash in the Jordan seven times to be healed of leprosy. Seven is the number of spiritual perfection. Leprosy represents sin and speaks of the cleansing of sin in the hearts of Christ's followers. 2) Elisha made the iron ax head float after it had fallen off its handle into the waters of the Jordan. This speaks of resurrection life. So, the two miracles Elisha performed in the Jordan symbolize the cleansing of sin and resurrection life. Both point to Jesus who cleanses our sin by His blood, His Word and His Spirit and is the resurrection and the life for all who follow Him.

The following are the 14 miracles God performed through Elisha:

1. *He divided the Jordan making the way for him to cross over in the center on dry ground.* (**2 Kings 2:14**) Elisha returned the way he came, just as Jesus returned to the place from which He came.....at the throne of God. Jesus parted the waters between heaven and earth making a straight path for all to cross over to the very presence of the Father.

2. *He healed the waters of Jericho destroying death and made the land fruitful.* (**2 Kings 2:20-22**) Jericho represents the condemned world. Jesus sent the waters of His Holy Spirit and Word to heal the nations of the world, destroy death and make the land of our hearts fruitful for His kingdom.

3. *He pronounced a curse over the young men who mocked him as he was going up to Bethel. As a result, two female bears came out of the woods and mauled forty-two of them to death.* (**2 Kings 2:23-24**) This is the only time Elisha cursed in scripture. Jesus also only cursed once in scripture. He cursed the unfruitful tree. (**Matthew 21:19**) Jesus expects His followers to bear fruit for His kingdom. Bethel means "house of God." Elisha was going to the place of the house of God to offer sacrifice. These young men mocked him taking the things of God lightly. Sin brought death. Christ also was mocked, spat upon and humiliated. (**Luke 23:11,36**)

4. *He supplied water for Jehoshaphat and the king of Israel's army and their horses so they could defeat the Moabites.* Jesus provided the water of His Word and His Spirit to defeat the enemy of His people.

5. *He multiplied the widow's oil as long as she had an empty vessel.* Jesus pours out the oil of His Holy Spirit as long as there is an empty vessel (person) to fill. Jesus must first empty us of our flesh life before He can fill us with His Holy Spirit.

6. *He raised the Shulamite's child from the dead.* Elijah breathed his spirit into the child and he came back to life. Jesus is the resurrection and the life. Jesus raised 1)Lazarus *(Jew)*, 2) the widow's son and 3) Jairus' daughter *(Gentile)* from the dead. In so doing, Jesus was showing us that His resurrection life is for all young and old, male and female. Lazarus was older so his stench was greater than the young boy and girl. Jesus breathes His Spirit into those who follow Him giving them new, resurrected life no matter what stage of life they come to Him.

7. *He made the poisoned pottage harmless.* Elijah put flour (bread) in the pot and made it harmless. It is the Bread of life, Jesus and His Word that purifies all and keeps us from harm.

8. *He fed 100 people with 20 loaves of bread.* Jesus fed 4,000 and 5,000 with five loaves of bread and two fish. Five is the number of "grace" and two is the number of "fullness of testimony in agreement"—truth. The supernatural message of these "natural" feedings of Jesus is that He fed the multitudes with grace and truth. Jesus is Grace and Truth. The Law came through a servant, but grace and truth through the Son. **John 1:14: And the Word became flesh and dwelt among us, and we beheld His glory, the glory as of the only begotten of the Father, full of grace and truth.**

9. *He cured Naaman(a Gentile) of leprosy.* Elisha told Naaman to go and wash in the Jordan River seven times and then his flesh would be restored and he would be clean. Leprosy represents "sin." The Jordan River represents cleansing and anointing. Seven is the number of spiritual completion/perfection. Jesus is God's spiritual perfection and the One who anoints and cleanses. Mankind with Jesus in his heart is God's spiritual perfection.

10. *He gave Gehazi, his servant, leprosy because he lied and was greedy.* The leprosy that was cured in Naaman was placed on Gehazi because of sin. We reap what we sow. Gehazi was bound in sin.

11. _He made the ax head float by cutting off a stick and throw-ing it into the water._ This is a picture of the cross of Jesus and its resurrection power. We must be felled by the ax and take up our cross to receive resurrected life. There must be a death before there is a resurrection. Our flesh must die so we can be raised in resurrec-tion power. The water represents the Word and the anointing of the Holy Spirit that will bring us to new life in Christ.

12. _Ben-hadad's plans to attack the Israelites was revealed to Elijah._ Jesus knows the thoughts and intents of everyone's heart. He will reveal the Enemy's plans to His prophets as a warning and for action.

13. _Because Elisha prayed, God struck the Syrians blind and they were defeated. He prayed again and they received their sight again._ Jesus thwarts all the plans of the Enemy for His people. Sin blinds people. When Elisha and the Israelites had taken the Syrians captive, the king of Israel wanted to kill them. But Elisha would not let him. **"Would you kill those whom you have taken captive with your sword and your bow?"** Instead Elisha fed them and sent them back to their master. We are not to "kill" sinners. They have been taken captive by the Enemy of their souls. Instead we are to feed them the bread and water of the Word so they will come to Jesus for salvation. Elisha did "good" to his enemy.

14. _Even after his death, Elisha's bones revived a man bringing him back to life._ Even Elisha's bones were anointed. Jesus, God's Anointed One, is the resurrection and the life. It was after Jesus died and was buried that He was resurrected and gave the power of the Holy Spirit to His disciples. God can take dry, dead bones, revive them and knit them together into His Body by the anointing of His Holy Spirit and Word.

As Elisha received a double-portion of Elijah's power and author-ity, Christians receive a double-portion in Jesus. We not only receive Jesus in our hearts, we also have the Holy Spirit to bring us into the fullness of Christ's resurrection power and authority within us. Elisha had to pick up Elijah's mantle in order to receive the spirit of Elijah's power and authority. In so doing, Elisha claimed the anointing, power and authority of this garment and crossed back over the Jordan to carry on God's work that had begun in Elijah. Christians also have to put on the garment of Christ's righteousness, anointing, power and authority in order to cross over the Jordan and fight the giants in the land and conquer it. It must be an act of our will.

Baptism and repentance is the first step in our journey to the promised inheritance in Christ. John the Baptist came out of the wilderness and began preaching repentance and baptism in the Jordan River area to prepare the way of the Lord. (**Matthew 3:5-6; Mark 1:5; John 1:28**) Jesus is calling His Bride to holiness and resurrection power to prepare the way of His return.

Elijah and Elisha were two mighty witnesses of resurrection life. In **Revelation 11:1-6**, there are two witnesses in Israel moving in great power and authority like Elijah and Elisha. These will be two mighty prophets of God who will witness of God's judgment over the earth and who will be killed and resurrected on the third day. God is now working through the witness of Yeshua's Body of believers made up of Jew and Gentile. He will raise up His Body in resurrection power in the end times as a witness of His blessing through Yeshua/Jesus and as a warning of His coming judgment to those who have rejected His saving grace through Jesus. In the endtimes, Christ's Temple will operate in the spirit and power of Elijah and Elisha before God's wrath is poured out. Christ's mighty army of believers full of the power of His Holy Spirit and Word will be large and mighty. His judgment will begin in the Temple with the elders and the leaders of God's people. (**see Joel 2:15-17**) The leaders will weep for God's people and ask God to spare them as Moses did the Israelites.**v17 "Let the bridegroom go out from his chamber, and the bride from her dressing room."v16** The Bridegroom (Yeshua) and His Bride (Temple) will be moving closer to the wedding. This speaks of the intimate relationship between the Bridegroom and the Bride just before the union. Repentance and cleansing will prepare this Bride, who is the spiritual army of God, for the work God has called them and raised them up to do.

Commander of God's army – Joshua 5:13-15

It was after the men had been circumcised and had celebrated

Passover that Jesus, the Commander of God's angelic host appeared to Joshua. Here the first and second Joshua met face to face. The Israelites had returned to the Lord in obedience to His Word (Law) that God had given to Moses. Jesus, the Living Word, had not yet come to earth, so God's people were under the authority of the Law at this time. Joshua had thought that he would be the commander of God's army, but he would soon learn that the battle was not his, but the Lord's.

God's grace called them out of Egypt through the Red Sea, but it was His faithfulness to His Word that brought them into Israel. Before they can enter the land of Promise, however, there is one more death that must take place – Joshua's. If Joshua is to lead God's people into victory and possession of the land, he must understand that the battle is the Lord's, not his. He must surrender his will, self-sufficiency and strength to Jesus, the Commander of God's army.

Joshua has not yet received direction from the Lord as to how he should proceed against the inhabitants of the Promised Land. As Joshua is nearing Jericho, he looks over the situation and plots his course of action. Joshua looks up *(eyes of faith)* and sees **"a man with a drawn sword in his hand." Joshua 5:13** A "drawn sword" represents judgment and battle in scripture. But to God's people it is an instrument of mercy, grace and victory. The sword of God's Word shows us the love, grace and mercy of the Father through His precious Son. Joshua and the Israelites would be God's instruments of judgment against His enemies and the enemies of His people. Joshua saw a "man" but this was no ordinary man. It was the preincarnate Jesus who is the Commander of God's angelic host. Jesus and His angelic host had already conquered the land for Joshua and God's people by His Divine power. Under the command of the Lord of the heavenly host, Joshua will be victorious. As leader of God's people, Joshua must die to his own strength and trust Jesus for the victory. He must take his orders from above. There can only be one Ruler in God's kingdom—Jesus/Yeshua. Joshua is merely a follower of the One who gives him the victory. The battle is the Lord's but Joshua must obey all that God commands. Then the victory will be his. Christ will lead Joshua through all the land in victory and in power. He will uphold Joshua with His righteous right hand—the place of power and authority. **(2 Corinthians 3:5;2:14)**

Jesus appeared to Joshua in the form of a "man," the same form He would come to earth to save the world. Jesus had to come in the fashion of a man to redeem mankind from the original sin of Adam because it was man who committed this original sin. Because sin entered the land through the disobedience and unbelief of man, it must be removed through the faith and obedience of God in the form of man. Adam was made "man" in the image and likeness of God. He was clothed in God's glory. Jesus came in the fashion of Man but had God's glory within Him. Jesus had to reverse the sin of the first Adam so man could once again come into God's presence without fear or shame.

In **Revelation 19:14-15,** Jesus comes with a sword in His mouth and the army of heaven follows Him. This is the sword of the power of His Word that He will use to destroy the enemies of God's people. In **Genesis 1:3** as the Word, Jesus created. But here in Revelation, by the power of His Word He destroys the enemies of His people. To God's people, the Word is a shield and a blessing, but to those who don't know Jesus, it is a vehicle of judgment.

Joshua asks this "man" if He is for them or against them. Jesus answers that He is neither but as Commander of God's army He has now come. Jesus doesn't "join" our side; we join Him as His servant and spiritual warrior. When we join Christ's army, the burden of the victory in battle is His, not ours. **(see 2 Corinthians 2:14;Philippians 4:13;Revelation 15:2)** Jesus didn't come to take sides but to save the world and to do spiritual battle with the forces of evil that hold humanity captive. Christ appears to Joshua as a mighty warrior armed for battle with His sword in His hand. This was the very position Joshua was about to take.

Joshua realizes that he is before the very presence of God so he falls down before Him in reverence, humility and awe. The person who bows the lowest in humility brings the greatest honor to Jesus.

Joshua was the commander of an earthly army, but Jesus is Commander of God's spiritual army. The Lord told Joshua to **"take your sandals off your foot, for the place where you stand is holy."**

And Joshua did so. Joshua 5:15 Wherever the presence of the Lord stands is holy ground. It is God's presence that sanctified this wicked land and made it holy, just as the presence of Jesus and His Holy Spirit in the heart of a person makes him or her holy. Only the blood of Jesus makes the land of Israel holy. All – both Jew and Gentile – have sinned and fallen short of the glory of God. We cannot achieve righteousness by our own work. It is strictly the blood of Jesus that makes a land and a people holy so no one can boast.

Taking ones sandals off is a sign of respect and honor. This act made Joshua a servant of the Lord. Sandals are dirty—full of the dust of the earth. Joshua must remove what is dirty in order to stand in the presence of the Lord. The disciples had removed their sandals and Jesus washed their feet. **(John 13:5)** It is Jesus who sanctifies and who will lead Joshua to victory. Joshua must take the position of servant and take his directions from Jesus, the Commander of God's army. Nothing or no one must take the glory away from Jesus.

If Jesus lives in our hearts, we must allow His cleansing hand to purify the land of our hearts so He can abide in them. All that is not of Him must be destroyed bringing unity and harmony to His Body. All that causes division or separation must cease. Denominational pride must go! Self-wills must go! Jealousy must go! Unforgiveness must go! Anger must go! Bickering must go! Insecurity must go! Greed must go! Arrogance must go! Pride must go! Followers of Jesus must be willing to lay aside every weight and follow Jesus. We must humble ourselves before Him and give all of the glory and honor to Him alone. Victory will only come through faith, submission and obedience. We were not created to function independently of God or to act as our own master. We must deny our self—our self-seeking, self-serving, self-justifying, self-glorifying, self-centeredness and self-confidence that serves the world, the flesh and the devil and take up our cross and follow Jesus. **(Matthew 16:24)** As we deny our self, we invite Jesus to fill the unoccupied land of our hearts with His life in us.

Joshua and God's people already had the victory because Jesus went before them with His army of angelic host. All Joshua and the people had to do to obtain the victory was obey God's commands. Joshua made the Lord's Word known to his leaders and God's people. He doesn't explain God's command nor does he alter it as strange as the command sounded in instructing them to walk around the city silently for six days blowing the trumpets of ram's horns and then seven times on the seventh day. The Israelites were to **"be still and know that God is God."**

CHAPTER 5

The Fall of Jericho – Joshua 6

G od told Abraham in **Genesis 15:16** that the Israelites could
not inherit the Promised Land because the sin of the Amorites
had not reached its full measure. The time has now come. The sins
of the people of Canaan has reached its full measure, just as it
happened in the days of Sodom and Gomorrah and as will happen
in the days of Revelation when the wickedness and sin in the world
will reach its full measure.

God's presence must be with His people if they are to have
victory. Jericho was to be the firstfruit to God of the Promised
Land. Everything that was not holy in that city must be destroyed.
The Law said that the firstfruits must be consecrated to God and
holy to the Lord. Therefore, everything in the city of Jericho must
be totally eliminated. Christ's Bride will be the firstfruit to the
Lord. She will be wholly consecrated to God and purified, "without
spot or blemish." There will be nothing of the world or flesh in Her.

Joshua has prepared God's people for the first battle. They have
circumcised their flesh, renewed their covenant with God, have
celebrated Passover—the memorial of their redemption and deliverance – and have eaten the fruit of the land. Now they will advance
into battle against the strong, fortressed city of Jericho.

Jericho is known as the "city of palm trees." **(see Dt. 34:3;2
Chron. 28:15))** Palm trees symbolize victory. **(see Ps. 92:12;SS
7:7-8)** The crowd took palm branches and went out to meet Jesus as

He rode into Jerusalem just before the Feast of Passover. They shouted, **"Blessed is he who comes in the name of the Lord! Blessed is the King of Israel." John 12:13** Jesus is the King of victory over the enemy and death and the King over His people. It is Jesus alone who will purify His Bride and bring His people victory.

Joshua lived by faith, not by sight. He had seen He who was "invisible" Yeshua/Jesus, the Commander of God's heavenly host. Jericho was to be conquered by faith and obedience to God, not through human wisdom and strength.

When God's people are crossing the Jordan and going into the land of Israel, they march behind the Ark. But now going into battle, the Ark is in the center of the marching army with a front guard of warriors before it and a rear guard behind it.

Front Guard = New Testament Saints
Ark = Yeshua/Jesus/Word of God
Rear Guard = Old Testament Saints

The front guard and the rear guard meet making a complete circle around the stronghold of Jericho. This represents the full circle of the Word of God (Jesus). The first and the last meet in Yeshua/Jesus forming the full circle of the Word. As we walk in unity with the full circle of the Word of God on our lips surrounding the strongholds of the Enemy, he is defeated. Jesus comes in Revelation with a sword in His mouth. This is the sword of the power of His Word, which will defeat the enemies of His people. To God's people, the Word is a shield and a blessing, but to the Enemy of God's people and to those who don't know Yeshua/Jesus, it is a vehicle of judgment.

These front guard and rear guard warriors in Joshua are the guardians of the Ark, the Law, the Rod of Aaron and the Golden Pot of Manna, which are hidden inside the Ark of God's Presence. The elect must guard the sword of God's Word who is Jesus when marching into spiritual warfare. The Word of God is holy and must be carried reverently and with caution making sure it is being rightly divided.

As I have stated previously, the Law, the Rod of Aaron and the

Golden Pot of Manna are all hidden in the True Ark of God's Presence Yeshua/Jesus. Jesus is the two tablets of the Law as the Word of God. He is the Rod of Aaron that budded as the Resurrection Life. He is the Golden Pot of Manna as the Divine Bread of Life. Those of us who follow Yeshua/Jesus must be the guardians of His Word, His life and His resurrection power. In the last days, Yeshua and His Word will spiritually circumcise all who go "into" Israel. Upon accepting Yeshua/Jesus as Lord, we are all "Israel"—"those who strive with God." We are not only tied to the physical land of Israel that Jesus has chosen as His final abode on earth, we are tied to spiritual Israel. Jesus will rule and reign from that land during the millennium. Joshua had to fight the Canaanites in order to conquer Israel for God's people. Christ's Bride has to conquer spiritual Israel for God's people through spiritual warfare and the Anointed Word. The same spiritual powers and principalities that ruled Canaan at the time of Joshua also rule today. **For our struggle is not against flesh and blood, but against the rulers, against the authorities, against the powers of this dark world and against the spiritual forces of evil in the heavenly realms. Ephesians 6:12**

Jericho is five miles from the Jordan River. God would show His grace indicated by the number five by defeating the enemies of His people. The city of Jericho was closed because the inhabitants were filled with fear at the advancing of God's people. No one was permitted in or out of the city. The walls of Jericho had to come down so God's people could begin the conquer of the Promised Land *(Israel)*. Jericho was the first hindrance to conquering all of the land. Jericho represents the world and pride. Pride is a strong fortress. God must conquer our pride so the walls around our hearts will come down. It is after God has broken our pride that He will begin to possess the land of our hearts. Our stony hearts full of pride will then become hearts of compassion, mercy and love. God must also take the "world" out of us so we will reflect the grace and mercy of Jesus, Our Commander.

The Lord said to Joshua, **"See, I have given Jericho into your hand, its king and the mighty men of valor." Joshua 6:2** Their new Commander, Jesus, had already given them the victory over the enemy. Victory only comes from the Lord through faith, submission and obedience. All God's people had to do was obey their commander, walk around the city once a day, no talking, blow the trumpets and carry the Ark in their midst for six days. The Lord gave the inhabitants of Jericho six days to surrender. This was God's grace. This represents the 6,000 years God has sent His Word out over the earth to call people to surrender their lives to His Son Yeshua/Jesus for salvation and eternal life. On the seventh day, God's people are to march around the city of Jericho seven times with the priests blowing the trumpets *(shofars)*. When the priests give one long blast of the trumpets *(shofars)*, the people are to give a loud shout and the walls of Jericho would fall down. This represents the seven trumpets of Revelation, which are blown just before the fullness of God's wrath is poured out over the earth and the Enemy is destroyed forever by Yeshua/Jesus.

Here in **Joshua 6**, there are seven priests with seven shofars before the Ark of God's presence sending God's warning to the inhabitants of Jericho. In **Revelation 1-3,** Jesus, the True Ark of God's presence, is revealed and is walking among the 7 menorahs *(candlesticks)*, as the Light and High Priest of His Church. These 7 candlesticks represent His entire Church made up of all nations and people. There are 7 angels over the 7 churches who are preparing His Temple to rule and reign in the land, just as Joshua prepared the Israelites before going into battle to conquer the land of Israel and defeat the enemy. There are only two "candlesticks" of the seven in Revelation who receive no correction ......Philadelphia, which is the church of brotherly love and Smyrna, which is the persecuted church. Smyrna means "myrrh" and represents burial, anointing, sacrifice, suffering and sweet fragrance. These two churches are the two olive trees of **Zechariah 4:3** who are filled with the oil of the Holy Spirit who carry the Divine Light of the Word Jesus Christ *(represented by the golden menorah)* and the fullness of the Holy Spirit to others. They operate in the power of the Holy Spirit, which is love and sacrifice. **"Not by might, nor by power, but by My Spirit," says the Lord Almighty. Zechariah 4:6** These two olive trees also represent the two testaments of the Word of God that reveal the Divine Light Jesus who is filled with the fullness of

God's Holy Spirit. The solid gold menorah in **Zechariah 4:2** repre-sents Yeshua/Jesus. **"I see a solid gold lampstand** *(menorah)* **with a bowl at the top and seven lights on it, with seven channels to the lights. Also there are two olive trees by it, one on the right of the bowl and the other on its left." Vv2-3** The bowl on top of the solid gold lampstand *(menorah)* and the seven lights represents Jesus as Perfect Divine Light who is the recipient of the fullness of the Holy Spirit indicated by the seven channels. The seven channels are the seven spirits of God, which is the fullness of the Holy Spirit. It is the blood of Jesus that poured out the golden oil of His Holy Spirit over all the earth.

In **Revelation 8,** there is silence in heaven just like there is in Joshua as God's people encircle Jericho for six days. In Revelation, there were 7 angels ready to blow the 7 trumpets of God's judg-ment. The first six were blown and then there was a delay before the 7th trumpet was sounded in heaven. **(Revelation 10:7)** In the delay, the Book of Prophecy (Word of God) is given to John the Revelator to eat. **(Revelation 10)** It was both sweet and bitter because the Word shows both God's love and His justice. To John, it was sweet to the taste but bitter in the inner working. **(Revelation 10:9-10)** John was told that he was to carry the Book of Prophecy (Word of God) to many peoples, nations, languages and kings. **(Revelation 10:11)** In the book of Daniel **(12:4),** the book was sealed, but here in Revelation it is an open book in the hand of the mighty angel who is Jesus. **(Revelation 10:2)** The Word of God has a veil over it that only Yeshua/Jesus can open. The mysteries of God are concealed (kept silent) until the day God says they should be revealed and shouted out.

Between the sixth and seventh trumpet of Revelation, the two mighty witnesses were also revealed. **(Revelation 11)** These witnesses were prefigured in the two spies Joshua sent to Jericho (world) before going into warfare. These two witnesses in Revelation will have the supernatural power of the Word of God in their mouths and the power of the Holy Spirit within to accomplish all that God sent them to do. When their ministry is through and they have been resurrected in the sight of the entire world, the seventh angel will sound the seventh trumpet, which will usher in the 7 vials of the fullness of God's wrath over the earth. These 7 bowl judgments are represented by the seven circlings of Jericho on the 7th day. As the seventh angel sounded his seventh trumpet, there were loud voices *(a shout)* in heaven which said, **"The kingdom of the world has become the kingdom of our Lord and of his Christ, and He will reign for ever and ever." Revelation 11:15** These seven trumpets are sounded in heaven before the True Ark of God's Presence Jesus just before He comes to earth to destroy evil. Just as Joshua exercised his authority over the enemy of God's people in Jericho, Jesus will exercise His authority over all the earth and will conquer the forces of evil. **Then God's temple in heaven was opened, and within his temple was seen the ark of his covenant.** *(Yeshua/Jesus).* **And there came flashes of lightning, rumblings, peals of thunder, an earthquake and a great hailstorm. Revelation 11:19** In like manner, when the loud trumpet sounded and the people shouted around the walls of Jericho, the walls came tumbling down and God's people went straight in and conquered all of the inhabitants and destroyed everything in the land.

As the ground shook and the walls of Jericho came tumbling down, God is also about to shake His Body of believers. He will raise up bold, courageous and anointed "Joshuas" who will urge the people to purify themselves and take the land for Christ. God needs uncompromising, faith-filled, courageous and bold warriors to lead His people into spiritual warfare and possess the land for Christ.

God punished the Canaanites because they were excessively wicked just as Yeshua/Jesus says the world will be before He comes again. These Canaanites were idolators, sexually promiscuous, practiced child sacrifice and lived degenerate lifestyles. They had to be totally exterminated. Such a wicked people must not influence God's people. So, under Joshua's authority, God's people destroyed the city and its inhabitants. But before Joshua and God's people destroy the city completely, Rahab and all in her house were saved. The Lord and His people have not forgotten Rahab's faith, service and obedience and their covenant with her. Rahab, the gentile, and all in her house were put in a **"place outside the camp of Israel." Joshua 6:23** However, eventually she would join Israel and marry a Jew. This, of course, speaks of gentiles in Christ's Church who were outside of the camp of Israel until the Jewish Messiah Jesus brought them in because of the rejection of Him by the majority of the Jews. All, both Jew and Gentile, will join "Israel" when they wed the Jewish Messiah Yeshua/Jesus. Every believer in Yeshua/Jesus upon accepting Him as Lord and Savior has physically and spiritually entered into "Israel," God's land of promise in the heavenly Jerusalem and must strive with God in building His spiritual kingdom here on earth.

God claimed all of Jericho, its inhabitants and all that belonged to them for Him as the firstfruit of the land He gave to His people. This is the only city that God claimed all for Himself. God's people were not to touch anything that belonged to the enemy. This is because Jericho represented the world and pride. He didn't want any remnants of these left to tempt His people because He knew pride and the world would destroy the people He loved. Pride is the root of all sin. God must remove all of it. **Otherwise you will make the camp of Israel liable to destruction and bring trouble on it. Joshua 6:18** Once God has conquered pride in the hearts of His people and taken the "world" out of them, He will own the whole land of our hearts. Everything in Jericho must be destroyed by the edge of the sword (Word) and by fire (Holy Spirit). Pride and "self" try to rebuild. But God says we must not let that happen. We must allow the sword of the Word and the fires of His Holy Spirit to cut off our pride and burn our flesh.

The gold, silver, bronze and iron were purified by fire. These were taken to the Lord's treasury for use in His kingdom. **(Joshua 6:19)** These metals represent the works of His refined believers who do His kingdom work on earth. Only that which is refined by the fire of God making it an enduring substance will live eternally in the kingdom of heaven. All else will be burnt up as wood, hay and stubble, just as Joshua and God's people were to burn up all that was left in Jericho. These metals that were used for weapons by the people of Jericho will be used for good in God's kingdom. God will turn their swords of destruction into plowshares. **Micah 4:3**

Seven is the number of spiritual perfection. The trumpets of ram's horns (shofars) represent the voice of God and His authority. The priests carrying the Ark of God's presence and blowing trumpets represent ministers who carry the Word of God and Yeshua/Jesus before the people. The Ark represents the presence and power of God among His people. Jesus is Immanuel, "God with us." All of the people encircling the city of Jericho represent the unity of the brethren walking in obedience to their Commander Yeshua and His Word.

After obeying all that God commanded him to do, Joshua cursed Jericho so the people would not be tempted to return there, as they were tempted to do with Egypt. Jericho was to remain a "heap" forever, never to be rebuilt. Anyone who did so would be cursed. The foundation would cost his firstborn son and the gates, his youngest son. **(Joshua 6:26)** This curse came upon Hiel of Bethel during King Ahab's reign because he rebuilt Jericho. **(1 Kings 16:34)** He lost two of his sons. The first son died when the foundation was laid and the second when he set up the wall and gates. Joshua speaking a curse over Jericho and having it come to pass also illustrates the power of our words to either bless or curse. Life and death, blessing and cursing, are in the power of the tongue. If God created through His Word and we are created in His image and likeness, then our words also have creative power. Our words will either bless or curse—build up or tear down.

Christ's Temple is not to be a "heap of ruins" but a building of "living stones" of committed, dedicated, obedient Christians who are knitted together in love, grace and peace, set in their God-given position and walking in unity as one Temple under the command and authority of Yeshua/Jesus. The unified army of God blowing the trumpet of God's Word and encircling the hardened heart *(represented by Jericho)* with love, prayer and peace will bring victory.

Physical and spiritual Israel will never fully possess the Promised Land or the world until Christ comes again and gathers His people and rules and reigns over a redeemed "Israel." However, Christ's Church made up of both Jewish and Gentile believers are to take the Good News of salvation in Christ Jesus to others and use the Word of God and the power of the Holy Spirit to defeat the enemy of the souls of humanity. Christ's kingdom is unfolding in the hearts of His true followers.

Shofars of Ram's Horns *(Trumpets)*

The trumpets referred to in Joshua were shofars, which were made from rams' horns. The ram's horn looks back to Genesis and forward to Revelation. The ram's horn of the ram that God provided as a substitute sacrifice for Isaac in Genesis was caught in the thicket symbolizing "sin." **(Genesis 22:13)** This ram took the place of Isaac as the sin-offering as Jesus takes our place and sets us free from bondage to sin. A ram is the father of a lamb! The fulfillment of the "lamb" had to wait. Isaac asked his father Abraham, **"Where is the lamb for the burnt-offering** *(sin offering)?* The first mention of the lamb in the New Testament is in **John 1:29** where John the Baptist answered Isaac's question saying, **"Behold, the Lamb of God who takes away the sin of the world."**

The shofar is a call to repentance and a warning of impending judgment. The forces of evil symbolized as the warriors of Jericho were in battle formation. The Israelites blew the shofars *(symbolizing the Word of God)* calling the wicked inhabitants of Jericho to repentance. God gave them six days to repent, just as God has been speaking through His Anointed Word for six thousand years calling humanity to repentance and to His saving grace through Yeshua/Jesus. The shofar will also call God's people to unity to prepare for the final battle at the return of Jesus, the Messiah **(1 Thessalonians 4:16),** as the shofar called the Israelites to unity under the command of their leader Joshua.

The shofar also signals God's presence. In **Exodus 19:19,** the long blast of the shofar ushered in the presence of God coming down upon Mount Sinai.

The shofar was also used to herald in a new king. **(1 Kings 1:34-41)** The blowing of the shofar will proclaim the coming of King Yeshua/Jesus. **Matthew 24:31** says, **"He will send His angels with a great sound of a trumpet, and they will gather together His elect from the four winds, from one end of heaven to the other."** (see also Zechariah 9:14)

Revelation 1:10 says that Jesus' voice was as the sound of a trumpet. The "voice" was a Person – Jesus Christ, the Word of God. So, trumpets also represent the Word of God. As Christ's followers send forth the Word of God throughout the land, Jesus will conquer the world, the flesh and the devil through us, His representatives on earth. **For the Word of God is living and powerful, and sharper than any two-edged sword, piercing even to the division of soul and spirit, and of joints and marrow, and is a discerner of the thoughts and intents of the heart. Hebrews 4:12**

In **Joel 2:1-11,** the trumpet is blown in Zion as a warning to the world that Satan's army of demons have been loosed throughout the world and that God's judgment was impending. God warns His people before He takes action. **Joel 2:12-14** is a call of God for all of His people to repent and return to Him with all their heart. **"Return to me with all your heart, with fasting and weeping and mourning. Rend your heart and not your garments. Return to the Lord your God for He is gracious and compassionate, slow to anger and abounding in love, and he relents from sending calamity. Who knows? He may turn and have pity and leave behind a blessing – grain offerings and drink offerings for the Lord your God.**

Next in **Joel 2:15,** the trumpet is blown in Zion again calling His people to holiness and blessing. The result of repentance, consecration, holiness and unity is in **Joel 2:18-30.**

1. God will take pity on His people and will answer their prayers. **Vv18-19**
2. He will fill us fully with the provision of His Word, new joy and anointing. **V19**
3. His temple will never again be scorned by the nations. **V19**
4. He will defeat the army of the enemy and drive them away from His people. **V20**
5. He will give new life and fruit. **V22**
6. He will send the autumn rain in righteousness. **V23**
7. The threshing floors will be filled with grain and the vats will overflow with new wine and oil. **V24**
8. He will restore all that the locusts (demons) have eaten. **V25**
9. He will fill us with His Word and we will praise His Name for the wonders He has worked for us.
10. His people will never be put to shame again. **V26**

11. All people will know that He is in us (Israel) and that He is the only True God.
12. He will send a great outpouring of His Spirit on all people. **Vv28-29**
13. His sons and daughters will prophesy and old men will have dreams and the young men will have visions. **V29**
14. There will be great signs and wonders in the heavens and the earth. **V30**
15. Everyone who calls on the name of the Lord will be saved. **V32**

Only the trumpets were blown for six days as the people marched around Jericho. As I said previously, this represents the 6,000 years the Word of God has been sounding and drawing people to new resurrected life in Jesus. In **1 Thessalonians 4:16,** the trumpet (shofar) will sound and the dead will be resurrected.

In Exodus when the Law was being given to Israel, the sound of the shofar grew louder and louder. God's Word has been sounding louder and louder over the earth in these end times preparing the way of the Lord's return.

In Joshua, on the 7th day, the shofar was to be blown in one long blast and then the people were to shout and the walls of Jericho would fall down. The 7th day represents the Day of the Lord in **Revelation 19:15** when the Word of God Jesus comes after **what sounded like the roar of a great multitude in heaven shouting (v1)** with a **sharp sword out of His mouth with which to strike down the nations.** Yeshua/Jesus, the Word of God, will come with the blowing of a trumpet and a loud shout to complete the redemption of the earth and destroy the enemies of His people forever. In Genesis 1 as the Word Jesus created. In Revelation with His Word of power and authority He destroys. The Word is double-edged!

CHAPTER 6

Defeat at Ai – Joshua 7

Ai was a small city compared to Jericho but it was 3,300 feet high with rocks and caves to hide in. Because of its smallness, God's people anticipated an easy victory. Instead of Joshua seeking God's counsel, he sent spies to Ai who came back and told him that Ai had so few people that Joshua should just send 3,000 men to defeat it instead of his whole army. Joshua listened to the counsel of men, not God. Unless we seek the mind of Christ and His Holy Spirit in a matter, we will make wrong decisions and suffer defeat. Trusting in the flesh rather than God did two things: 1) They over-estimated themselves and their strength, and 2) they underestimated the enemy. "**Do not weary all the people, for the people of Ai are few.' Joshua 7:3** The victory at Jericho had made God's people overly confident. They were flushed with their tremendous victory at Jericho so they felt Ai would be an easy triumph. They had forgotten that it was God who gave them the victory, not the arm of flesh. They had also forgotten that Jericho was defeated because all of God's people were unified and obedient to God's command. Instead of all Israel going into war in unity here at Ai, they only sent a part of God's army. Victory can only come through unity, not division. Dividing God's army weakened its strength. The result was God's people were soundly defeated! Why?

1. Joshua trusted in the counsel of men rather than seeking

God's direction as he did at Jericho.

2. They underestimated the strength of the enemy. Satan and his demons are too powerful for the flesh. Only the power of God and His Word can defeat them.
3. There was sin in the camp of God's people (Israel). Sin separated them from God's blessing. Achan from the tribe of Judah had disobeyed God's commandment.
4. The Israelites were "self" confident instead of depending on God for the victory.
5. They acted ahead of God through impatience.
6. They depended on the strength of man instead of the power of God.

This was Israel's only defeat in the seven-year conquest of the Promised Land. Joshua and God's people gave into the flesh. The Bible tells us that we are to **"have no confidence in the flesh" (Philippians 3:3)** but are to be strong in the Lord and His mighty power. It is the little selfish acts of the flesh that bring defeat. It's the little, baby sins that spoil the vineyard. **"Catch for us the little foxes, the little foxes that ruin the vineyards, our vineyards that are in bloom." SOS 3:15** Foxes are sneaky and destructive. They hide in holes and eat the fruit of the crops. God is warning us in the Song of Songs to be watchful for the little sins in our lives, so they won't rob us of our fruit. The result of God's people giving into the flesh was defeat and humiliation. They were demoralized and discouraged. Their actions not only brought discouragement and humiliation upon themselves, they also brought dishonor to God.

In disgrace and humiliation, full of self-pity and pride, Joshua and the Israelites fall on their faces before the Ark of God's Presence. Joshua even seemed to blame God for their defeat and wanted to turn back to the other side of the Jordan. The cause of the defeat was with Israel, not God. However, it is the tendency of the flesh to blame God for the consequences of our own sin and defeat. **"O Lord, why did you ever bring this people across the Jordan to deliver us into the hands of the Amorites to destroy us? If only we had been content to stay on the other side of the Jordan! O Lord, what can I say, now that Israel has been** routed by its enemies? The Canaanites and the other people of the country will hear about this and they will surround us and wipe out our name from the earth. What then will you do for your own great name?" Joshua 7:7-9** Can you hear the self-pity, blame and wanting to give up and quit? Joshua and the people were concerned with their self-image. Listen to how God answers Joshua. **"Stand up! What are you doing down on your face?" v10** In other words, "Arise! You are My chosen leader. What are you doing down on your face in defeat?" God had told Joshua that He had given him every place the sole of his feet touched. Joshua should have surmised that the fault was not God's, who is all-powerful, but his and the peoples' fault.

Next God tells Joshua why they were defeated. There was sin in the camp! **"Israel has sinned; they have violated My covenant, which I commanded them to keep. They have taken some of the accursed things; they have stolen; they have lied, they have put them with their own possessions. That is why the Israelites cannot stand against their enemies; they turn their backs and run because they have been made liable to destruction. I will not be with you anymore unless you destroy whatever among you is devoted to destruction." Joshua 7:11-12** This is a sobering thought. God would not be with them until they destroyed the sin in the congregation. Sin destroys and brings defeat. God who is holy cannot reside in the same place as sin. Sin and holiness can't mix! Sin must be searched out and removed.

God gives Joshua the solution.

1. They are to consecrate themselves to God.
2. The sin must be acknowledged and brought to the light.
3. The sin must be put away forever.

"Go, consecrate the people. Tell them. 'Consecrate yourselves in preparation for tomorrow; for this is what the Lord the God of Israel says: That which is accursed is among you, O Israel. You cannot stand against your enemies until you remove it." Joshua 7:13 God's people cannot stand against the enemy with sin in the camp. It must be removed. All sin must be confessed. We must call it by its right name and bring it to the Light of God's love. Sin must be stripped of its disguises and forced out of its hiding place so you can never be deceived by it again. God will surround you with His love and meet you with an even bolder assurance of victory and blessing if you will be honest with Him with your sin and put it away.

God told Joshua that the spoils of Jericho were to be placed in His treasury but Achan disobeyed and took some for himself. Joshua said in **6:18, "But keep away from the accursed things, so that you will not bring about your own destruction by taking any of them. Otherwise, you will make the camp of Israel liable to destruction and bring trouble on it."** Achan, the sinner's name, means "troubler." He lived up to his name! This one person's sin would bring destruction and defeat to the whole congregation of Israel. This is the effect of one single sin in the camp of God's people. Because of this one man's sin, God's wrath burned against the whole nation. **"The Body is a unit, though it is made up of many parts; and though its parts are many, they form one Body." 1 Corinthians 12:12** God sees those who love and follow Yeshua/Jesus as "one man" – one Body. The sin of one member of the Body affects the whole Body. **"Therefore, I urge you, brothers, in view of God's mercy, to offer your bodies as living sacrifices, holy and pleasing to God—this is your spiritual act of worship." Romans 12:1** This Chapter of Romans goes on to say that we are to **"weep with those who weep and rejoice with those who rejoice"** and **"live in harmony with one another." V14-21** What affects one member of the Body affects the whole Body. Thankfully, we have an Advocate with the Father, our Savior Jesus Christ, whom we can come to in sincere confession and repentance and He will remove our sin even erasing it from the Father's sight as if it never happened. As in Joshua, those of us who follow Yeshua/Jesus must acknowledge our sin before Him and repent. **"If we confess our sins, He is faithful and just and will forgive us our sins and purify us from all unrighteousness. If we claim we have not sinned, we make Him out to be a liar and His Word has no place in our lives." 1 John 1:9-10** You cannot stand against the Enemy with unconfessed, unrepented of sin in your heart. God will not go into battle with you if sin exists. Sin is not a little matter to God. He hates it because He knows it will defeat those He loves.

Instead of confessing his sin, Achan attempted to hide it, nor did he show any remorse for it. God used an unusual way to reveal the sinner probably to give Achan a chance to confess and repent. But Achan remained silent. Instead of having the best interest of the whole congregation of God's people in his heart, Achan satisfied his own selfish, greedy desires. The result was defeat and shame for the whole Body. First God showed Joshua the tribe of the sinner. Then He showed him the clan; then the family and finally the individual. When the process of elimination dwindled down to Achan, he finally confessed but it was too late! He received the penalty of death. God wants a willing confession. Sin destroys and brings death. It is a good idea to keep short accounts with God and confess sin speedily so you can go forward in His work. Joshua and all Israel destroyed the "accursed thing" and stoned Achan and his family to death. Obviously, Achan had drawn his family into his sin, so they were equally guilty. Oh that Christ's Body would learn from the mistake of Achan.

Once the sin was removed, God encourages Joshua once again. He tells Joshua to take the **"whole army"** *(unified)* and go up and attack Ai. They must return to their place of defeat and try again. God is a God of second chances. This time, God would be with them to lead them into victory. Jesus as Commander of God's army must be Lord over our lives. He is our Savior, but He must also be our Lord (Master) if we are to be successful. The battle must be fought His way according to His Word not by the strength of the flesh. Death of the flesh and sin and obedience to God's Word is the power of God to destroy the Enemy. Jesus showed us this on the cross. Jesus came to do the will of the Father even in dying on the cross for our sin. It is the crucified life that will be the power of God to defeat sin and the devil.

God said "all Israel" and the "whole army" nine times in this account of scripture to stress the need for unity before going into warfare. All of God's people must be cleansed of sin and all must go into the battlefield if there is to be victory. If Joshua is to be successful, he must give 100% effort in obeying God and must go with all of God's people as one unified army.

After Israel repented and removed the sin and punished the sinner, God opened the way to victory. Jesus came to die for the sin of the world and open the way for victory over sin, death and the Enemy for all who receive His grace. Yeshua/Jesus, however, did not take sin lightly in His Father's House. He went to the Temple to cast the sinners out! The object of Joshua and the victory of God's people were to blot out sin and purify the earth by fire. The object of the True Joshua, Jesus, is to also blot out sin through the power *(fire)* of His Word and Spirit.

Achan's sin brought dishonor to God and shame and defeat to His people before their enemies. Achan represents "death of the flesh." The death can only be conquered through crucifixion for **the desires of the flesh are against the Spirit, and the desires of the Spirit are against the flesh." Galatians 5:16** God was about to redeem His people and restore their honor because they removed the sin and the sinner. Thankfully, in Yeshua/Jesus we need not receive the death penalty. However, sin must be removed from our hearts and His Body. At Jericho, God fought the battle. But now, God's people have a part in the victory also. Jesus, like God did at Jericho, defeated the world, the flesh and the devil at the cross. But, it is the responsibility of His spiritual army to do spiritual warfare against the enemy of our souls and bring in the victory and His kingdom on earth.

Joshua has learned from his defeat. He will use his defeat to set a trap for the inhabitants of Ai. Joshua moved his troops into position at night (in darkness). Joshua and the Israelites surrounded Ai. He set some of the troops behind the city to ambush them. At daylight, Joshua and some of the army would be in front. When the army of Ai advanced toward them, Joshua and his army would pretend fleeing to draw them out of their stronghold and weaken them so his rearguard could rush into the city and ambush them and burn the city. Joshua conquered the enemy by "yielding," just as Yeshua/Jesus conquered the Enemy by yielding His life on the cross of suffering defeating the penalty of death and the Enemy forever. When Joshua held up his spear, God's people were to attack the enemy from all sides. A "spear" symbolizes that which pierces.

(see John 19:34;Psalm 57:4;Hab. 3:11) It represents the Word of God. Joshua (Yeshua) held up his spear until the victory was complete. The Body of Christ is to lift up Jesus Christ, who is the Word of God, and use His Word to pierce hearts and defeat the Enemy of peoples' souls.

Joshua singled out the king of Ai to emphasize the curse upon him and his followers. The king of Ai is a "shadow" of Satan who is cursed indeed. Joshua hung the king of Ai from a tree. To be hung from a tree meant that you were cursed. According to the Law, a dead body could not hang overnight because it would desecrate the land. **(see Deuteronomy 21:23)** So, at sunset, Joshua ordered his men to take down the body and throw it down at the entrance of the city gate and bury it under a heap of stones. This "heap of stones" bore witness of the evil king's defeat. Sunset is just before darkness. That which operates in darkness remains in darkness. The enemy's camp is a heap of ruins without order, but Christ's Temple should be made of "living stones," knitted together with each member in his God-given position as One Temple with Christ as the Chief Cornerstone and the Capstone....the Head and the Foundation.

At Jericho, all of the spoils of the war were to be given to God. But here at Ai, God said that His people could divide the spoils to keep and support Israel throughout the conquest of the land. It is interesting to note that had Achan just waited upon God and His goodness, he would have received the desires of his heart at Ai. Instead of waiting on God to give him his reward, Achan took it upon himself to reward himself in direct disobedience to God. God is the Rewarder of His people. Jesus said in **Matthew 16:27, "For the Son of Man is going to come in His Father's glory with his angels, and then He will reward each person according to what he has done."**

Achan was buried in the Valley of Achor which means "trouble." Because the majority of God's people, the Jews, have rejected Yeshua, they have had much trouble. In **Hosea 2:15,** God promises the Jews that He will make the Valley of Achor a "door of hope." One day, Yeshua will reveal Himself to the Jews and they will turn to Him and find hope. Let it be so soon, Lord. Let it be so soon!

CHAPTER 7

Renewed Covenant on Mount Ebal and Mount Gerizim

Joshua 8:30-34

In times of victory, it is easy to forget God who gave us the victory. So, Joshua now takes time out from the battles to return to the Valley of Shechem between Mount Ebal and Mount Gerizim, the mounts of cursings and blessings. Mount Ebal and Mount Gerizim are exactly in the center of the land. You could see the Promised Land in every direction from these mounts. Abram in obedience to God had left the land of his father to go to a land that he did not know, but a land God had said he would take him. Abram did not enter Canaan until his father had died. **Genesis 11:32** The "old" must pass away before entering into the "new." The same is true in Joshua. Moses had to die so Joshua could lead God's people into their promised inheritance. The Lord appeared to Abram at the site of the great tree of Moreh at Shechem and said He would give Abram this land. Abraham received his first promise of the land from God on Mount Ebal. At the foot of this mountain in Shechem, Abram built the first altar to God in the land. **Genesis 12:6-7** This was the beginning of Abram's hope of possessing the land as an inheritance. Joshua would bring God's people into the land God showed Abraham.

The Israelites had gone their own way and sinned against God.

They must renew their oath to God. So, Joshua takes them back to where they began their journey at Shechem, which is the Valley of Decision. Joshua's ministry began at Shechem and ended at Shechem. He is buried there. **(see Joshua 24:32) The first will be last, the last will be first.**

Shechem is 30 miles from Ai. The True Joshua, Yeshua/Jesus began His ministry on earth at the age of 30. 30 is the number of spiritual maturity. Yeshua/Jesus walked this earth in ministry for 3 ½ years. He will come again after the last 3 ½ years of the tribulation of Revelation to rule and reign and to establish His earthly, spiritual kingdom from the land of Israel for 1,000 years. The True Joshua, Yeshua/Jesus, will bridge the gap between the mount of cursings and the mount of blessings. The Valley of Shechem symbolizes the great chasm that separated the rich man and father Abraham in heaven. **(Luke 16:19-30)** The rich man chose the wrong way. His money could not help him escape death or buy a place in heaven. Only Yeshua/Jesus can bridge the gap. You will either see the Promised Land from afar from Mount Ebal, the mount of cursings or you will be across the great chasm and be in the presence of the Everlasting Father *(whom Abraham typifies)* through accepting the True Joshua, Yeshua/Jesus, as your Lord and Savior.

Joshua took **"all Israel, foreigners** *(gentiles)* **and citizens** *(Jews)"* back to Shechem where he obeyed the commandment of God through Moses in **Deuteronomy 27:4-26, 28.** All Israel was one. All Israel, both Jews and Gentiles, stood by the Ark of God's Presence in the Valley of Shechem. **(Joshua 8:33)** Six tribes stood next to the Ark on the side of Mount Ebal, the mount of cursings and six tribes stood next to the Ark on the side of Mount Gerizim, the mount of blessings, facing the priests who carried it. **(Joshua 8:33)** Six is the number of man in scripture because man was created on the sixth day. Man must decide whether he will choose blessings through Yeshua/Jesus or cursings by rejecting Him. We must also choose whether we will receive blessings through obedience to God's Word, or cursings through disobedience. God gave man freewill. The choice is ours. Joshua said that he and his house would serve the Lord. **(Joshua 24:15)** Joshua was a Godly leader who kept God's people serving God in faith and obedience. Notice that God's people faced the priests (Levites) who carried the Ark of God's Presence as Joshua read both the blessings and cursings of the Law. God's ministers must teach the full counsel of God in His Word – both its blessings and cursings, God's love and His justice, grace and Truth.

According to God's Word in **Deuteronomy 27:5,** Joshua built an altar to God on Mount Ebal, the mount of cursings. Where the curse was put was the place the altar must be built. This is the shadow of the cross of Yeshua/Jesus who would become the curse for all. This altar must be built of fieldstones *(uncut stones)*. No iron tool must be used on these stones. In other words, nothing of man (flesh) must touch this altar. It must be built of God-made stones, not manmade. Building an altar of sacrifice to God is worshipping and exalting Him. As the following diagram indicates, this altar was lifted up and had three parts of the cross in it. On this altar, Joshua offers a sin-offering for atonement and repentance and a peace-offering for fellowship. God eventually provided this altar Himself at the cross of Jesus/Yeshua. He is the sin-offering for atonement of sin for all who repent and the peace-offering who brings us back into fellowship with God.

We are to present our **"bodies a living sacrifice to God"** and allow Him to shape and form us into His image and likeness. **(Romans 12:1)** This is the greatest sacrifice of worship any human can give to his/her Creator. In thankfulness for the defeat of the enemy and the salvation and victory of his people, Joshua brings God's people back to their place of beginning to remind all Israel that the victory was theirs only by God's grace and His everlasting love covenant with His people. In like manner, when a person who follows Jesus sins, we must bring our sin back to the cross in confession and repentance.

This is a diagram of a gigantic altar, which was found by an archeologist on Mt. Ebal. **This altar is the uncompleted picture of the cross of Yeshua/Jesus that passes through the two testaments removing the curse of sin (Mt. Ebal) by His sacrificial death.** *The author inserted the broken lines completing the cross to illustrate that God was using the scriptures of the first Testament to point to their completion in Yeshua. God built His own altar on the mountain of cursings – the cross of Yeshua/Jesus. Man had no part in it.*

Shechem has a prominent place in Israel's history. At Shechem, Abram had a tree, a promise and an altar. **(Genesis 12:1-7)** This, of course, pointed to the tree of life, Yeshua, who was the altar of sacrifice and the giver of the "new covenant" God promised to His people.

In **Genesis 14:17-24** Abram meets Melchizedek, the king-high priest, at Shechem. Melchizedek was the first one to visit Abram after defeating the enemies who had captured his nephew Lot. Abram had been successful in warfare as he rescued backslidden Lot from the hands of the enemy. Melchizedek means "King of righteousness." He was from Salem, which means "peace." Melchizedek is called "the priest of God Most High." In Hebrew, this is El Elyon, which means Sovereign Lord. Abram also uses that name except he added Yahweh (Lord) and **"the Possessor of heaven and earth."**

Melchizedek was a priest but he offered no sacrifice. He gave Abram bread and wine. It was after Abram drank the wine and ate the bread that Melchizedek ratified the covenant God had given Abram. Then he blessed Abram and gave glory to God for the victory over the enemy. Bread and wine symbolize the body and

blood of Yeshua/Jesus. Melchizedek was a theophany of Jesus, God's High Priest and Prince of Peace and Possessor of heaven and earth. **Hebrews 5:5-6 says, "You are My Son, today I have begotten You." As He also says in another place, "You are a priest forever according to the order of Melchizedek." (see also Psalm 110:4) For this Melchizedek, king of Salem, priest of the Most High God, who met Abraham returning from the slaughter of the kings and blessed him, to whom also Abraham gave a tenth part of all** *(tithe)***, first being translated "king of righteousness" and then also king of Salem, meaning "king of peace," without genealogy, having neither beginning of days nor end of life, but made like the Son of God, remains a priest continually. Now consider how great this Man was, to whom even the patriarch Abraham gave a tenth of the spoils." Hebrews 7:1-41..........**
Therefore, if perfection were through the Levitical priesthood (for under it people received the law), what further need was there that another priest should rise according to the order of Melchizedek, and not be called according to the order of Aaron? Hebrews 7:9-11 It is after we accept Jesus' sinless blood as the perfect sacrifice for our sin and eat the Bread of His Word that God ratifies the promise of the New Covenant. When we partake of the Lord's Supper as Jesus instructed as a remembrance of Him, we are partaking anew of the Bread of Life (Word of God) and the cleansing power of the blood of Jesus of the New Covenant. In other words, we take a fresh impartation of spiritual life to ourselves. The early Christians ate the Lord's Supper daily, because they understood the spiritual power in it. In eating the Bread and drinking the cup, we partake of the bread of life broken for us and drink the cleansing, empowering blood of the New Covenant.

God appointed the new priesthood of Jesus. His priesthood supersedes the Levitical order, which was appointed by God as a temporary order because it proved it could make nothing perfect. The Levitical priesthood had to offer sacrifices, but Abraham paid tithes to Melchizedek and was blessed by him without a sacrifice being given. Jesus, God's Eternal and Permanent High Priest, meets the sinner at Shechem in the valley of decision. Jesus, the Great High Priest, is the Minister of the sanctuary and of the true tabernacle of heaven, which the Lord erected, not man. **Hebrews 8:2**

God will judge through the Gospel of Jesus Christ, not the Law. **(see Romans 2:16)** He gives no preference to those who received the Law. God says that He does not show favoritism. **(Romans 2:11)** All of humanity is God's special creation. He wants that none should perish... neither Jew nor Gentile. Both share in the blessings and the responsibilities to God through His Son Yeshua/Jesus. God is calling all to Him through the precious blood of Jesus.

Abram, like Joshua, built an altar at Shechem. Shechem is from the Hebrew word "sekem" which means "shoulder." By building an altar, Abram and Joshua are giving an open confession of their faith in God and worship of God. It also memorializes the place of God's promised blessing. Yeshua/Jesus who holds the government of the Kingdom of God on His shoulder **(Isaiah 9:6)** was crucified on a tree for all to see. The cross is the Christian's altar. It memorialized the place of God's blessing through His Son. Jesus' sacrifice gave all people a New Covenant of promise of a heavenly land, a heavenly kingdom and a heavenly home for all eternity. He is the One to be worshipped and glorified as the One who fulfilled God's Covenant blessing to Abraham, Isaac and Jacob. Our promised inheritance is to begin right here on earth as Jesus transforms us from glory to glory into His image and uses us to reach out to a lost and dying world filled with sin and sorrow, spiritual death and decay and lacking in hope.

Yeshua/Jesus' first missionary work was near Shechem at Jacob's well. Jacob had purchased a piece of land at Shechem, set up an altar to God and dug a well. **(Genesis 33:18-19)** Jacob had given this piece of land to his son Joseph as his inheritance. Joseph represents Jesus as the Suffering Servant who was exalted to the Right Hand of the throne of God.

The "well of salvation," Jesus, was sitting and resting from His journey at Jacob's well. **(Isaiah 12:3)** Jesus was leaving Jerusalem because the Pharisees *(Jewish keepers of the Law)* were jealous that He and His disciples were baptizing more people than John the Baptist. Jesus used every circumstance in His life on earth to touch the heart of someone or the multitudes with the knowledge of His saving, healing, resurrecting grace and love. Jesus was returning to

Galilee but went out of His way to go to Samaria to save this one woman who was living in sin and in need of rescue. This woman had obviously experienced much rejection. Five husbands had rejected her, probably because she was barren. Had she committed adultery according to the Law she would have been stoned to death. So, these husbands left her for another reason. In those days, a woman was considered cursed if she couldn't have children. No doubt this woman probably even felt that God had rejected her because of her barrenness. The Jews too had rejected her. Jews had nothing to do with Samaritans at the time of Jesus because they considered them half-breeds because they had intermarried with gentile heathens. Now she was with a man who was not her husband, which probably brought more rejection and condemnation her way. Her shame was so great that she went to the well when no one else was around to draw water. Much to her chagrin I am sure, this Samaritan woman sees a Jewish man sitting by the well of her forefather Jacob. Jesus looked beyond her sin and saw her need. He saw her heart with His heart of compassion and love.

It was unheard of for a Jewish Rabbi to speak to a Samaritan let alone a woman! This woman said to Him, **"How is it that You being a Jew, ask a drink from me, a Samaritan woman? For the Jews have no dealings with Samaritans." John 4:9** Jesus went there not only to rescue this sinner, but also to show and teach that He was above all religious, racial and gender prejudices and that true worship was a matter of the heart.

The woman wanted to talk about the hostility between the Samaritans and the Jews **(John 4:19). "Our fathers worshiped on this mountain** *(Mount Gerizim – the mount of blessing)* **but you Jews claim that the place where we must worship is in Jerusalem."** Only Mount Gerizim is referred to in this account because Jesus became Mount Ebal, the curse, for us. Jesus tells her that it is the spirit of worship not the place of worship that pleases the Father. **"Believe me, woman, a time is coming when you will worship the Father neither on this mountain nor in Jerusalem." V21** True worship is not in a place but in the heart of His followers. There will be a day when we will no longer worship the Father on earth but will worship Him in the heavenly sanctuary in Spirit and in Truth. We will be in the presence of Truth.

"For salvation is of the Jews……." v22 Jesus, the salvation of the world, came through a Jewish woman. Salvation is indeed of the Jews. God used the Jewish people, places, circumstances, tabernacle, feasts, law, and the nation of Israel to paint a picture of His salvation through His Son Yeshua/Jesus. Originally, Jesus told His disciples that they could not go to Samaria to preach because He was sent for the **"lost sheep of Israel."** (Matthew 10:5-6) Israel had not only been scattered throughout the world because of their disobedience, they were spiritually lost. Jesus came to save them. Salvation must be extended to the Jews first to fulfill scripture. When Jesus was rejected by a majority of the Jews, He then went to Samaria to this woman.

Samaria is the name of the Northern Kingdom of Israel. **(1 Kings 21:1)** Samaria means "watch mountain." In **Acts 1:8,** Jesus told His disciples to wait for the gift of the Holy Spirit and then they could preach the Good News of salvation through Christ to all people. The blood of Jesus and the Holy Spirit are a spiritual oneness. It was the Holy Spirit that kept Jesus in the will of the Father and gave Him the strength to endure the cross that gave the gift of the Holy Spirit to all who accept Him as their Lord and Savior. Without the Spirit there would be no blood and without the blood there would be no Spirit given to His followers to lead, guide, teach and protect them.

Jesus wanted to tell this Samaritan woman about the gift of God that would set her free. **"If you knew the gift of God, and who it is who says to you, 'Give Me a drink,' you would have asked Him and He would have given you living water."** John 4:10 The One standing in front of her asking her for a drink was Yeshua/Jesus, God's free gift of grace, who would give her the well of His Living Water (His Holy Spirit). Those who drink of Yeshua's blessing and mercies will have a fountain of living water through His Holy Spirit. This Samaritan woman was taken aback by Jesus' remark about Jacob's well. **"Sir"** the woman said, **"you have nothing to draw with and the well is deep. Where can you get this living water? Are you greater than our father Jacob, who gave us the well and drank from it himself, as did also his sons and his**

flocks and herds?" John 4:11 This Samaritan woman understood literal, earthly water, but she does not understand "living water." **Jesus answered, "Everyone who drinks this water will be thirsty again, but whoever drinks the water I give him will never thirst. Indeed, the water I give him will become in him a spring of water welling up to eternal life." John 4:13-14** The greater One than Jacob was the One who would give her this Living Water from the deep well of His salvation, Spirit and Word. A well of earthly water will run dry, but the living well of Yeshua will never run dry. The water that Christ gives not only flows into a person, it flows out of a person. In **Jeremiah 2:13 and 17:13,** God Himself is called a spring of living water. Jesus by saying that He is the Giver of living water is saying that He is God. At Jacob's well, this woman met Jacob's Star *(Light in the darkness)* and Jacob's Ladder *(bridge between heaven and earth)*. The water of the Holy Spirit that flows from the throne of God and of the Lamb will free the soul from sin and be a spring of water that regenerates and gives everlasting life. Jesus, the One who gives the Holy Spirit is now standing at Jacob's well offering a sinner His living water. **Revelation 22:17** shows us that this living water is for everyone. **The Spirit and the Bride say "Come!" And let him who hears say, "Come!" Whoever is thirsty, let him come; and whoever wishes, let him take the free gift of the water of life.** Those who drink this deep well of living water through Christ will have true joy and blessed hope.

This Samaritan woman asks Jesus to give her this water. But first Jesus must bring her to confession. He tells her to go and bring her husband and come back to Him. She confesses, "I have no husband." She speaks the truth to Messiah Jesus. He does not condemn her. Instead, He leads her into deeper truth. Her truthful confession removed the blinders from her eyes. Then He reveals Himself as the Messiah (called Christ). Jesus' unconditional acceptance did away with the stronghold of rejection, insecurity and sin. In His presence she felt love, acceptance and joy. So, she quickly goes to the town and told the people about the "Man" who had told her everything she ever did. Then they came to Him and heard His Word and believed. **(John 4:39)** They saw Jesus for themselves.

The excitement of this one woman brought an entire town to Jesus.

At Shechem in **Genesis 12:1-7,** we have father Abraham, a tree, an altar and a promise. At Shechem in **John 4:4-26,** we have 1) fulfillment of promise- a Son 2) a sinner 3) a Savior 4) a well and 5) living water. *(#5- God's grace)*

Joshua read both the blessings and cursings of the Law to God's people as He instructed Moses, then he carved them on stones on the altar on Mount Ebal. The altar and the Word go together. Jesus who is the Word was also the altar of sacrifice. The altar and the scriptures stand together as one in Christ as the revelation of God's redemption of mankind. By writing the Law on stones, Joshua was testifying that this was now the Law of the land. Jesus writes His Word on our stony hearts so He can turn our hearts of stone into hearts of His compassion, love, grace and peace. Like the Israelites, we can choose blessing through faith and obedience to God's Word or cursing through unbelief and disobedience. Faithfulness to God's Law would bring blessing and victory to God's people. Jesus who is the Word of God will bless those who are faithful to Him and obey His Word. These are the ones who will have victory in spiritual warfare. The Ark of God's Presence – Yeshua/Jesus—is in the center of the two testaments drawing them together by His blood.

While Joshua and God's people are building an altar and worshipping God, the five Canaanite kings are joining forces to make war against them. Satan has a counterfeit kingdom. Christ has given His Body the fivefold ministry gifts to war against Satan's counterfeit kingdom. The battle between good and evil will go on within each of us and in the world until Jesus comes again to bind Satan and establish His kingdom on earth. We must not give up in discouragement and defeat but press on toward the goal. Jesus will fill us with His power and strength through faith and His Word and Spirit to defeat the enemy of peoples' souls. However, we must walk as a unified army without division. The battle has already been won. Jesus has given us the victory!

CHAPTER 8

Gibeonite Deception – Joshua 9

God's people have just renewed their covenant with God and heard the blessings and cursings of the Law. What happens? The enemy deceives them! Moses told God's people that they were to make no treaty with the inhabitants of the land or to allow any of them to remain alive. **(Deuteronomy 7:1-3; 20:16-18)** The Gibeonites were of the nation of the Hivites. The name Hivite in Hebrew means "the serpent," and like the serpent who controlled them, they deceive God's people.

The Gibeonites must have been aware that the Israelites could make peace with cities that were far away from the Promised Land. **(Deuteronomy 20:10-18)** They also knew that if they could get God's people to make a peace treaty with them, the Israelites would be bound by God to keep it. No oath made in God's name can be broken, even if it is entered into foolishly.

The Gibeonites knew the power of Israel's God. They had heard about God's defeat of the city of Jericho and Ai. They knew they wouldn't be able to stand against Israel in open warfare, so they resorted to deception and flattery. They would appeal to Joshua and his leaders' pride. The walls of Jericho and the weapons of Ai couldn't stop God's people, so the Gibeonites decided to appeal to the Israelite's carnal nature. They made themselves look like they had just come from a far journey by putting old sacks on their donkeys and taking used wineskins that had burst and been mended back together. They put old, worn-out sandals on their feet and dressed in old, worn-out clothes. The only provision they had with them was dried-up bread that was crumbling. The devil is a great compromiser, deceiver and counterfeit. **2 Corinthians 11:14** shows us that the devil even transforms himself into an angel of light in order to deceive. If he cannot defeat you in open warfare, he will use deceit and flattery. Everything about this incident was false. Everything these Gibeonites carried and wore was defiled and ugly, not beautiful and radiant like the garments of those who follow God. God's people are to take off the garment of flesh and put on the beautiful garment of Christ. Jesus says we will know who are His by their fruit. **(Matthew 7:20)** The Gibeonites were clothed in filthy, old rags. The bible says our righteousness is as filthy rags in God's sight. **(Isaiah 64:6)** The heart of man is ever deceitful but the heart of God is forever Truth and Faithful. Both the Gibeonites and God's people sinned against God. The Gibeonites in their deceit and the Israelites in not seeking God's counsel and will. They were equally guilty.

Things are not always what they seem. The Gibeonites used six things to deceive God's people. The number six is the number of man/flesh, so these things represented the works of the flesh, not the Spirit. These Gibeonites "seemed" to be telling the truth. They also "seemed" to be spiritual. They bragged about Israel's God. The Bible warns us that we are to be ever watchful for the **"wiles of the devil."** These Gibeonites lied to God's people. The father of lies is Satan. **(John 8:44)** God gave us His Word to search out the truth. Though something "seems" true does not mean that it is truth. God's people are obligated to search out the Truth through the study of His Word.

Jude 1:4 warns us that false teachers, prophets and apostles will slip into God's House. It is important to know the Word of God and seek His counsel so we will not be deceived. Joshua and the Israelites didn't seek God's counsel on the matter of the Gibeonites. Instead they judged by the outward appearance. Had they asked God, He would have warned them. As it was the Israelites no doubt had a "check" in their spirit because they were hesitant to believe the Gibeonites. The Israelites said, **"How do we know that you don't live here among us? If you do, we don't want to make a covenant with you." Joshua 9:7** The Israelites should have trusted their instincts. But, the Gibeonites appealed to man's desire for power over others and offered to be their servants. Even Joshua had doubt. He asked them, **"Who are you and where do you come from?" Joshua 9:8** The Gibeonites never gave Joshua an exact answer as to the country they were from. But what they did was seem to exalt Israel's God by saying how they had heard about all God did in Egypt and how he defeated the kings across the Jordan. However, they never mentioned the recent victories at Jericho and Ai. To do so would have shown Joshua that they were from nearby.

Instead of taking time to search out the truth and consult God, the men of Israel sampled their provisions of old, stale bread and old wine in old wineskins. Old fermented wine is symbolic of false teaching. The wineskin is that which holds the wine. Old wineskins symbolize the harlot church, which is described in **Revelation 17** as being drunk with the wine of impure doctrines and fornication. It is important for God's people to eat the fresh Bread of God's Word and the pure doctrine, which is produced by proper study of the word. If we open the door to Satan by tasting impure doctrine, he will weaken us and rob us of the fullness of the blessing that is ours in Christ Jesus.

Those who follow Yeshua/Jesus cannot be married to the Law and Grace at the same time. **"No one sews a patch of unshrunk cloth on an old garment, for the patch will pull away from the garment, making the tear worse. Neither do men pour new wine into old wineskins. If they do, the skins will burst, the wine will run out and the wineskins will be ruined. No, they pour new wine into new wineskins, and both are preserved." Matthew 9:16-17** If we follow Yeshua/Jesus, we become a new creation *(wineskin)* and must be yoked to Him not the Law. We cannot put old wine into new wineskins. Jesus set us free from the yoke of the Law by paying the penalty of death for us on the cross. If a person disobeys just one point of the Law, he is guilty of breaking all of it. **(James 1:10;Galatians 3:10)** Thus, he/she is under its penalty of death. Since the flesh is weak and all of us sin, we all break the Law. The only remedy for this is the sinless blood of Yeshua/Jesus. In order to step into our inheritance of the land, we must enter into the life in the Spirit through Yeshua/Jesus. The first testament revealed Yeshua in type and shadow. Yeshua is the Substance of the shadow. Yeshua is to receive all honor, glory and power. It is important that God's people not exalt the "shadow" of the Law over the Substance, which is Christ.

Joshua and the Israelite elders rushed into a treaty with them on the same day. Patience is one of the fruits of the Holy Spirit. Had they been patient, sought God in the matter and waited upon Him, there would have been a different result. Instead, three days later God's people heard that these Gibeonites were neighbors in the land of Canaan. But the Israelites could not touch them because they had made a treaty with them sworn before God. Breaking an oath before God would be like breaking a promise to God and would eventually bring His wrath upon them. **(see Ezekiel 17:12-19)** Those who follow Yeshua/Jesus are to give no place to the devil so he cannot gain a foothold in our hearts. **(Ephesians 4:27-31)**

The whole congregation of Israel grumbled against their leaders. However, Joshua and the elders could not go back on their oath. They decided to make the Gibeonites their slaves. They were to chop wood and carry water for God's house and the whole community. They served both God's people and God in the tabernacle and the temple. The Gibeonites were not their own. They belonged to God and His people in perpetual service. The Gibeonites' lie put them into bondage to God and His people. God had saved them by His grace in spite of their deception. Though they lied to receive mercy, God allowed them to join Israel as servants. Then He protected them from their enemies by having His people fight on their behalf. The Gibeonites represent compromising and backslidden Christians. Christ's true followers must do spiritual battle with the forces of evil who have taken these backslidden Christians captive.

We who are saved by grace in Yeshua/Jesus are His servants and the servants of His people. As His servants, we must do the work of His kingdom and His House. Like the Gibeonites, those who follow the True Joshua, Jesus, must force our flesh to serve others and God. We must carry the cross *(wood)* and the water of His Word and Spirit to both the Jews and the Gentiles. The Apostles called themselves "servants of Jesus Christ." Like the Gibeonites, we once contended against God and Christ and His people, but now we fight with Him.

These Jews and Gentiles went into battle side by side against the five evil kings and their armies. The Israelites (Jews) and the Gibeonites (gentiles) with Joshua as their leader met foe after foe and had victory after victory until the whole land was successfully conquered. Christ overcomes the world by the world. He takes vile sinners and turns them into the army of God, just as Joshua took the deceiving Gibeonites and turned them into the army of God. God is calling His spiritual army together...both Jews and Gentiles....into unity of purpose to defeat the Enemy of all mankind's souls. With Jesus as our Leader and unity among His Body, we will meet foe after foe and have victory after victory until the whole land is conquered for Christ. As the book of Joshua shows us, victory can only come through unity. We cannot separate into little groups, i.e. Methodists, Pentecostals, Messianics, Baptists, etc. and expect to have the victory. It is time to take down the dividing walls and march together with one Holy purpose to defeat the Enemy and bring souls to salvation and life in Christ. There is much unoccupied territory because God's people are fighting amongst themselves and over doctrine rather than walking humbly with their God and in unity. God can only trust greater works to those who walk in humility, obedience and faith, not to the arrogant, proud and divisive. God wants us to repent of everything worldly and fleshly and live in complete abandon to His will and to unity of purpose.

The Gibeonites had told Joshua that they were willing to be subordinate to God's people. As a subordinate, God's people were obligated to protect them. In the very next chapter of Joshua, the Israelites had to go and defend the Gibeonites against the five evil kings of the land who wanted to keep them from their inheritance.

God can turn what Satan means for evil to good. Even though the Gibeonites used deception to join Israel, God did not destroy them. As a matter of fact, some 400 years later when Saul massacred the Gibeonites, God's wrath brought a famine on Israel for three years. David sought the Lord to find out the reason for the famine and God said it was because the blood of the Gibeonites (gentiles) was on Saul's hand. David avenged them, reconciled with them and restored relationship with them. **(2 Samuel 21:1; 2 Samuel 21:2-9)** God would turn their hearts toward Him and His people. The Gibeonites several years later helped Nehemiah rebuild the wall around Jerusalem. **(Nehemiah 3:7)**

The Gibeonites were weak compared to this vast army coming against them. So, they called upon Joshua and the army of God's people to rescue and defend them. We are to come to the aid of a weaker brother or sister and rescue them from the hand of the Enemy. **(1 Thess. 5:14)** When we are weak, then the True Joshua (Yeshua) is strong. He will send His army to our defense and rescue us. Calling upon Joshua for rescue was a sign of their repentance. Though they came to Israel unworthily, now as servants of God and His people their peace treaty is binding.

Joshua has shown God's love and grace to the Gibeonites. Now he will show God's power and might to the evil kings and their armies who came against the Gibeonites.

Joshua and God's people found their hiding place and strength in God. But these five kings hid in caves. These five kings represent the hidden spiritual kings of Satan in the supernatural. Their names have significance and a message.

1) **Adoni-Zedek, king of Jerusalem** – this name means "lord of righteousness." He represents self-righteousness that must be destroyed that we may become the righteousness of God in Christ. This king wants to steal your peace indicated by the name Jerusalem which is the place of peace.

2) **Hoham, king of Hebron** – this name means "he crushed" and Hebron means "fellowship;friendship." Hoham represents independent spirits, which crush fellowship with God and with other believers. The independent spirit must be crushed if there is to be unity in the Body of Christ.

3) **Piram, king of Jarmuth** – this name means "a wild donkey" and Jarmuth means "he will be lifted up." He represents rebellious pride that exalts itself. Rebellious pride must be destroyed and replaced with humility.

4) **Japhia, king of Lachish** – this name means "causing brightness" and Lachish means "the walk of a man." This one will get you to shine the light upon yourself rather than God. Pride must be destroyed as well as the carnal mind. We must have the mind of Christ and the ways of Christ if we are to receive revelation knowl-

edge and walk in the light of God's truth.

5) **Debir, king of Eglon –** this name means "the speaker" and Eglon means "a bull calf." He represents the accuser of the brethren and stubborn, accusing and critical mouths that must be destroyed if we are to walk in the meekness of the Spirit of God and speak Truth.

God's Word has many levels of truth. The names of these five kings also have the message of Christ hidden within their meanings. "The Lord of Righteousness will crush a wild donkey and be lifted up causing Light. He is the revelation of Truth (oracle) and power and strength (bull calf)." When we crown Jesus Lord of our lives and walk in accordance to His Word by the power of His Spirit, we will defeat these five kings.

Joshua threw these five united armies of the enemy into confusion by surrounding them with a surprise attack. The cross of Jesus Christ and the power of His Anointed Word in the mouths of His servants will throw the Enemy and his demons into confusion. After Joshua and God's people surprised the enemy by attack, the Lord stoned the enemies of His people to death with huge hailstones. These hailstones touched no Israelite but spared no Canaanite! God killed more of the enemy by the hailstones He threw down than were killed by the swords of God's people. In **Revelation 8:7,** God will again throw hailstones from heaven to earth. God was fighting on His peoples' behalf, as He will during the events of Revelation. In **Revelation 6:15-17, the kings of the earth, the princes, the generals, the rich, the mighty, and every slave and every free man hid in caves and among the rocks of the mountains. They called to the mountains and the rocks to "Fall on us and hide us from the face of him who sits on the throne and from the wrath of the Lamb! For the great day of their wrath has come, and who can stand?"** Like these enemy kings in Joshua hid in caves, the enemies of God and His people will also hide in caves again in Revelation. They will hide in vain those who try to hide from God! In Revelation the kings of seven nations gathered against Israel. **There are also seven kings. Five have fallen, one is, the other has not yet come. Revelation 17:10** There were a total of seven kings and nations that Joshua defeated first. It began at Jericho, then to Ai and now these five for a total of seven. These represent the spiritual perfection of evil. In Revelation, there are also 7 kings that Jesus will defeat and destroy.

God performed a miracle so His people could defeat these five enemy armies. Joshua boldly called the sun to stand still in the presence of Israel, **"O sun, stand still over Gibeon, O moon, over the Valley of Aijalon." Joshua 10:12** Joshua had faith to believe the impossible and God honored that faith. It also again shows the power of our spoken Word to create what we speak. **The sun stopped in the middle of the sky and delayed going down about a full day. There has never been a day like it before or since, a day when the Lord listened to a man. Surely the Lord was fighting for Israel! Joshua 10:13-14** God stopped the universe in its course so His will could be accomplished through Joshua and His people. God responded to their faith and their willingness to fight for the salvation of others. The Light of the Sun of Righteousness, Yeshua/Jesus, has been shining throughout the earth for 2,000 years. He has made His Son stand still for 2,000 years while He fights our true Enemy. When Jesus died on the cross, the sun was darkened for three hours and then the greatest victory of all time was fought and won – the victory over sin and death. Here in Joshua, the light of the sun stood still and prevented the darkness so God's people under the leadership of Joshua (Yeshua) could defeat the enemies of peoples' souls, just as Jesus/Yeshua has done for 2,000 years. In Revelation there will be no more light of the sun and moon, for the Lord God will give them light. **(22:5)**

These five kings had escaped, fled and hid in the cave at Makkedah. Makkedah means "place of shepherds." These five kings wanted to rule over the Lord's House and flock by replacing the true Shepherd Jesus. We must be alert and watch for the wiles of Satan and his hidden spiritual princes who are constantly trying to use our flesh to bring us to defeat and weaken God's House.

The first thing Joshua did was bind them by placing a large rock over the entrance of the caves they were hiding in. Then he set a guard over them. Having bound and guarded these evil kings, Joshua told God's people to pursue the rest of the enemies and attack them from the rear so they couldn't regroup and become powerful again.

Then Joshua and God's people destroyed these enemies completely. **Joshua 10:16-21** God gave them the total victory.

Jesus came to the enemy's house –earth— to bind the strongman (Satan) at the cross. **Jesus said in Matthew 12:29, "How can anyone enter a strong man's house and carry off his possessions unless he first binds up the strong man? Then he can rob his house."** Though Satan is still alive and working, Jesus bound him at the cross. When we make Jesus Lord of the battle and walk according to His commandments, He will give us the victory. Jesus said, **"How can Satan drive out Satan? If a kingdom is divided against itself, that kingdom cannot stand." Mark 3:23-24** In other words, our flesh which is controlled by Satan cannot stand against Satan. And if there is division in the army of God, we will also be defeated. Like Joshua did with these five evil kings, Yeshua/Jesus will guard our hearts if we are willing to obey Him so the enemy will remain bound and will not be able to return to the strongholds he once held in us. Jesus will also bind Satan during His 1,000-year millennial reign. There will be peace on earth during that 1,000 year period.

After all of the spiritual warriors of the enemy were completely defeated, Joshua instructs his army commanders to bring the five evil kings to him. Then Joshua told his army commanders to **"put your feet on the necks of these kings."** In other words, take authority over them. **"The God of peace will soon crush Satan under your feet." Romans 16:20** The foot is the lowest member of the body and the head and neck are the highest place on the body. Putting one's feet on the neck is a sign of total victory. A snake's head must be cut off at the neck in order to kill it. We must cut off our carnal mind, which is the spiritual battlefield and put on the mind of Christ to defeat the enemy. God has given us our full armor for the battle. **(Ephesians 6:10-18) And God placed all things under His *(Jesus)* feet and appointed Him to be Head over everything for the church, which is his body, the fullness of him who fills everything in every way." Ephesians 1:22-23** Christ has conquered our enemies for us. However, we must not give place to the devil. We are to put our feet on his neck and stand in victory. Jesus has given us His authority over serpents and scorpions. All things are placed under His feet including the enemy and our flesh. Joshua told God's people not to be afraid or discouraged by these five evil kings but that they should be strong and courageous. **This is what the Lord will do to all the enemies you are going to fight. Then Joshua struck and killed the kings and hung them on five trees, and they were left hanging on the trees until evening. At sunset Joshua gave the order and they took them down from the trees and threw them into the cave where they had been hiding. At the cave, they placed large rocks, which are there to this day. Joshua 10:25-27** Jesus was hung on a tree for all to see. Then He was put into a cave tomb and a large stone was placed on the entrance. The enemies of Jesus tried to bind Him and His authority. But this stone was rolled away and Jesus is alive. He conquered the curse, death and the grave for us and put Satan under His feet. He is the Light of the world. In Him there is no darkness at all. Like Joshua showed God's people that he had authority over these evil kings, Jesus showed us on the cross that through Him we also have authority over all the works of the enemy. Because Jesus was raised in resurrection power, He gives that power to those who love and obey Him.

Next Joshua attacked Makkedah putting its king and people to the sword and totally destroyed everyone in that city. He left no survivors. As I said before, Makkedah means "place of shepherds." It represents God's House. Everything that is not holy and of God must be destroyed completely in God's House. God and His House cannot begin to possess the land until He first possesses the land of our hearts and sin is removed from the camp.

The Israelites continued in warfare and battled with a total of 31 kings and destroyed their people and possessions completely. These 31 kings represent the enemies of our souls that keep us from our full promise in Christ. We must face each one of these when they come before us and daily defeat them. Joshua and the Israelites conquered the high places of Canaan but the plains and the fertile valleys remained unconquered. The battles were quick and decisive, but settling in the land would not be completed in Joshua's lifetime. The big battles were over and Joshua was advancing in years so God tells Joshua to begin to divide up the land among His people.

There were still battles to be won and a land to be conquered, but the Israelites would now receive their reward *(blessing)*. Christians who have overcome will also receive their rewards from Jesus. There are five crowns Christians can receive as their reward: The crown of joy **(1 Thess. 2:19)**, righteousness **(2 Tim. 4:8)**, life **(James 1:12)**, glory **(1 Pet. 5:4)** and incorruptible **(1 Cor. 9:25).** We will cast our crowns before Jesus, however, for He alone is worthy of glory and honor and praise. **(see Revelation 4:6)**

The Israelites did not possess the full land of Canaan until hundreds of years later under David's reign. David was a conquering King and mighty warrior who pointed to Jesus the King of Kings and Mighty Warrior.

The tribes of Reuben, Gad and the ½ tribe of Manasseh were the first to ask for their inheritance but the last to receive next to Joshua. It was only after all of the other tribes had received their inheritance that Joshua dismissed these 2 ½ tribes and sent them home to their wives and children in the land outside of Israel with blessings. Jesus said in **Matthew 19:30** that **many who are first will be last, and the last first.** Joshua was the first to enter the Promised Land but the last to receive his inheritance.

CHAPTER 9

God's People Receive
Their Reward

Caleb – The Faithful Servant who "wholly followed God."

Caleb was a Gentile (a Kennizite) who crossed the Red Sea with Moses and God's people. He joined the Tribe of Judah. Caleb proves that those who come into "Israel" do not have to be born into it. Caleb, the Gentile, and his adopted tribe of Judah were the first to receive their inheritance. Because of Caleb's faithfulness to God and His people, this Gentile turned Jew will receive a piece of the land first. In like manner, the Bride of Christ made up of both Jews and Gentiles who have loved and obeyed Yeshua/Jesus in faithfulness to Him and His people will be the first to receive their blessed inheritance. The Bride of Christ will be the firstfruits to Jesus.

Joshua, the Jew, and Caleb, the Gentile, were the only two spies out of the twelve that Moses sent to Canaan who came back with the faith that they could take the land because they had the God of Israel with them. Joshua and Caleb saw the giants in the land as well as the fruit and the milk and honey of the land just as the other 10 did. However, the ten brought back a compromising, unbelieving word, but Joshua and Caleb brought back a faith-filled and honest word. The result was that the unbelieving, compromisers perished in the wilderness without entering the land. Joshua and Caleb were the only two to enter into the fullness of their inheritance in the Promised Land. They were the remnant that represents the remnant Bride of Christ. Caleb didn't let the spirit of unbelief in the hearts of God's people influence his spirit. In the midst of a faithless generation, Caleb had a spirit of faith. God testified in **Numbers 14:24** that Caleb had **"a different spirit."** The Bible says six times that Caleb **"wholly followed the Lord."** He was totally committed to God and lived his life according to the Word of the Lord. Caleb believed God's promises and obeyed His commandments fully. As a result, God used Caleb mightily.

Together Joshua and Caleb represent Yeshua/Jesus and His Bride of both Jews and Gentiles. God trained Joshua and Caleb in the wilderness quietly and secretly as He did David in the shepherd's field. Joshua and Caleb were tried, tested and proved faithful. Like Joshua and Caleb, God is purifying and preparing His Bride now until every impurity is gone and she is fit for a King. The parable of the wheat and tares in **Matthew 13:24-30** is about the Church. "Wheat" symbolizes "Godly ones." Tares represent the "ungodly ones." Jesus is talking about a separation that will take place in His Body. The Bride will rise to the top. Christ's Bride will first establish His kingdom in Her heart through purity and then She will bring in the end time harvest for Christ. She will bring Jesus a rich inheritance. Like Joshua *(Yeshua)* and Caleb *(Bride of Christ)* by faith, boldness, strength and power Christ's Bride will lead God's people into victory as they destroy the enemy's strongholds and capture the land. With Jesus as Commander of God's army, His Bride must take down the strongholds of the enemy by force destroying every evil work. She must lead God's people into spiritual warfare and take Satan's kingdom by force. Wherever an enemy stronghold is cast down, the kingdom of God is established.

It is now time for Caleb to receive his reward in the Promised Land. Caleb is now 85 years young. He is still strong and courageous and ready to take on the giants of Hebron. He doesn't ask for an "easy" inheritance. Instead he asks for Hebron which was the place full of giants that Joshua and he had seen 40 years before. **"The people are stronger and taller than we are; the cities are large, with walls up to the sky. We even saw the Anakites there."**

Dt. 1:28 Caleb was well aware of the task ahead of him. But he also knew it was the choice piece of the land full of fruit, milk and honey. Hebron would be a hard-won victory. Caleb wanted God's best even though it would require further warfare. Caleb wasn't afraid of the giants of Hebron forty years before and he isn't afraid of them now. In the wilderness he said, **"Let us go up at once and take possession, for we are well able to overcome it. Numbers 13:30** Caleb wanted a "higher" inheritance. He wasn't content with little but wanted the best of the land. Instead of waiting for his share to be determined by "lot" as the others did, Caleb reminded Joshua of his faithfulness and boldly asked for the very place Joshua and he had spied out 40 years before. **"Now, therefore, give me this mountain that the Lord promised me." Joshua 14:12** Caleb knew that the best piece of the land would be where the strongholds were the strongest but he also knew it would be the very place where he would receive the greatest reward *(blessing)*. Caleb also had faith in God and believed His promise. God had promised him this mountain, so he wanted it! He would hold God to His promise. If God promised it to him, then God would give him the strength and power to fight the giants and possess it. **(see Joshua 14:12b)** Caleb would be an overcomer with God's help.

Joshua blessed him *(Caleb)*, **and gave Hebron to Caleb the son of Jephunneh as an inheritance. Hebron therefore became the inheritance of Caleb the son of Jephunneh the Kenizzite to this day, because he wholly followed the Lord God of Israel. Joshua 14:13-14** Joshua *(Yeshua/Jesus)* gave Caleb, the faithful servant, the desire of his heart. Hebron is a mountain that overlooks a wide area of the Promised Land. It is full of fruit and plantations. Caleb has been faithful to God's leader and people throughout the wilderness wandering, has fought side by side with God's people against the kings and inhabitants of Jericho, Ai and the other enemies that unified against God's people. He has waited patiently for God to fulfill His promise and give him his reward. Now he will receive it. Through all of his experiences, suffering, sacrifice and warfare, God was training Caleb and spiritually maturing him for His highest blessing.

Even though there are still battles to be won, the reward will be the choicest piece of the land, which is full of fruit. Caleb represents those who want to go higher with God. God has a choice piece of the land for choice spirits. Only those who wholly follow the Lord in obedience to His Word and faithfulness can rise higher into a deeper and closer relationship with God and inherit these choice territories. The devil, of course will try to stop your advance into the higher place, just as the giants of Hebron tried to stop Caleb from possessing this choice spot.

God has much more for us than just being saved and sanctified. He has choice inheritances for choice spirits. But, he lets each one of decide for ourselves how much we will receive. Hebron is the choicest spot in the land, but it is also the hardest won victory. It takes sacrifice, hard work, self-denial, suffering, persistence, obedience and patience. And most of all, it takes great faith. We must hold tight to all of God's promises and wait. Blind faith is the hardest of all the virtues. In our flesh, we want instant results and immediate action. But Our Father says that if we wait on Him, we will be blessed. Hebron became Caleb's inheritance because he was faithful and obedient. It is when we obey God that we please God. **John 14:21 says three times: "Whoever has my commands and obeys them, he is the one who loves me. He who loves me will be loved by My Father, and I too will love him and show Myself to him."**

Hebron was the city of Abraham, the friend of God, and of David, the man after God's own heart. It represents fellowship with God in an intimate and mutual love relationship. Hebron is the place of the betrothal of the Bride awaiting the day of the wedding. Our hearts are connected to the heart of the Bridegroom. And our hearts are also connected to the other members of the Body—heart to heart, bone-to-bone—making it one Body without division. This Christ-like love has no respect for persons but sees each through the eyes of God through Christ. This is a simple, unselfish love that sees others in the light of Christ's perfect love and grace. This love may see the sin in another but covers it with prayer, faith and hope for Christ's healing. Like the Apostle John, we must lean close to God's heart so we can hear the whisper of His love and share it with others. We must carry the burden of the sorrows of others, share in their joy and carry on the work of the kingdom together as One

Body with One Lord. A selfish, insensitive heart that lacks compassion, love, gentleness, patience, long-suffering, kindness, goodness, faithfulness, self-control will stop you from reaching your Hebron. Faith and obedience is the prerequisite of this higher call.

Prior to being named Hebron, which means "friendship," it was called Kiriath-Arba, which means the "City of the strength of Baal." God can take a person who is controlled by the world, the flesh and the devil and transform him into a "friend to God" and "a man after His own heart." Then he will bear much fruit unto the Lord. We must come to Hebron the place of Christ-like love and fellowship before we can go to Jerusalem, the city of God and His throne where we see Jesus face to face. David made his capital in Hebron before he moved to Jerusalem and brought the Ark of God's presence there.

It is driving out these evil kings in the land of our hearts that will bring us to this Christ-like love and an intimate relationship with God. Caleb himself drove out of Hebron first Arba, the greatest man among the Anakites, then Anak and then the three sons of Anak. The names of these five have a spiritual message:

1. Arba means "self-masterful" and represents Satan.
2. Anak was Arba's son and means "long-necked" and represents pride.
3. Sheshai means "free" and represents a rebellious spirit.
4. Ahiman means "brotherhood" signifying humanism (flesh).
5. Talmai means "bold" signifying arrogance.

Caleb was not only fighting a physical battle, he was also fighting a spiritual battle against the powers and principalities controlling these evil kings. These same powers and principalities are at work today and must be conquered. Satan, pride, rebellion, the flesh and arrogance must be conquered before we can possess God's finest and best blessing for each of us.

Having captured and destroyed the inhabitants of Hebron, **Joshua 15:15** says that Caleb went up higher to the inhabitants of Debir formerly known as Kirjath Sepher. Caleb always went up higher. He wanted all that God had for him.

Debir means "the speaker" and represents the tongue, and Kiriath Sepher means the "city of the book" and represents the Word of God. It is the Word of God in our mouths that will conquer the enemy and possess the land. The tongue is the most difficult thing for Our Lord to conquer in us. Kirjath Sepher represents both the mental source of thought and the outward expression of it. This is where Satan loves to work. He tempts through the mind and expresses it through the mouth. The temptation can slip in so cleverly disguised that even the mature Christian can be tricked. We must take our thoughts captive to Christ before they are spoken. We must put any thought that is not from God to death immediately so that it will not linger and create its own character in our spirit. Our Father says **For as a man thinketh in his heart, so is he." Proverbs 23:7** The Word of God is full of warnings about the evil of the tongue. Our tongue has the power of life or death. We can speak blessing or cursing. And, Our Father, says we are not to speak both through the same mouth. In **James 3:2,** Our Lord says, **If anyone is never at fault in what he says, he is a perfect man, able to keep his whole body in check.** A person who wins the victory over the tongue will have little trouble living a triumphant life in every other direction. A tongue that has learned to be silent for self and Satan will become the instrument of God's messages and the channel of His glorious power. But first, Our Father must know that He possesses it. God's symbol at Pentecost was a divided tongue. God wants to use our voice as His instrument of power and authority. But He will not use it until He knows He controls it absolutely.

Kirjath Sepher comes after Hebron. We must have the love of God before we can speak God's Truth in love.

Instead of Caleb conquering Kirjath Sepher, he put out a challenge to whoever attacked and captured Kirjath Sepher, he would give his daughter Acsah in marriage. Acsah means "grace." Jesus is Grace. Othniel, which means "the power of God" and represents the Holy Spirit, took up the challenge and won the city. Jesus and the power of the Holy Spirit will conquer our sins until the whole city of our heart is captured — grace upon grace. Then He will use us to set the other captives free. As Othniel would receive a Gentile/ Jewish bride (Acsah) because of his willingness to attack and conquer Kiriath Sepher, Jesus will also receive a Gentile/Jewish Bride from the Holy Spirit. The Holy Spirit is purifying and preparing a Bride for Christ. Through his bride, Othniel received a rich inheritance and a double portion from Acsah's father.

Acsah was born during the last ten years of God's people wandering in the wilderness. While the others were dying in the wilderness, Caleb was fruitful and was receiving God's grace *(Acsah)* because of his unfailing faith and obedience.

Acsah *(grace)* moved her husband *(Jesus)* to ask great things of her father. And Acsah *(the grace of Jesus Christ)* asked even more of her father *(Our Father)* than what Othniel *(the Holy Spirit)* asked for himself. **Now to Him who is able to do exceedingly abundantly above all that we ask or think, according to the power that works in us,...Ephesians 3:20** The grace of Jesus Christ will move the Father through the power of the Holy Spirit to give us more blessings than what we could ever ask or hope for. This is the abundant grace of Our Lord Jesus Christ to His Bride.

Caleb gave his daughter and her husband the upper *(high)* and lower *(deeper)* springs. God is always willing to take those who stoop in grace and have thirsty hearts to the heights and depths of His love, His Word and His blessings. All our fountains are in Him. **(Psalm 87:7)** These spiritual springs water the fruitful life. **On the last day, that great day of the feast** *(Feast of Tabernacles),* **Jesus stood and cried out, saying, "If anyone thirsts, let him come to Me and drink. He who believes in Me as the Scripture has said, out of his heart will flow rivers of living water." John 7:37-38** This living water will carry you to the mountaintops but it will also flow in the valley of trouble to lift you up and encourage you. This living water not only flows into you, it flows out of you to others. The heights and depths of faith, hope, love, joy, praise and prayer reach the very throne of God.

Caleb understood the purpose of God's anointing upon his life. It was not just to bless Caleb and make him feel good. His anointing was to give him victory in battle against the enemy. No weapon formed against Caleb would prosper. **Numbers 23:19-20**

Caleb's example shows us that if we are to claim our inheritance, we must be:

1. wholly submitted to God
2. know His Word and obey it
3. live by faith in God, not by sight
4. know His promises and believe them
5. be under the authority of Joshua (Yeshua) the commander of God's army and leader of his people
6. keep our eyes on the vision not the circumstances
7. depend upon God for the victory

Othniel, Caleb's son-in-law, became the first judge of Israel. **Judges 3:9** Caleb fought the good fight and was blessed.

Caleb and the tribe of Judah received their inheritance first. David who would eventually conquer all of the Promised Land came from the tribe of Judah. The second tribe to inherit their share of the Promised Land was Joshua's tribe of Ephraim. And the third was the ½ tribe of Manasseh. Two and ½ tribes receive their inheritance first in Israel and the 2 ½ tribes of Reuben, Gad and ½ tribe of Manasseh received their inheritance last on the east side of the Jordan outside of Israel. **Many who are first will be last, and the last first. Mt. 19:30** Joseph received his double-portion through his two Jew/Gentile sons who had been adopted by the father Jacob. Joseph represented Jesus as the Suffering Servant who was eventually exalted to the right hand of the throne. Christ adopts both the Jew and Gentile who follow Him as His own and gives us our inheritance. Ephraim and Manasseh received a united inheritance, which included Bethel which means "house of God." **(see Joshua 16:1-4)** Judah, Ephraim and the ½ tribe of Manasseh represent Christ and His Bride. Reuben, Gad and the ½ tribe of Manasseh who received their inheritance outside of Israel represent the unsaved Jews and Gentiles.

One of the descendants of Manasseh had no sons but five daughters. Joshua gave these five daughters their father's inheritance. The names of these five daughters have a message:

1. **Mahlah** means "song" *(praise)*
2. **Noah** means "rest" *(peace)*
3. **Hoglah** means "festival" *(joy)*

4. **Milcah** means "counsel" *(wisdom)*
5. **Tizrah** means "benevolent" *(love)*

These five attributes will build Christ's kingdom.

God told Joshua they must totally annihilate the inhabitants in the land. However, **Joshua 15:63** says that **Judah could not dislodge the Jebusites, who were living in Jerusalem** and in **Genesis 16:16,** the Ephraimites **did not dislodge the Canaanites living in Gezer.** Instead they made these Canaanites their slaves. **Genesis 17:12-13** says that the Manassites **were not able to occupy these towns, for the Canaanites were determined to live in that region.** The Manassites also subjected these Canaanites to forced labor but did not drive them out completely. Because these two and ½ tribes disobeyed God and compromised His Word, they were not able to fully possess the land. Their compromise of God's Word eventually backfired on them because the Canaanites eventually enslaved God's people. This is the nature of sin and disobedience to God's Word. If we compromise God's Word even a "little," we open the door of our hearts for Satan to come in. Eventually that one sin if not confessed and repented of will grow into many and we will be enslaved to Satan once again.

The Manassites and Ephraimites also complained to Joshua that their inheritance was too small. Joshua's answer to them was in essence "work for it!" These tribes wanted an "easy inheritance," but Joshua said to them, **"You are numerous and very powerful. You will have not only one allotment but the forested hill country as well. Clear it, and its farthest limits will be yours; though the Canaanites have iron chariots and though they are strong, you can drive them out." Joshua 17:17-18** God's blessings and grace require hard work if we are to inherit the land. Though the enemy is strong, God with us will drive them out. But it will require faith and hard work.

There were still seven tribes left to inherit a part of Israel. Joshua told them to appoint three men from each of these tribes to go and survey the land and write a description of it. Then they were to divide the land into seven parts. **Judah was to remain in its territory on the south, and the house of Joseph in its territory**

on the north. Joshua 18:5 Jacob, the father, had prophesied that Judah and Joseph would share the blessing of the firstborn. **(see Genesis 49:8-12; 22-26)** Judah would be the kingly tribe of leaders and mighty warriors. Judah received the scepter *(authority;ruler-ship)* but Joseph received the birthright and blessings that come with it through his sons. Joseph was a prince among his brothers. Though he was in a dry, thirsty, hungering land, he bore fruit because he trusted God in all the circumstances of his life. Though Joseph suffered at the hands of many, **"his bow remained steady, his strong arms stayed limber, because of the hand of the Mighty One of Jacob, because of the Shepherd, the Rock of Israel....."** Genesis 49:24-25 Jacob prophesied that Joseph would be fruitful and have both material and spiritual blessings and victory in God. Together Judah and Joseph represent Christ as the Suffering Servant and Mighty King and Warrior. Jesus was both a Priest who in compassion and love suffered for His people and a King who is mighty and victorious in spiritual warfare.

Joshua put God's people first. He was the last to receive his inheritance. Joshua did not give himself an inheritance, the people did. In like manner, the True Joshua Jesus will receive His inheritance of the land and a kingdom through His people. With Yeshua/Jesus as our Leader and Mighty Warrior, we will inherit the land for Him. The people gave Joshua Timnath Serah in the hill country of Ephraim. Timnath Serah means "the city of the sun." The "city of the Sun" is the place of light, life, power, warmth and love, guidance from error and healing. It represents Yeshua/Jesus and the heavenly Jerusalem. Those who follow Yeshua/Jesus will also inherit the City of the Son where we will abide with Him forever and where the Lamb is its Light. **(Revelation 21 and 22)** The Light of the Son will fill the New Jerusalem with brilliance and glory. **Revelation 1:16** describes Jesus as **"One like the shining sun in all its glory."** And **Malachi 4:2** says, **"the Sun of Righteousness shall arise with healing in His wings."**

Believers must be transparent before God allowing His Light to shine forth into our innermost being and filling us with His glorious light and presence. We are His jewels and will reflect the light of His glory in the New Jerusalem – the Bride of Christ. Christ is looking for men and women who are willing to conquer the giants in the land in order to gain the highest places in His kingdom. Jesus asked His disciples, **"Can you drink the cup I am going to drink?" Matthew 20:22** In other words, are you willing to die to the flesh and suffer for His kingdom. If we want to be seated with Christ on the throne, we must first be willing to go through the cross of suffering.

As the Israelites received rest after their conquests, followers of Christ will also find eternal rest in our heavenly sanctuary. We will rest from our labor and our deeds will follow us to our heavenly home. **(Revelation 14:13b)**

CHAPTER 10

Cities of Refuge — Joshua 20

God told Joshua to designate cities of refuge **so that anyone who kills a person accidentally and unintentionally may flee there and find protection from the avenger of blood. V1-3** There was three on the west side of the Jordan **(Kedesh, Shechem and Hebron)** and three on the east side of the Jordan **(Bezer, Ramoth and Golan).** There was a total of six in the first testament. The 7th was yet to come. The 7th city of refuge would be a "city built by God." Jesus and His Body of believers would partially fulfill the 7th city, but the "New Jerusalem" would ultimately be fulfilled in Revelation. God invites us to receive His High Priest Jesus so we can escape death. Abraham died looking for the **"city built by God." Hebrews 11:10**

All legal business was transacted at the gates of these cities. These cities were the only place of salvation for a sinner. They illustrated God's care and concern for the sinner and the lost. These cities never closed their gates to people in trouble. They were all mountain top cities, could be seen from a great distance and were only a half-day's journey from any Israelite. There were no weapons in these cities! They represent the Body of Christ in the New Testament. The Body of Christ should be a place of safety and refuge for all who enter it. These cities of refuge were not places that gave license to sin. Instead they were places where a person could be delivered from sin restoring them to right relationship with both God and man. The same is true of Christ and His Church. Jesus does not give us a license to sin. On the contrary! He gives us the power of His Holy Spirit and Word to deliver us from sin. We must not take the grace of God through Yeshua/Jesus lightly. Our deliverance came at a cost. It cost Jesus His precious, sinless blood through suffering on the cross.

These cities were not havens for murderers but were a place of safety from the law that showed no mercy through its demand of an eye for an eye and a tooth for a tooth. These cities allowed a place for one who accidentally took the life of someone to plead his case before the priests(Levites) who were experts in the Law of God and the elders. These cities of refuge protected the innocent until guilt was established. The accused could plea his case to the elders. If there were doubt as to his guilt, he would be given asylum in the city of refuge until a trial could be held. If more than one witness testified of his guilt of premeditated murder and the elders found him guilty, he was put to death. But, if he was found innocent, he was kept within the city walls until the death of the high priest who was anointed with the holy oil. **(Numbers 35:25)** The death of the anointed high priest atoned for his sin setting the sinner free to return to his family and his own property. This, of course, pointed to Yeshua/Jesus, the Anointed One and our Great High Priest who atoned for the sins of all with His death on the cross. The atoning blood of Jesus met every requirement of the sinner's debt. Like the gates of the cities of refuge, Jesus' arms are always open to receive a sinner. Jesus is our refuge, our only safety against death and God's judgment. He assumed the death penalty for us. **(Romans 8:1-2)** As the manslayer in the first testament had to go to the city of refuge for salvation, the sinner must come to Jesus and accept his payment for sin in order to be rescued from the death penalty.

The roads (way) to these cities of refuge were always kept in good repair and signs were posted pointing to the way. The way to Christ and salvation is just as open and easy to find as these cities. God has left the road to salvation through His Son open for over 2,000 years. Christ is accessible to all who come to Him. The gates of His mercy and grace are ever open. No one needs to be lost. The only obstacle in the road to the safety of Jesus' arms is our will and flesh.

If a person killed another unintentionally, he must run to a city of refuge without delay. Joshua 20:3 says the sinner must **"flee to one of these cities"** and then he was to stay within its walls for protection. In like manner, sinners must run to Christ for salvation from the penalty for sin, which is death. We must be in the arms of Jesus if we are to **"flee from the coming wrath of God" (Matthew 3:7)** The accused in the Old Testament was only safe as long as he stayed inside the walls of the city of refuge. **(Numbers 35:26-27)** Sinners are to run into the arms of Jesus for salvation and remain there for protection. If the sinner went outside the walls of the city of refuge, the **"avenger of blood,"** who would be a relative of the slain one, may kill him even though he is innocent. Remaining in Jesus and within the walls and boundaries of His Word and His House will protect us. When we go outside of these boundaries we are in danger of being taken captive by Satan and even put to death.

The names of these six cities of refuge have meaning also:

1. **Kedesh** means "holy"
2. **Shechem** means "shoulder"_
3. **Hebron** means "friendship;love"
4. **Bezer** means "fortress"
5. **Ramoth** means "high place;exalted"
6. **Golan** means "circle"

These six cities of refuge represent Jesus the Righteous One who is our strength and the one we love and have fellowship with. He is a strong fortress who is exalted to the right hand of the Father and is the circle of the Word of God._These earthly six cities of refuge pointed to the 7th and ultimate city of refuge in the New Jerusalem whose maker is God. We will live in this Eternal City with Jesus and the Father forever. **Revelation 22:17**

The names of these cities are what Christ's Body should be. A holy place that gives strength to the weak sinner and fellowship with God and each other. It should be a strong fortress of protection against danger—a high and exalted place of praise and rejoicing and filled with the teaching of the full circle of the Word of God.

The more we understand God's grace, the humbler we become and the lower we will stoop to extend God's mercy to those who fall, and extend His grace and love to the lost.

These six cities of refuge also speak of the maturation of a follower of Christ. At Kedesh, Jesus imputes His righteousness (holiness) onto us making us right with God. Then at Shechem, He strengthens us and helps us along the way carrying us upon His shoulders as He bears our burdens with us. Then at Hebron and Bezer, Jesus establishes us in our love for Him and for others binding us to Him heart to heart in a personal relationship. We are also established in our faith and hope in Him. He is our strong fortress. At Ramoth, He brings us into the higher Christian life to the heights of His love and glory and His resurrection power. And finally, we reach the circle of everlasting life that never ends when He comes to gather us to Himself forever in the Eternal City of Refuge—the New Jerusalem.

CHAPTER 11

Priestly Inheritance

Towns for the Levites: Joshua 21

God chose the Levites for holy service. **(Deuteronomy 10:8)** Jacob prophesied that Levi's tribe would be scattered among the other tribes because of their murder of the Shechemites. **(Genesis 49:5-7)** This prophesy of Jacob was fulfilled here in Joshua. Because the Levites obeyed Moses after the golden calf incident, God reversed the curse upon the Levites and set them apart for service to Him and His people and blessed them. Moses prophesied in **Deuteronomy 33:10** that because Levi observed God's Word and kept His covenant **"they shall teach Jacob Your judgments, and Israel Your law."** The Levites were murderers (sinners) who turned from their evil ways and obeyed God's Word. They prefigure sinners who repent and come to Jesus and then obey His Word. We are all priests in Christ. Christ said that we did not choose Him, He chose us for holy service in His kingdom. In the above-referenced scripture in **Deuteronomy 33:10,** "Jacob" refers to the sinner because it means "deceiver." "Israel" represents the regenerated, spiritual Jacob who has been transformed into "one who strives with God." To the sinner, the Levites would teach God's judgments, but to the spiritual man, Israel, they would teach God's Word (Law). Moses also said that the Levites would serve in the sanctuary. The Levites offered their lives in service to God and His people, as those who follow Jesus are to offer their lives a **"living sacrifice"** to Him and His people.

God gave the Levites as "gifts" to Aaron, the high priest, and his sons, the priests, to do the work of the sanctuary on behalf of His people and make atonement for the people so no disease would strike the Israelites when they go near the sanctuary. **(Numbers 8:19)** God also sends people with gifts into His body to help in the work of His kingdom and serve His people and ministers. The Levites were divided into families with each family having an assigned task in setting up, taking down and carrying the tabernacle from place to place. They were also to teach the Word of God and oversee the cities of refuge. The Levites represent committed and set apart servants of Christ who in unity and purpose and in their God-given positions are to build the spiritual house of God and carry it to others. We are called to Jesus to be used and be a blessing to others. We are to surrender unconditionally and joyfully our will, our voice, our bodies, our deeds and our possessions to God's ownership and control. It is complete surrender to His will and ways that brings the fullness of His blessing to us and blesses others through us. All who follow Jesus are priests and kings—a royal priesthood – who serve King Jesus by ministering to others with love and compassion as a priest and in power and victory as a king using our God-given gifts. **(Romans 12:4-8)**

The Levites made God their all. In giving up all to God, they received more than all the other tribes had received. All of the tribes of Israel were to allot towns and pastureland to the Levites. They were given a total of 48 towns, six of which were cities of refuge. These towns scattered throughout the land gave the people access to God's servants who taught the Law, served in the sanctuary, oversaw the cities of refuge and also judged righteously. **Now to Him who is able to do exceedingly abundantly above all that we ask or think, according to the power that works in us, to Him be glory in the church by Christ Jesus to all generations, forever and ever. Amen. Ephesians 3:20-21** The power that works in each of us who belong to Christ will do more than we could ever hope for or ask if we trust and obey Him. As the Levites were supported and provided for by the other tribes, the New Covenant also states that God's ministers should be supported and provided for by God's people. **Even so the Lord has commanded that those who preach the gospel should live from the gospel. 1 Corinthians 9:14**

Each of the nine and one-half tribes has received a portion of the land of Israel as their reward for their faith and obedience to God. The possession and conquering of the land of Israel is still as important to the Jews today as it was in the days of Joshua. God, however, is not only interested in the conquering and possession of the land of Israel, but also the conquering and possession of the land of every heart and every nation on earth through His precious gift of grace through His Son Yeshua/Jesus. Dividing the land foreshadows the gifts of the Holy Spirit given to Christ's Body to conquer the land of earth for Christ. The whole land is before us. Like Israel in the days of Joshua, the body of Christ has fallen desperately short in possessing our inheritance. Just as full possession of the land would not be completed in Joshua's lifetime, possession of the earth will not be completed until Yeshua/Jesus comes again to destroy the forces of evil and set up His kingdom. The forces of evil that were at work during the time of Joshua are still at work today. And, the way of victory in spiritual warfare is the same today as it was in the days of Joshua. We must walk by faith in God, be under the Lordship of Jesus and obey His Word if we are to be **more than conquerors through him who loved us. Romans 8:37**.

CHAPTER 12

Tribes of Reuben, Gad and 1/2 Tribe of Manasseh Receive Inheritance – Joshua 22

Joshua releases the 2 1/2 eastern tribes – Joshua 22

These tribes of Reuben, Gad and ½ of Manasseh have spent 7 years helping their brethren conquer the land. They have put God and His people first before their own inheritance. This should be the heart of every Christian. The Apostle Paul gave acclaim to Timothy for having this heart for Yeshua/Jesus and His people. **"I have no one else like him, who takes a genuine interest in your welfare. For everyone looks out for his own interests, not those of Jesus Christ." Philippians 2:20** Like these 2 ½ tribes of Israel, followers of Christ are to bring glory and honor to Christ and have the interest of the whole Body at heart. We must be sold out for Christ and His people.

Because these 2 ½ tribes obeyed God's Word through Joshua and Moses and have fought the good fight on behalf of their brethren, they will now receive their reward. They can return to their inherited land and their families. Not only are they to receive their inheritance of the land, they have the increase of the spoils of the warfare to take with them. **(Joshua 22:8)** Joshua tells them, however, that they must share their gained wealth with their brothers who stayed home to care for the women and children. The "spoils" of the spiritual warfare Christians receive are souls that are presented to Christ for His eternal family.

Joshua's love and concern for these tribes is illustrated in the warning he gives them before they return to their land outside of Israel. He tells them to:

1. *Keep* the commandments of the Law — *honor and preserve the Word*
2. *Love* the Lord your God — *love*
3. *Walk* in all His ways — *follow*
4. *Obey* His commands — *obedience*
5. *Hold* fast to God – *faith and trust*
6. *Serve* Him with all your heart and soul – *service*

God's love is unconditional, but His promises are conditioned on an action on our part. "If you do (this), then I will do (this)." Jesus gave only three unconditional promises: 1) **"I will send the Comforter;** 2) **"I will build My Church;** and 3) **"I will come again."** These are the three "I wills" that Jesus spoke to His disciples.

Yeshua/Jesus, the One to whom the earthly Joshua pointed, also gave a similar warning to His disciples. Before He was crucified, Yeshua/Jesus told His disciples to love Him and keep His words **(Joshua:47-50; John 14:23)** Then Jesus washed His disciples feet to illustrate our need of His cleansing so we will walk in His ways and serve Him and others. In **John 13:34,** Jesus gave a new command to His disciples, **"Love one another. <u>By this</u> all men will know that you are My disciples, if you love one another."** Then Yeshua/Jesus illustrated the need for His disciples to cling to Him in faith in the comparison of the Vine and the branches. **(see John 15: 1-12)** When asked by the Pharisees and Sadduces which is the greatest commandment in the Law, Yeshua/Jesus quoted Deuteronomy 6:5, **"Love the Lord your God with all your heart and with all your soul and with all your mind. This is the first and greatest commandment."** Then Yeshua/Jesus added to this, **"And the second is like it: 'Love your neighbor as yourself.' All**

the Law and the Prophets hang on these two commandments. Matthew 22:37-40

God gave Moses ten commandments, but Yeshua/Jesus reduced them to two. If we walk in these two, we will fulfill all of the others. God is love. We must love God wholly and fully, and then we must love others as we love ourselves. These two fulfill all of the Law and the Prophets. In other words, we must walk our talk. We can't speak one set of beliefs but live a different set. We are not to be like the Pharisees who made demands on others that they themselves were not able or were unwilling to do themselves. We can be full of impressive spiritual talk, but be deficient in walking it in our every day lives. Yeshua/Jesus gave a whole sermon on this very matter to the Pharisees in **Matthew 23.** The Truth without being motivated by the Spirit of love kills. The Pharisees and Sadduces illustrated this fact well. They knew the Law well. They even memorized all 39 books of the Bible. But, they were lacking in the Spirit of God behind the Law, which is love. As a result, Yeshua/Jesus pronounced awful woes upon these self-righteous, false teachers who were full of inner corruption including pride, hypocrisy, greed and misdirected priorities. The heart attitude of how these Pharisees held Truth blinded them to the Truth Yeshua/Jesus who was standing in front of them. The Pharisees were harsh and preached a God that was full of fire and brimstone over disobedience to the Law, when infact these Pharisees were disobeying the Law themselves at times. Christ's disciples also fell into this attitude in the story of the Samaritans who refused to receive Jesus. Two of His disciples wanted to **"command fire to come down from heaven and consume them?" Luke 9:54** Jesus said, **"You do not know what kind of spirit you are of; for the Son of Man did not come to destroy men's lives, but to save them."** This spirit is widespread within the Body of Christ now. We argue over doctrine while millions of people are spiritually dying without Jesus. The various conversations between Jesus and the Pharisees should teach us that it is possible to be committed to Truth and yet not be walking in the greatest of all God's commandments, which is love.

The Sadducees were wealthy. They sat around and discussed philosophical ideas.....kind of like a wealthy mens' club! Their money gave them more power than the Pharisees. They lived a life of compromise. Their reputation among men was more important than their personal relationship with God. The Body of Christ also has "Sadducees" among it today also. There are those in the body of Christ who will kill you over what they consider "incorrect doctrine" just like the Pharisees in Jesus' time and there are those in the Body of Christ who like the Sadducees will compromise God's Word until it is hardly recognizable as God's Word. All followers of Christ must be watchful that these heart attitudes do not creep into our lives and reduce the effectiveness of our service for God and His people. Jesus hated sin but operated in love and compassion. He was pure (holy) and motivated by love. We are to follow His example! We must understand the love of God before we can speak the Truth of God in love! All followers of Yeshua/Jesus are the benefactors of God's love and grace. We must remember His tender mercies toward us and extend that same love and mercy to others.

The Pharisees and Sadducees didn't practice what they preached so Jesus issued seven "woes" *(calamities)* that would befall them. Blessings from God for obedience and faithfulness do not make us immune to His correction and consequences for disobedience. Because God is faithful to His promises, He is also faithful to His judgments.

Faithfulness and obedience to God gave Israel the land. Faithfulness and obedience to God would keep them in possession of the land. Joshua warns both the 2 ½ tribes on the east side of the Jordan and the 9 ½ tribes in the land of Israel that as long as "Israel" was faithful and obedient to the Lord, He would continue to fight for them and bring in the victory. Christ has conquered our enemies for us. However, we must not give place to the devil. We must remain faithful and obedient to God's Word if we are to have the victory and possess the land.

The Jordan River was the natural barrier between the tribes in the east and the tribes in the land of Israel. When these 2 ½ tribes crossed back over the Jordan River, they decided to build an altar to God. They feared that their children and future generations would forget God's goodness and miraculous power in giving them the land. They also wanted to use this altar to remind their children and subsequent generations of their connection to the tribes in Israel. **(Joshua 22)** However, the tribes in the land of Israel misunderstood the intent of these tribes on the other side of the Jordan in building this altar. The nine and one-half tribes remembered the golden calf incident **("the sin of Peor" v 17)** in the wilderness and God's judgment for the sin causing them concern over the actions of their brethren on the other side. Sacrifices for atonement were only to be made on the altar in the tabernacle as God commanded Moses. **(Dt. 12:13-14)** The immediate reaction of the tribes in Israel was to go to war against these 2 ½ tribes. They had misjudged the action of the others. Their zeal for the honor of God and the purity of worship could have ended in division and hostility. Cooler heads prevailed however and the Israelites sent Phinehas, son of Eleazer the priest, with 10 of the elders to investigate the matter so they could make a "righteous" judgment. The sin of Achan, which brought the wrath of God upon all Israel, was fresh in their minds. **(see Joshua 22:20)** They must confront their brothers so the whole Body would be protected from God's anger.

Jesus tells us in **Matthew 18:15-17** that if a brother/sister sins against us, we are to go to him/her and show him/her their fault. This is to be kept between the two parties. We are not to judge by outward appearance but are to go to our brother or sister and discuss the matter with a view toward salvation, reconciliation, restoration, peace and unity. We must approach a brother or sister in the Spirit of love and gentleness, not arrogance or a judgmental, condemning spirit. If the person listens to you, you have won your brother over. In other words, you have restored him to you and to the Lord. If he will not listen, we are to take one or two other witnesses along so that **"every matter may be established by the testimony of two or three witnesses." V16** We are not to judge rashly but are to take two others to hear not only our complaint against another but also the accused party's response. If these two witnesses agree that the brother or sister has sinned and he/she then still refuses to listen, we are to tell the Body of Christ (Church). **Deuteronomy 17:6** says, **"On the evidence of two or three witnesses, he who is to die shall be put to death; he shall not be put to death on the evidence of one witness."** And again in **Deuteronomy 19:15, "A**

single witness shall not rise up against a man on account of any iniquity or any sin which he has committed; on the evidence of two or three witnesses a matter shall be confirmed." Confirming evidence must be found and attested to by two or three others before conviction. The Apostle Paul did this in hearing an accusation against a leader in **2 Corinthians 13:1 and in 1 Timothy 5:19.** If he/she still refuses to listen even to the church, then he/she is to be treated like a pagan or a tax collector. Phinehas and the 10 elders in Joshua lived out this commandment. They went to their brothers to seek out the truth and to allow them to explain their action.

It is interesting to note the attitude and response of these 2 ½ tribes who have been misjudged by their brethren. Instead of reacting in anger, resentment and retaliation, they react meekly, gently and calmly. They agreed with the others that any deviation from pure God-ordained worship deserved judgment, so if they were guilty, let God require atonement from them for it. **(vv22-23)**

These accused tribes use the three names of God in their response and repeat it twice. (El, Elohim, Yahweh – The Mighty One, God, the Lord) In other words, they swore before Almighty, Sovereign and Everlasting God. They said that God knew their hearts and the motivation behind their action. This altar was to be a "witness" to God and to future generations of their shared faith and unity with their brothers on the other side of the Jordan. They wanted their children and future generations to understand that they too were a part of Israel and worshiped the same God of Israel. Their response turned a "curse" into a blessing. They spoke the Truth and trusted God to defend them.

Because Phinehas and the leaders used Godly judgment and Godly ways by going to their brethren for an explanation, they are convinced that these tribes are not sinning against God and therefore the Lord's Hand would not be against all Israel. **(Joshua 22:31) "A gentile answer turns away wrath, but a harsh word stirs up anger." Prov. 15:11** Instead of war and division, there was reconciliation, restoration and unity among the brethren. Phinehas and the elders acted as peacemakers between the brethren as Jesus commanded in **Matthew 5:9.** The elders were **"pleased"** when they heard the explanation. **(Joshua 22:30)** They were motivated by love and unity not vengefulness. Phinehas and the elders **"did not rejoice in iniquity, but rejoiced in the truth."** **1 Corinthians 13:6** Their heart attitude was not to delight in another's downfall but to bring peace, unity and reconciliation among God's people. Even the rest of Israel was **"glad to hear the report and praised God. And they talked no more about going to war against them to devastate the country where the Reubenites and the Gadites lived." V33**

Jesus and His glory are revealed through the love between the brethren who live for the unity and common good of His Body. **(see Psalm 133:1-3)** The sweetest witness anyone can give God is a trans-formed life that reflects the love, grace and beauty of Jesus Christ. Jesus will take all of your past hurts and even your present ones, heal them and give you the grace to forgive and love those who have spite-fully used you. The result will be freedom, joy and blessing.

Jesus Himself was spit upon and **"when they hurled their insults at Him, He did not retaliate; when He suffered, He made no threats. Instead, He trusted Himself to Him who judges justly." 1 Peter 2:23** Jesus never defended Himself against His accusers. He remained silent. He knew that God knew His heart and His motive and that God would be His defense. Instead of retalia-tion, Jesus offered forgiveness and love as He suffered on the cross of Calvary. This love, grace and mercy are the "memorial (witness)" of God's undying love and the altar that brings unity and peace among the brethren. Our common ground is that we are all guilty but He has declared us "not guilty" by His precious, sinless blood.

Because these 2 ½ tribes were outside of "Israel," their enemies eventually attacked them repeatedly. Their land was taken and they fell into idolatry. Those who survived were integrated into the other tribes of Israel. This was the result of living too close to the pagan nations (*world*). Their influence and their defeat of God's people drew these tribes into worshipping their false pagan gods. Followers of Jesus are in the world but they are not **of the world. (John 17:14-16)** Jesus chose us **"out of the world." (John 15:19)** We are His set apart ones who are to reflect the light and love of Jesus to a lost and dying world. His Word of Truth becomes a sanc-tifying light preparing us for greater measures of His Spirit and work. **(John 17:17-19)** Then He sends us out into the world to bring others into His saving grace. Followers of Christ must be careful not to get too close to worldly ways or we too may be snared by the Enemy and miss our full inheritance in Christ.

CHAPTER 13

Joshua's Farewell Addresses – Joshua 23 & 24

God has given the Israelites rest from all of their enemies. Joshua has advanced in years. He knows his time on earth is nearing an end. Unlike Moses, God does not tell Joshua to appoint a successor as his death approaches. This resulted in a void in leadership, which shortly thereafter resulted in a seesaw of sinning, being oppressed, being saved by a Godly leader (*judge)* and then only to sin again. The Book of Judges chronicles this pattern.

Because God's people are surrounded by pagan nations, Joshua was concerned that they might fall into apostasy and idolatry. So, Joshua calls "all Israel" to Shechem , the valley of decision, between Mount Ebal the mount of cursings and Mount Gerizim, the mount of blessings, where they had begun their journey fifteen years hence. Shechem is an important place in the history of Israel. It was the place where God first made His covenant with Abraham. **(Genesis 12:6-7)** It was also the place where Abraham met Melchizedek, the King-Priest. **(Genesis 14:17-24)** Jacob purchased a piece of land at Shechem to abide in, built an altar to God and dug a well. **(Genesis 33:18-19)** At Shechem, Jacob renewed God's covenant after he told his family to put away their idols. **(Genesis 35:2-4)** Shechem became a "city of refuge," and Joseph is buried there. As we can see by this, Shechem is not only the place of decision, it is also the place of covenant, the place of safety and the place of burial. Yeshua/Jesus began His first missionary work at Shechem when He went to rescue the Samaritan woman at Jacob's well there.

At Shechem, Joshua delivers two speeches to a unified Israel before he dies. He reminds them of God's delivering, saving, victorious power for His people. They had seen it firsthand. Joshua always gave the glory to God for the victories, not himself. It is remembering God's goodness in the past that encourages our faith in the present and future. Because God has been faithful and loyal to them, Joshua tells the Israelites that they should be faithful and loyal to God and serve Him only. Joshua calls the Israelites together to warn them not to depart from God and His commandments or they would lose their inheritance.

Joshua assures the people that even though all of the inhabitants have not been completely driven out of the land, God would drive them out little by little as He promised Moses. **(Exodus 23:30)** Jesus also drives our sins out little by little. It would be devastating if God revealed the filth of our flesh to us all at once. He must do so gradually, grace upon grace. God's people must destroy everything that would entice them to worship false idols. **"Do not associate with these nations that remain among you; do not invoke the names of their gods or swear by them. You must not serve them or bow down to them." Joshua 23:7** If they mingled with the heathen nations, they would become a snare and a trap for God's people and would also result in the loss of the land *(blessing).*

God had instructed Joshua to **"be strong and courageous and be careful to obey all of the Law of Moses"** when He chose him to lead His people into the land of Israel. Joshua had learned the value of listening to and heeding this word of God. God had been faithful to Joshua, as Joshua had been faithful to God's Word. Now Joshua gives this same message to God's people before he dies. God would continue to fight for His people and give them victory over their enemies if they:

1. are **strong and courageous. (Joshua 23:6)**
2. **are careful to obey all that is written in the book of the Law of Moses, without turning aside to the right or to the**

left. Joshua 23:6 They must not allow anything to turn them from obeying all of God's commandments.

3. God's people are not to swear to, serve or bow down to heathen gods. **(Joshua 23:7)**
4. They are to hold fast to the Lord.
5. They are not to marry an inhabitant of the land or associate with them. **(Joshua 23:12)**

If they forsake God and His Word, the inhabitants of Canaan will become snares and traps that will entangle God's people, whips that will cause pain and punishment and thorns that will fly back in their faces stabbing their eyes and causing spiritual blindness until eventually they lose the land God gave them. There was no middle ground. They must be "sold out" to obedience to God and serving Him only. He is a jealous God who doesn't share His people with any other god. They must count the cost.

Joshua reminds the Israelites that God had driven out great and powerful nations on their behalf. **"No one has been able to withstand you." Joshua 23:9.** Why? Because as long as Israel was faithful to God and His Word, God fought for them and gave them the victory. It was the Divine Warrior who gave them the victory and the land. With God at their side, they were a thousand times stronger than their enemies. **(Joshua 23:10)**

Joshua's ministry is coming to a close, but God's work must continue. Joshua reminds them that God has not failed on any of His promises. **"Every promise has been fulfilled; not one has failed." Joshua 23:14** Next Joshua reminds God's people that just as God is faithful to all of His promises, He is also faithful in His judgments. **"But just as every good promise of the Lord your God has come true, so the Lord will bring on you all the evil He has threatened, until He has destroyed you from this good land He has given you." Joshua 23:15** Joshua told them of the continued blessing for obedience, but he also had to warn them of the consequence for disobeying God. Joshua was afraid the people would become careless and not finish the job of totally eliminating the inhabitants of Canaan as God had commanded.

The message to be faithful to God and obey Him was so important that Joshua repeated it three times. **(Joshua 23:3-8, 9-13, 24:14-16)** Joshua reminds them that God gave them a land for which they did not labor and cities that she didn't build. She received vineyards and olive yards that she didn't plant. **(Joshua 24:13)** It was God's gift to His people because of His grace and love, not because of the peoples' works. Therefore, they should fear God and be committed to serve Him with all faithfulness. **(v14)**

From **Genesis** to **Joshua,** God reminds His people of His faithfulness and deliverance. Joshua reviews the history of God's work on Israel's behalf beginning with His calling Abram out of idolatry in Ur of Chaldee. Abram believed in the True God and was willing to leave all to follow Him. It was not because of Abram's goodness but because of God's grace and love and Abram's faith and obedience that God gave him the land of Israel and made him the father of all children of faith. God said, **"Long ago your forefathers, including Terah the father of Abraham and Nahor, lived beyond the River and worshiped other gods. But I took your father Abraham from the land beyond the River and led him throughout Canaan and gave him many descendants. I gave him Isaac, and to Isaac I gave Jacob and Esau. I assigned the hill country of Seir to Esau, but Jacob and his sons went down to Egypt."** Joshua 24:2-4 Notice God said, **"I took; I gave; I assigned."** It was all God's doing, not man's.

Next God says that He **"sent Moses and Aaron, and I afflicted the Egyptians.......and I brought you out."** Joshua 24:5-7

Then, **"I brought you to the land of the Amorites.........I gave them into your hands. I destroyed them........and you took possession of the land. Joshua 24:8** Balaam was sent to put a curse on you, but **"I would not listen to Balaam, so he blessed you again and again, and I delivered you out of his hand. Joshua 24:10** When you crossed the Jordan, **"I gave"** all of your enemies into your hands. **(24:11-12) "I gave you the land......."** **(v13)** All of this was God's work lest any man should boast. **(Ephesians 2:9)**

Joshua obviously knew that the people had a divided heart, so he tells them to **"throw away the gods your forefathers worshiped beyond the River and in Egypt..." Joshua 24:14**

They must rid their homes of these false gods and genuinely repent before the Lord. **"A house divided against itself cannot stand."** **Matthew 12:25** They must choose whom they would serve. **(Joshua 24:15)** They cannot serve two masters. **(Matthew 6:24)** Joshua gave them three choices:

1. They could return to the idols their forefather's served in Ur of Chaldee.
2. They could serve the idols of the Amorite gods in the land that they were now living.
3. They could repent and follow God with their whole heart.

Joshua's choice was clear. He and his house would serve God only. The Israelites immediately promise to be faithful and serve God. But obviously Joshua knew the fickleness of the people. He had seen their disobedience and compromise over the years. So, Joshua says, **"You are not able to serve the Lord. He is a holy God; He is a jealous God. He will not forgive your rebellion and your sins. If you forsake the Lord and serve foreign gods, He will turn and bring disaster on you and make an end of you, after He has been good to you." Joshua 24:19-20** Joshua knew that obedience was impossible in the strength of the flesh. He had developed a close, personal relationship with His Savior. But the people thought that they could serve God in their own strength. Again the people said they would serve the Lord. **"The spirit is willing, but the flesh is weak." Matthew 26:41** The remedy for this condition is in **Acts 2** when Jesus poured out His Spirit upon all flesh giving them His power to become holy and serve Him. Serving God fully and obediently can only be done by His grace and power. Without Jesus, we can do nothing. We are helpless, weak and prone to temptation. Our failures show us our inability and the weakness of our flesh so we will learn to depend upon Christ's all-sufficiency in our insufficiency. We must develop and establish our own personal relationship with Christ and not totally lean upon a Godly leader. The Israelites made this mistake time and again. After their leader died, they fell into idolatry and sin once again. Like Joshua, we must learn to stand alone with God in faithfulness to the end.

Making an oath to God is serious and should not be taken lightly. Joshua said to them, **"You are witnesses against yourselves that you have chosen to serve the Lord." V22** According to the Law, there was no forgiveness for intentional sin. **(Numbers 15:30-31)** The Israelites say they are witnesses against themselves of their oath to God. Thankfully, the grace of Jesus Christ forgives all of our sins if we confess and repent of them. We are not to take the grace of God through Jesus lightly. Joshua was right in saying that the people could not serve the Lord in their own strength. The flesh is weak. But Jesus came to give us the power of the Holy Spirit to bring us to obedience and faithful service. **This is how we know that we love the children of God: by loving God and carrying out His commandments. This is love for God: to obey His commands. And His commands are not burdensome, for everyone born of God overcomes the world. This is the victory that has overcome the world, even our faith. Who is it that overcomes the world? Only he who believes that Jesus is the Son of God. 1 John 5:2-5**

Again, Joshua tells them to **"throw away their foreign gods that are among you and yield your hearts to the Lord, the God of Israel." Joshua 24:23** Idolatry was one of Israel's repetitive sins. Joshua confronts them again on their idolatry. Jacob made his family bury the idols of their father Laban under the oak tree at Shechem. **(Genesis 35:4)** Now Joshua tells the Israelites they too must get rid of the false gods of their forefathers at the same place in Shechem.

God's people have spoken their oath to God, now they must take action upon their words. There must be no compromise. They need to genuinely repent and commit themselves to God only. Sin and holiness cannot mix.

Jesus also reminded His people of his love and commitment to them. He gave them His all......His love, His life, His Word, His peace, His joy, His rest, His wisdom, His power and authority and His kingdom. He has given us all we need to live life abundantly and in the fullness of His blessing. The choice is ours. We will either serve Him or serve another. He assures us that He is with us

"always, even to the end of the age." Matthew 28:18-20 The Israelites could lose their inheritance because of sin, but followers of Jesus cannot be plucked from His hand. **(John 10:28-30)**

For the third time, the Israelites promise to serve God and obey him. God's people have established their word of covenant with God three times, so Joshua renews the covenant at Shechem recording all that had taken place in the Book of the Law of God. **(Joshua 24:25-26) Then he took a large stone and set it up there under the oak near the holy place of the Lord. "See! He said to all the people. This stone will be a witness against us. It has heard all the words the Lord has said to us. It will be a witness against you if you are untrue to your God." Joshua 24:26-27** Joshua memorialized their place of commitment to God. This God-made stone heard all of their words and would be a witness against them if they broke covenant with God. The foreign gods have been buried and a "rock" has been set up on the altar (holy place). This would be a constant reminder of God's grace and delivering power and their covenant with Him. This "rock," of course, represents Jesus Christ. As this stone reminded God's people of their vows, the Lord's Supper reminds us to be cleansed of sin and obedient.

The Book of Joshua ends with three burials: Joshua, Joseph and Eleazar. All three of these Godly men were great deliverers of God's people. Joseph saved them from starvation in Egypt and Joshua led them into their inheritance of the Promised Land, gave them the "new food" of the land as Jesus did and victory over their enemies. Thirdly, when Eleazar, the high priest, died, all those who had fled to the cities of refuge were set free. **(Joshua 20:6)** All three of these Old Testament saints pointed to Yeshua/Jesus who saved us, gave us our inheritance and victory over the Enemy and died on the cross to set us free. These three men had all once lived in a foreign land where they received God's promise to take His people back to Israel. They were now in the land and at rest. God had been loyal. Jesus said that He had to leave this earth **to prepare a place for us** so we can be where He is. **(John 14:2-3)** Jesus will take us into our land of Promise in the heavenly land and will give us eternal rest. All of God's promises are "yea" and "amen" in Christ. **"If we are faithless, He will remain faithful, for He** cannot disown Himself." **2 Timothy 2:13** Those who love Yeshua/Jesus are one with Him—His Body. He cannot disown Himself.

The failure of Israel to remain faithful and possess the land is also true of Christ's Church. There is only One who has been Faithful and True. The Apostle Paul wrote many letters to the early churches and disciples admonishing them and appealing to them to walk in the ways of the Lord so they would inherit the fullness of God's precious promises and conquer the land for Christ. Jesus also admonished the churches in Revelation calling them to holiness. Instead of love and unity filling Christ's Body, strife, division, denominationalism, jealousy and controversy have crept in. **"Awake, awake! Put on your strength, O Zion; Put on your beautiful garments O Jerusalem, the holy city! For the uncircumcised and the unclean shall no longer come to you. Shake yourself from the dust, arise; Sit down, O Jerusalem! Loose yourself from the bonds of your neck, O captive daughter of Zion. Isaiah 52:1-2** God is telling His Church that we must wake up and put on His power from on high and change our garments into beautiful garments of holiness. The unclean must no longer touch us. We must shake off the dust (unclean) and claim liberty from the things that bind us. He has given us His power from Zion *(His throne)*. We must have swift and willing feet shod with good news, salvation and peace. **(v7)** Jesus is speaking to His Bride who has allowed His preparation and sanctification. She will prepare the way of the Lord before He comes the second time. She must cross the Jordan and put the flesh to death. She must "watch" and not let any "accursed thing" touch Her. Jesus said that His Bride must come out of the harlot church and the Babylonian (worldly) system in **Revelation 18:4. "Come out of her My people!"** When Christ's Bride obeys this command of Jesus, She will stand in purity and power and will draw others to Her Lord. The True Joshua, Jesus, will lead her into victory over every Enemy and will use Her to bring in the end time harvest.

God is shaking down His Church as He sifted Gideon's army until there were only 300 out of 30,000 left (*10%-firstfruits*). These 300 won the victory. **"Once more (it is a little while) I will shake**

heaven and earth, the sea and dry land; and I will shake all nations, and they shall come to the Desire of All Nations, and I will fill this temple with glory," says the Lord of hosts. "The glory of this latter temple shall be greater than the former," says the Lord of hosts. "And in this place I will give peace," says the Lord of hosts. Haggai 2:6-9

When Christ's followers have dealt with both unintentional and intentional sin in their life and walk in total surrender and dedication to Jesus, God will use them in a greater way to uplift and feed others. Just as the Promised Land had everything the Israelites needed for food and drink, we have everything we need for life in Christ. Jesus laid down His life for us. His Seed went into the earth to produce fruit. We must lay down our life for Him by dying to self so His life will be manifested in us. Then we will inherit the Land.

There will be a "Hebron" of fellowship and love for every faithful and courageous Caleb. There will be wisdom, boundless knowledge and courage for every "Othniel" who will rise to the call and challenge to conquer strongholds. There will be a fountain of life for every "Acsah" who dares to ask for a double portion from the Father and claim her full inheritance in Christ. And finally, there will be a Timnath Serah, the "city of the sun," full of Christ's glorious light and power for every faithful, courageous and obedient Joshua. We have a heavenly calling and purpose. We have His past faithfulness and love to encourage us and we have a glorious and everlasting life to look forward to. Therefore, we should live a life worthy of the calling we have received in Jesus Christ.

Then Jesus will return to Israel not to bear sin but to complete the salvation of those who are waiting for Him. **(see Hebrews 9:28b)** With Him will be His called, chosen and faithful followers. **(Revelation 17:14c)** God will give His **"little flock"** the kingdom. **(see Luke 12:32)** It is those who have served, suffered and overcome who will receive the crown of victory and glory that Christ has promised to the faithful. God continually tests His people to see if they can be trusted with a crown

God's people served the Lord faithfully during all the days of Joshua. **(Joshua 24:31)** What a testament to this man of God.

God has been faithful. **"Not one of all the Lords' good**

promises to the house of Israel failed; every one was fulfilled." Joshua 21:45 All of God's promises throughout scripture are "yea" and "amen" in Christ. To His prepared and pure Bride, He says, **"Who knows but that you have come to royal position for such a time as this." Esther 4:14**

LaVergne, TN USA
24 February 2011
217817LV00002B/69/A